His eyes stared straight through her as his finger pressed the bright red stop button on the wall of the elevator.

"Did you just stop——?"

The rest of what she was going to say ended up muffled beneath firm lips as she was guided back against the wall and lifted to her toes. Unlike Riley's gentle hunt and pecks, this man went straight to the good stuff. And the good stuff was the best she'd ever had. She tried to remember what she was going to tell him, but his kiss wiped all thought from her mind. He devoured her hungrily, leaving no room for breath or refusal...

Acclaim for
Hunk for the Holidays

"4½ stars! Sharp, witty dialogue, a solid sense of humor, and a dab hand at sizzling sex is going to push Lane far, if this is an example."

—*RT Book Reviews*

"Lane's contemporary series launch sizzles from the moment Cassie McPherson's hired escort appears to accompany her to the company Christmas party... The romance is inevitable, but Lane makes the couple work for it, writing with warmth and humor. [Readers will] adore James, Cassie, and the affectionately jocular McPhersons."

—*Publishers Weekly*

"I was interested from the first page to the last...There was enough chemistry between Cassie and James to set the place on fire."

—Romancing-the-Book.com

"Katie Lane is an author who has the ability to create romantic magic with her words. Ms Lane bring characters to life that readers love to bring into their lives."

—The Reading Reviewer
(MaryGramlich.blogspot.com)

Praise for **The Deep in the Heart of Texas Series**

A MATCH MADE IN TEXAS

"4½ stars! Lane's outlandish sense of humor and unerring knack for creating delightful characters and vibrant settings are on full display...She does a marvelous job blending searing heart and surprising heart." —*RT Book Reviews*

"Engaging and really enjoyable...a funny and quirky romance." —HarlequinJunkie.com

"Fun-filled and heartwarming...a wildly sexy romance with a beautiful love story [that] old and new fans definitely do not want to miss." —BookReviews andMorebyKathy.com

FLIRTING WITH TEXAS

"4½ stars! [A] complete success, blending humor, innovative characters and a wonderfully quirky town with an unlikely and touching love story. [Lane's] insight and humor are pitch-perfect, making the sizzling chemistry between her leading couple a constant surprise and a delight...[The] misadventures and romance of Jenna and Beau are utterly engaging." —*RT Book Reviews*

"*Flirting with Texas* is an extremely entertaining and amusing tale of a feisty little hellcat of a woman. Every turn of the page is an unexpected journey full of humor as well as emotion...[Katie Lane's] writing is stimulating and doesn't allow the reader to put the book down." —FreshFiction.com

TROUBLE IN TEXAS

"Sizzles with raunchy fun...[Elizabeth and Brant's] dynamic provides the drama to complete this fast-paced novel's neatly assembled package of sex, humor, and mystery."
—*Publishers Weekly*

"This trip to Bramble, Texas, brings a close to the mystery of Cate's Curse with humor, romance, heart-warming affection and some mighty intriguing characters. Readers are in store for some fine surprises and a glimpse at stories yet to be told."
—*RT Book Reviews*

"I really enjoyed reading *Trouble in Texas*. The small-town feeling with its grudges, history, and eccentric residents was a blast. I spent a lot of my time giggling and wondering what the henhouse ladies were going to do next."
—TheBookPushers.com

"Lots of fun and games, enticing intrigues with tidbits of wisdom here and there make *Trouble in Texas* a tantalizing tale...Katie Lane's writing style keeps the reader turning pages."
—LongandShortReviews.com

CATCH ME A COWBOY

"4½ stars! This is an emotional story that will bring the reader to laughter as well as tears and spark a desire to see more of the characters, both new and old, who live here."
—*RT Book Reviews*

"Lane gives readers a rip-roaring good time while making what could feel like a farce insightful and real, just like the characters themselves."
—*Booklist*

"Nosy townsfolk, Texas twangs, and an electric romantic attraction will leave readers smiling." —*BookPage*

"Katie Lane is quickly becoming a must-buy author if one is looking for humorous, country romance! This story is an absolute hoot to read! The characters are real and endearing...the situations are believable (especially if one has ever lived in a small town) and sometimes hilarious, and the romance is hot as a June bug in July!

—*Affaire de Coeur*

MAKE MINE A BAD BOY

"A delightful continuation of *Going Cowboy Crazy.* There's plenty of humor to entertain the reader, and the people of the town will seem like old friends by the end of this entertaining story." —*RT Book Reviews*

"Funny, entertaining, and a sit-back-and-enjoy-yourself kind of tale." —*RomRevToday.com*

"If you're looking for a romance true to its Texas setting, this is the one for you. I simply couldn't put it down."

—*TheSeasonforRomance.com*

"I absolutely loved Colt! I mean, who doesn't like a bad boy? Katie Lane is truly a breath of fresh air. Her stories are unique and wonderfully written...Lane, you have me hooked." —*LushBookReviewss.blogspot.com*

"Another fun read and just as good as [*Going Cowboy Crazy*]...a perfect example of small town living and the strange charm it has. I really enjoyed reading this one and hope that Katie Lane is writing a third."

—*SaveySpender.com*

Ring *in the* Holidays

Ring *in the* Holidays

Katie Lane

FOREVER

NEW YORK   BOSTON

Copyright © 2014 by Cathleen Smith
Excerpt from *Hunk for the Holidays* copyright © 2012 by Cathleen Smith
Excerpt from *A Match Made in Texas* copyright © 2014 by Cathleen Smith

Forever
Hachette Book Group
237 Park Avenue
New York, NY 10017

HachetteBookGroup.com

Printed in the United States of America

OPM

First Edition: September 2014
10 9 8 7 6 5 4 3 2 1

Forever is an imprint of Grand Central Publishing.
The Forever name and logo are trademarks of Hachette Book Group, Inc.

The Hachette Speakers Bureau provides a wide range of authors for speaking events. To find out more, go to www.hachettespeakersbureau .com or call (866) 376-6591.

The publisher is not responsible for websites (or their content) that are not owned by the publisher.

To my L-Sisters, Lori Tillery, Lu Loomis,
and Linda Chambers,
thanks for all the Love and Laughter: o)

Ring *in the* Holidays

Chapter One

I guess you know that what happens in Vegas, stays in Vegas."

Ellie turned to find a man wearing a glittery "Happy New Year" tiara and an ugly plaid jacket that looked like it belonged at a salesmen's convention in the '70s. And if his pickup line and ridiculous clothes weren't bad enough, his gaze was pinned on her breasts.

"Really?" She held out a hand. "Ellie Simpson, reporter for the *National Enquirer*." That brought his gaze up. She smiled sweetly and nodded at his hand resting on the bar. A hand with a distinct white tan line on the ring finger. "Recently divorced?"

His eyes widened for a fraction of a second before he realized that she was screwing with him. Then he mumbled the word jerks always used when women put them in their place—bitch—and walked off to Ellie's best friend's shout of laughter.

"Now that was cruel," Sidney said. "Cruel, but funny as hell."

"I prefer men who look me in the eyes."

Sidney shot her an exasperated look as she accepted her lemon-drop martini from the bartender. "With boobs like yours, that's not going to happen. So get over it." She took a sip of the martini. "And speaking of getting over things, it's time to get over Riley. While I don't blame you for turning down the guy in the ugly jacket, you need to get back in the dating ring. It's been months since Riley broke it off with you. Months of sob-fests, ice cream bingeing, and one very lame suicide attempt—"

"It was not—"

Sidney held up her hand. "I told you before, I'm not falling for that dumb excuse about slipping and slicing your wrist open while shaving your legs. You're smart enough to know that's an impossibility."

Sidney had a point. A woman who had completed her doctorate of clinical psychology should be smart enough to know not to slick up her body with baby oil before she bent over to shave her legs. Ellie had slipped and nicked her wrist with the razor on the way down. Thank God it wasn't a straight-edge razor or she might've died. But instead of her life slowly trickling down the drain of the tiny bathtub, the dull twin blade only caused Ellie to bleed enough on the torn-down shower curtain for Sidney to assume the worse.

Before Ellie could get over the sight of her own blood, she was being raced to the emergency room where Sidney harassed the cute physician's assistant into giving Ellie stitches. Or not stitches as much as one. One tiny little stitch that hurt more than the actual cut. And while Ellie was getting her stitch, Controlling Sidney decided on the perfect Christmas gift for her best friend: two airline tickets to Las Vegas, Nevada.

Sidney was convinced that what Ellie needed was a vacation. And between her broken engagement, trying to build a medical practice, and getting her dissertation published, Ellie did need a vacation. She just didn't need it in Vegas on New Year's Eve. She needed peace, quiet, and relaxation, not a crowded nightclub filled with drunk, happy people who were looking to get lucky at more than just the slot machines.

"Come on, Elle," Sidney said as she handed her the Cape Cod Ellie had ordered. "You need to make the effort. I thought for sure that if any place could snap you out of it, Vegas could. Look at all the energy around you. People live here—really live."

Ellie coughed as a cloud of smoke drifted over from the group of gorgeous Amazonian women next to them. "Yeah, they know how to live, alright. They really live and then they probably really die from lung cancer." She took a sip of her drink, and her eyes watered. "And cirrhosis of the liver." Her gaze drifted to the couples gyrating on the dance floor. "Not to mention sexually transmitted diseases."

Sidney sipped on her martini. "Yeah, but at least they will die with a smile on their faces. At the rate you're going, you'll live to be a hundred. A hundred-year-old, unhappy, nonsmoking, teetotaling virgin."

"You don't have to broadcast it." Ellie glanced around before she realized no one could hear anything over the loud conversation and music.

Sidney shrugged. "Why not? I thought you were proud of the fact that you're a thirty-year-old virgin. If you wait much longer to get laid, they'll canonize you. Or make a movie about you."

"Very funny. There is nothing wrong with abstinence."

"True. I think all teenagers should practice it. But once you get past your mid-twenties, it's just plain weird. Especially for a woman who specializes in relationship counseling and sex therapy. How do you expect to help people with their sex lives if you don't have one of your own?"

"I know plenty of good psychiatrists who don't have any personal experience in their field of expertise," Ellie said. "Dr. Fletcher isn't bipolar. Dr. Holmes isn't schizophrenic. And Cindy Maitland doesn't have any children, yet she's getting her doctorate in child psychology."

"That's because she *is* a child. Don't tell me you haven't seen her Disney backpack?" Sidney pulled the lemon rind spiral out of her drink and nibbled on it. "And as for Dr. Holmes, the jury is still out. During sex, he wanted me to call him Gertrude."

"You had sex with Dr. Holmes? When?"

"Halloween night," Sidney said. "I have a thing about pirates. The earring and bandanna did me in. You've got to admit he looked just like Johnny Depp."

"Johnny Depp?" She moved closer to Sidney to make room for the two guys who were trying to hit on the gorgeous Amazonian women. "Holmes is over six foot and pencil thin with stringy blond hair. He looked more like Ichabod Crane on crack than a pirate."

Sidney laughed. "Yeah, Bud Goggles screw with your mind. But don't try to get away from the subject. Which is . . . why you're still a virgin." Ellie opened her mouth to explain, but Sidney held up a hand. "I know. Some lunatic motivational speaker convinced you to take a pledge of abstinence in high school, and you took it seriously. Then after college you met Riley the Self-Righteous, and you both wanted to wait until you were married. Or, at least, you did. But what I don't get is why—"

Ellie grabbed her arm. "What do you mean, at least I did?"

Sidney sent her a resigned look that made Ellie extremely uneasy. "I wasn't going to tell you—especially after what happened in the shower. But maybe it's best if you realize what a jerk Riley is." She downed the rest of her martini and then released her breath. "Riley didn't break off your engagement because he wasn't ready to commit to marriage. He broke it off because he's been screwing around with Valerie Sawyer."

The glass slipped from Ellie's fingers and thumped to the bar as her knees gave out. Fortunately, one of the Amazons had vacated her barstool for the dance floor, so Sidney guided Ellie down to the plush velvet seat.

"How did you find out?" Ellie said in a voice that didn't sound like her own.

Sidney grabbed a cocktail napkin and wet it with a glass of water. "There were rumors going around even before you broke up, but I didn't pay much attention to them. If all the rumors about me were true, I'd have screwed half the men, and women, in Lawrence, Kansas." She handed Ellie the wet napkin. "But then I overheard Valerie when I was standing in line at the Starbucks bragging to her friends about how great Riley was in bed.

And I figure if he screwed her, then he probably screwed the other women."

Other women? A wave of nausea swept over Ellie, and she bent at the waist and tried not to puke all over the new shoes she'd bought herself for Christmas.

Sidney awkwardly patted her back. "I'm sorry, Elle, but you need to realize that not everything fits into your perfect little black-and-white world. Some things are gray—and dirty brown. I mean, shit happens." She stopped patting. "Look, if you want to leave we can. We can even pack up and head home. But I don't think we should. I don't think we should give the bastard the satisfaction of ruining your vacation. Or your life. I mean, where does he get off—"

Sidney continued to rant, but Ellie was no longer listening. With the wet napkin clutched in her hand and her crumpled body perched on the barstool, it took all her focus to continue to breathe. While her emotions were racing around inside like Olympic speed skaters, her body had completely shut down, frozen with shock and disbelief. She wanted to scream. Oh, how she wanted to scream, so loudly that it would break all the bottles behind the bar. And after that, she wanted to call Riley every bad word she'd ever heard but never said. Then she wanted to hit something. Really hard. Like Ugly Jacket who had stared at her breasts without giving one thought to how it made her feel. After she hit him, she wanted to kick him. Repeatedly. Over and over again until he was nothing but a bloody—

She released the breath she'd been holding, along with the tight grip on the napkin.

My God, she had to get a hold of herself. If she didn't, she'd be carried away in a straitjacket. And if they put her in a straitjacket, she really would go crazy. She wasn't claustrophobic; she just freaked out when she was confined to small, tight places. She had gone to the bad place and needed to get back. And if anyone should know how to get through an emotional crisis, she should.

Taking a deep breath, Ellie tried to remember that anger was just a by-product of much deeper emotions. Usually pain. She was hurt. Not only at the thought of Riley having sex with Valerie, but also because he'd been doing it the entire time he was calling her his sweet little virgin and spending hours discussing her theories on abstinence and its importance to a strong, healthy relationship. She had truly believed that Riley was nothing like all the high school boys who went straight for her breasts after a cheap dinner at Mickey D's. He had convinced her that he was a man who valued monogamy in a relationship and understood the true meaning of love and trust.

A man the complete opposite of her father.

Opening her eyes, Ellie stared down at the pointed toes of her shoes as the anger drained out of her body, to be replaced with a flood of depressing resignation. After countless hours spent researching case studies that supported her theory that strong relationships were built on friendship and compatibility, not sex, the truth finally came out.

Pushing sex from her life hadn't strengthened her relationship. It had only weakened it. Riley hadn't broken off their engagement because he wasn't ready to make a commitment. He'd broken up with her because he wasn't willing to make a commitment to a woman who wouldn't give him sex.

"Elle?" Sidney interrupted her thoughts. "Have you been listening to a word I've said? So do you want to leave? Or what?"

Ellie looked around the Vegas nightclub at all the patrons with their party hats and drunken smiles. Yes, she wanted to leave. She wanted to go home to the cozy, little apartment she shared with Sidney and strip off the tight, strapless bra and uncomfortable shoes and bundle up in her comfy sweats and the afghan her grandmother had crocheted her. Then she wanted to fall apart. Except she'd already done that after Riley broke up with her. And Sidney was right: He didn't deserve a second more of her time.

Not one second.

She looked at her best friend's concerned face and made a feeble attempt at a smile. "No. I want to stay. In fact, I want a drink." She motioned to the bartender. "A double."

Sidney looked skeptical. "Are you sure you're okay?"

All she could do was nod as she pulled the credit card from her bra and paid for her drink. She had just taken a sip when someone tapped her on the shoulder. She turned, expecting to see another guy with another lame pickup line, but instead it was one of the tall, gorgeous Amazons who had all the men drooling.

The pretty brunette pointed at Ellie's breasts. "Hey, are those real?"

Since nothing else in her life seemed real at the moment, Ellie found deep satisfaction in answering. "One hundred percent."

"No shit? Mind if I touch?" Before Ellie could utter a syllable, the woman in the skintight dress with the perfect body reached out and cupped Ellie's breast. "Hey, Dee, you gotta feel these," she called back to her friend. "Now I'm really pissed at my plastic surgeon."

Life is strange, Ellie thought. If someone had asked her a month ago what she'd be doing on New Year's Eve, she would've answered without hesitation, "I'm having a quiet dinner with Riley at our favorite Italian restaurant." She knew this because the dinner had been written in her planner since the beginning of this year. Along with the appointments for cake tastings, flowers, and wedding dress fittings. Almost every white block of the planner had been filled with flourished handwriting using sherbet pink and spring green pens—pens she had bought to match her bridal colors.

Vegas hadn't even been in her planner.

Yet, here she stood, the woman who usually freaked out when anyone entered her twelve-inch perimeter of personal space, letting a gorgeous Amazon feel her up. Yes, it was strange. Almost like it was happening to someone else. Someone who hadn't wasted five years of her life, or countless squares in her planner, on a lie.

Maybe that was exactly who Ellie wanted to be tonight... someone else. Someone who drank doubles, let strange women fondle them, and didn't care if men stared at her boobs. Someone who, for one night, could throw caution to the wind and completely immerse themselves in the decadence of Sin City.

And why not?

After all, Vegas knew how to keep a secret.

Chapter Two

"Would ya look at that? Shi-i-it, I love Vegas."

Matthew McPherson glanced up from the label he was methodically peeling off his bottle of beer and followed his friend's gaze down to the lower level of the club. It only took a second to spot what Tubs was referring to. Standing at the bar were the two women Tubs had pointed out earlier. One of the women was fondling another woman's breast. Not her friend's, but a different woman's. A petite, big-busted woman with really ugly hair.

While his other two friends joined Tubs and leaned over the railing of the VIP section, Matthew went back to peeling. At the moment, the job of pulling the beer label off in one perfect piece was more important than a little lesbian action. Which probably should concern Matthew, but didn't. He had grown weary of girls going wild. These days, everywhere you looked women were kissing or fondling women. At clubs, strip joints, and spring break beaches around the world, the opposite sex had figured out exactly what two women kissing and rubbing around on each other did to men.

Made men go wild.

And, at one time, he was no different from Tubs or his other buddies who were transfixed by the women's entertainment for the evening. But not anymore. Now it just bored him. Of course, lately, everything bored him. The condo he lived in, the women he dated, the car he drove, and the job he worked at. All of it was boring. Which made no sense whatsoever. He could understand it if he was an Average Joe who drove a Honda Civic, worked as an accountant, and was married to his high school sweetheart who had put on a few extra pounds after the birth of their third child. If he were that guy, it would make perfect sense. But he wasn't.

No, he was the youngest son of Big Al McPherson who owned M&M Construction, a multimillion-dollar company. The same company where Matthew worked as a top corporate lawyer and had a huge office with a panoramic view of downtown Denver. An office only miles away from his trendy condo where a Range Rover and brand-spanking-new Porsche Carrera GT sat in his double garage.

What more could he possibly want? He was young, single, and wealthy with the uncanny ability to make women fall at his feet and money collect in his bank account. How could a man be bored with that?

Yet, he was.

Bored and completely out of his mind.

Matthew stopped peeling when he remembered another McPherson who had gone Looney Tunes. Poor Uncle Rudy had become bored with life and had given away all his money to live on the streets. After he was caught in a Chicago park wearing nothing but his birthday suit while roasting a squirrel for supper, the family slapped his ass straight into a mental ward. Every year at Christmas, his aunt Marsha still received a death threat written on three squares of toilet paper.

Matthew preferred stationery. Nice, clean, expensive stationery with the company letterhead printed across the top. Besides, it wasn't his friends' fault that he was bored with life. They had come with him to Vegas on New Year's Eve expecting to party, not peel labels off beer bottles and ruminate with him about not having any adventure in his life.

"So you think those are real?" Stan asked.

Trying to appear interested, Matthew looked down at the women who stood at the bar. "What ones are we talking about?"

"The petite blonde's that just got felt up."

He examined the breasts in question. He had to admit they were impressive. Impressive, but about as genuine as his last girlfriend's. "Fake."

Always a sarcastic drunk, Mitch turned to him. "And just how can you tell that from this far away, O Great One?"

"Simple. Very few petite women have real breasts that big."

"What about Ronda Letterman?" Stan asked.

Matthew shook his head. "The only thing Ronda had

in common with this woman is height. The bone structure is completely different."

Tubs laughed. "Bone structure? Only you, Mattie, would notice some woman's bone structure."

It was true. Matthew did notice more about women than their obvious physical traits. To him, women were like works of art. In order to enjoy the piece, you first needed to study every nuance: The butterfly sweep of a hand. The musical pitch of laughter. The gentle slope of a naked shoulder. These were all part of the entire package. A package that, when appreciated, could offer a man hours of enjoyment.

"Who cares about her bone structure"—Stan rested his arms on the railing—"I just want to get my hands on those sweet chest puppies."

Matthew shook his head at such ignorance. "Which is exactly why you never will. And why most men strike out. They don't take the time to really study a woman before they approach her." He nodded at the bar. "Take her for example. You've been watching her for a while now. So what can you tell me about her—besides the sweet chest puppies?"

Stan seemed befuddled by the question, but Tubs chimed in. "For being so short, she has nice legs. And her face doesn't look too bad. Although her hair looks like mine after I went to SuperChop. With the way she's downing that drink, I'd say she's out for a good time. Of course, letting her friends fondle her breasts is a dead giveaway on that count."

Matthew took a moment to study the woman. "As far as pickup lines go, you need to throw out the boobs and legs," he said. "But you're on the right track with the hair. Her haircut is flat-out ugly. Which leads me to believe that she's more concerned with what's inside a person than what's outside. An intelligent woman who isn't interested in what people think...or in men who are after only one thing."

Which made him wonder why she let her friend feel her up. She didn't dress like a tease. In fact, the simple black dress she wore could just as easily work for a funeral. It said the exact opposite of the tall brunette's tight, short dress. One shouted, "I'm ready for a night of hot sex," while the other whispered, "Get ready to work for it."

Tubs laughed. "You kill me, Mattie."

Matthew pulled his gaze away from the woman and smiled. "It's a gift."

"A gift of bullshit," Mitch said. "So now tell us how this information will get that woman in bed?"

Matthew shrugged. "Information is a building block. Once you have it, you have to know how to use it. Take law for example. A court attorney can have all the information about a case in the world, but if he doesn't know how to present it, it becomes nothing but a pile of notes. In this case"—he nodded down at the bar—"I would appeal to her intellect. Ask what she does for a living—where she went to college."

"What if she doesn't work or go to college?"

He studied the woman in question. "Doubtful. But, in that case, I would have to rely on my charm."

"Fuckin' Prince Charming," Mitch grumbled.

Matthew grinned. "Most women believe in the fairy tale. Which is exactly what I give them. They want a man who looks at them as more than just a pretty face and a nice body. A man who cares about their feelings and emotions and really listens when they talk. A man who fits into their illusion of a happily-ever-after."

"A man full of shit?"

"Aren't we all, Mitch? Especially in the hunt for the prize." Matthew's cell phone rang, and he pulled it out of his pocket and glanced at the number. "Excuse me." He got up from the table and moved away before he answered. "Hey, gorgeous."

His great-aunt Louise snorted. "Don't pull that flirty playboy stuff with me, Matthew McPherson, especially when you've fallen down on the job. You told me that you would introduce that reclusive brother of yours to your harem of women, and here you are in Sin City without Patrick."

"Hold on, Wheezie," Matthew said. "I invited Patrick, and he turned me down."

"So use some of that charm of yours and change his mind. Or does that only work on women?"

"Pretty much."

Another snort had him smiling. "Well, I guess it's too late to worry about it now. You're there getting plenty, and he's here getting none. But when you get back, I expect you to make more of an effort. Patrick is next in line to find his perfect match, and he won't find her amid all those construction workers he hangs out with. I'm not getting any younger, and I refuse to leave this world until all of Big Al's kids are happily married."

Which explained why Matthew wasn't making more of an effort to get his brother to the altar. Besides keeping his feisty aunt around, he wasn't about to become her next target and be manipulated into spending his life with just one woman. It would be like spending his life with just one van Gogh. But he couldn't deny Wheezie, either. Despite being the worst kind of matchmaker, she was the funniest and most endearing relative he had.

"Okay, I'll do my best to fix Patrick up when I get back," he said. "But I can't make any promises. Paddy seems quite content with his bachelor's life."

"No man is content without a woman," Wheezie said. "They just need to find the right one to prove it to them. Now try not to break too many hearts in Vegas, and I'll see you when you get back. Happy New Year, handsome."

"Same to you, gorgeous."

Matthew was still grinning when he hung up and took his seat back at the table where the guys were placing their orders with the waitress. A waitress who, after bringing their drinks, slipped Matthew a cocktail napkin with her number on it. The gesture gave Mitch a perfect mark for his pent-up anger.

"You are so full of it, McPherson," he said. "And that napkin is a perfect example. Here you are spouting off all kinds of shit about collecting information and charming women, when it all boils down to one thing: physical attraction. You haven't said one word to that waitress, besides the name of that damned Scottish ale you drink, and she still gave you her number. Which means that everything you've just told us only works for guys like you, guys with more looks and money than they know what to do with."

Matthew shook his head. "You're wrong. Women don't

care about physical looks as much as personality. Make them laugh and feel good about themselves, and they're yours."

"I don't know," Tubs said. "I make girls laugh like crazy, and I still can't get as many as you do, Mattie."

"I must concur." Stan tipped his glass at Matthew. "Women do seem to love your looks. In fact, I think you could out-and-out ask and that woman at the bar would let you pet her sweet puppies."

Mitch pulled out his wallet and tossed some money onto the table. "Let's bet on it, shall we?"

Matthew stared down at the hundred-dollar bill. "You're betting a hundred bucks that I can walk up to the woman and ask to feel her breasts and she'll let me?" He sat back in the chair. "Sorry, but that's not my style."

"Because you know I'm right." Mitch took the hundred back and slipped it in his wallet. "Women care about looks as much as the rest of us."

Matthew never went in for petty bets, but he really wanted to prove Mitch wrong. Not only to save face with his buddies, but also because just the thought that he had wasted his time and energy all these years on being charming and witty when brutal honesty would've gotten him in the same number of bedrooms was horrifying. It was also doubtful and ridiculous. But no one could ever accuse Matthew McPherson of not looking at things from all the angles.

Or of backing down from a challenge.

"Fine," he said. "But I refuse to be the only one proving my theory." He nodded at the bar. "While I'm getting slapped by the short one, you need to approach the tall brunette in the white dress and try talking to her about something other than her great body parts. If you score and I get slapped, I win. And if you get the shaft and I get a feel, you win. And if it's one or the other, we call it a draw."

"Deal." Mitch shook Matthew's hand.

While Stan and Tubs took sides and joined in on the wager, Matthew looked at the woman in question. The fondling had long since stopped, and she was now chatting it up with some guy who couldn't seem to take his eyes off her breasts. She wasn't even close to being Matthew's usual choice. She was too short on hair and legs. But there was something about her that was cute and...he watched as she went to take a sip of her drink and poked herself in the chin with the stirring straw...awkward. And maybe that was exactly what he needed to help him win the bet: A cute, smart, awkward woman who was not used to Vegas nightclubs or being treated rudely. A woman he would never have to see again when the experiment fell flat.

And it would fall flat.

Matthew smiled. He'd make sure of it.

Chapter Three

Ellie was having fun.

The three Cape Cods probably had a lot to do with it. Or the celebratory atmosphere. But some of it had to do with finally being able to let Riley go. For months, she had held on to the hope that he would get over his commitment issues and come back. Now she knew that would never happen. And as angry as she was by his cheating, she was thankful that he had broken up with her before they'd gotten married—and before children were involved.

While Sidney flirted with some guy who looked like he'd needed a fake ID to get in, Ellie got up from her barstool and headed for the dance floor. Having never been much of a dancer, it took her a while to find the rhythm of the Bruno Mars song. She bounced and jiggled for three straight songs before the music stopped and the DJ's voice blasted through the speakers, starting the countdown for the New Year. Surprised that it was already midnight, she tried to make her way back to the bar to celebrate with Sidney. But as the countdown continued, even more people flooded the floor, leaving no room to take a breath, let alone move.

With nothing else to do, Ellie counted down with everyone else. With each shouted number, she released the pain of the previous year and pinned her hopes on the coming one. After a loud chorus of "Happy New Year," she watched as couples kissed amid the colorful balloons and confetti that fell from the ceiling. Depression was about to set in when a man appeared out of nowhere. Ellie batted a blue balloon out of her face. No, not man. Men, even nice-looking ones, had at least one or two flaws. But from what Ellie could tell, this man didn't have a one.

From the top of his thick, wavy black hair to the tips of his polished brown leather shoes, he was pure perfection. His light green button-down shirt tapered just enough to showcase nice shoulders, a muscled chest, and flat stomach, while his designer jeans defined long legs and lean, muscular thighs. Topping off the well-proportioned body was a face that would make a modeling agent weep: Strong chin with a tiny cleft. Firm lips with just enough plump. And a nice-size nose that complemented high cheekbones and thickly lashed eyes.

Eyes that appeared to be staring directly at her.

Although she figured it had to be a trick of the flashing strobe lights. Greek gods did not go for average women who couldn't dance. Fortunately, Ellie had never gone for Greek gods, either. She had discovered a long time ago that the prettier the face, the more arrogant and obnoxious the man. So instead of bowing down and worshipping at his feet like most women, Ellie waited for him to move on.

Except he didn't move on. He just stood there looking at her as if he wanted to say something.

While her Cape Cod–soaked brain tried to figure it all out, the music started back up, and a wild dancer bumped her from behind. She stumbled on her heels and would've disappeared into the sea of balloons and confetti if the Greek god hadn't caught her. He lifted her clear off her feet and pulled her against a body as hard as it looked.

Suddenly, sexual attraction became something more than just a definition in a textbook. Like iron filings to a magnet, every cell in her body shifted toward the man. Her heart thumped like crazy, her breath paused, and the pit of her stomach felt as if she had just reached the top peak of the highest roller coaster.

For a moment, his eyes seemed to beg her forgiveness before he leaned closer and whispered something in her ear. At the touch of his warm lips, chill bumps spread through her, and liquid heat pooled in the crotch of her panties. She had this thing about her ears. Something Riley hit on a few times but never really figured out. If he had, it was doubtful she would still be a virgin. And with the way she felt at the moment, she might not be one by the time she got off the dance floor. Especially when the man released her and her body did a slow slide down soft denim and hard male. The sensations that assailed her brought her within seconds of orgasm.

And if anyone knew about orgasms, Ellie did. She hadn't had sex, but she'd had orgasms.

A lot.

And alone.

Embarrassed by her reaction, she took a step back. His eyes remained on her face as if waiting for something. Probably a reply to whatever he'd whispered in her ear. The logical answer would be no. But for some reason— Riley's infidelity or the sexual desire that flooded her body—Ellie wasn't thinking logically.

Slowly, her head bobbed up and down.

A frown tipped the corners of his mouth. He looked puzzled, then after a few seconds, resigned. Without another word, he took her hand and led her off the dance floor. And she followed. Somehow her body had gone on autopilot and wasn't about to let her logical brain get in the way of what it had been denied for thirty years. And wasn't this exactly what she'd wanted? To be someone different? Someone who could immerse herself in the wicked wiles of Las Vegas? Well, what could be more wicked than leaving a bar with a hot stranger? A hot stranger who had chosen her. Not Sexy Sidney. Or the gorgeous Amazons. Or Valerie Sawyer. But her—Virginal Ellie Simpson.

Once they reached the entrance, one of the bouncers directed them to an elevator located in a corner. An elevator far away from the set of elevators she had arrived on. The bouncer held the door and discreetly accepted the tip her escort offered him.

The doors slid closed, and suddenly, Ellie came face-to-face with her own reflection in the highly polished gold. It was like a cold slap in the face. For as much as she wanted to be someone else, it was the same Ellie Simpson who stared back at her. The same Ellie who made the hotel bed every morning and hung up all the towels. The same Ellie who kept water, a PowerBar, and blankets in the backseat of her Honda Civic in case she got stuck in a fluke blizzard. The same Ellie who, despite Riley's betrayal, couldn't have sex with a man she didn't know.

And no amount of Cape Cods or heartbreak would change that.

Or even a perfect god of a guy.

She dropped her gaze and cleared her throat. "I'm sorry, but—"

The elevator came to a jerky stop, and she glanced over and forgot what she was about to say.

While the bright lights highlighted her flat hair and mascara-smudged eyes, they made him appear even more of a god. A god in vivid color. His skin was a smooth, even brown that no tanning product could duplicate. His lips a subtle, tempting rose that held a trace of moisture as if his tongue had just swept over them. His hair expertly cut waves of black velvet that begged for a woman's caress. All set off by a pair of piercing green eyes. A green so vibrant and intense it reminded her of the eighteenth hole at her father's golf course after a light spring shower. Those eyes stared straight through her as his finger slid away from the bright red stop button on the wall of the elevator.

"Did you just stop—?"

The rest of what she was going to say ended up muffled beneath firm lips as she was guided back against the wall and lifted to her toes. Unlike Riley's gentle hunt and pecks, this man went straight to the good stuff. And the good stuff was the best she'd ever had.

She tried to remember what she was going to tell him, but his mouth wiped away all thoughts from her mind like a damp paper towel on a dry-erase board. He devoured her hungrily, leaving no room for breath or refusal. Not that she wanted to refuse him. At least, not yet. Once he ended the kiss, she would put a stop to things. But for now, she was quite happy doing exactly what she was doing. She liked how his lips molded to hers and how his long fingers flexed at her waist with each sexy flick of his tongue. But she especially liked the way his body held her in place, the hard press of his chest, stomach, and thighs papering her against the wall.

Unfortunately, all good things must come to an end.

Ellie tensed as one of his hands released her waist and crept toward her breasts. It was inevitable. No boy had ever kissed her without wanting to feel her up. And once they were allowed access to her breasts, attention to all other parts of her body ceased in their sheer enthusiasm for such a plentiful bounty.

Except this man didn't seem that enthusiastic. In fact, his hand stopped a good two inches from her breast. With a nip of her bottom lip, he ended the kiss and nibbled a heated path to her ear. It was only after his tongue and lips had turned her into a quivering mass of incoherent female that she felt a light caress on her breast. So light that she barely felt it through the material of her dress and bra. But she did feel the brush of his warm fingertips when they reached the top of her dress and came in contact with naked skin. He painted a slow heated path over the top of one breast to her cleavage, where he dipped inside the crevice before caressing the top of her other breast. And with each back-and-forth stroke, he pushed the bodice of her dress lower and lower. And made her heart rate higher and higher. When he finally exposed one breast, Ellie was ready for the groping to begin. Instead, he gently cradled it in his hand, his thumb lightly strumming the nipple.

"I'll be damned." His words vibrated through her earlobe and clear down to her cramped toes. His breath rushed out as his hips flexed against her. She might not understand what his words meant, but she understood what the hard bulge in his jeans did. And after an entire lifetime of denying her sexuality, she suddenly embraced it.

With a deep, satisfied moan, she buried her fingers in his thick, wavy hair, pulling his mouth back to hers. This time, she was the one to devour him, swirling her tongue along the edges of his perfect, even teeth, exploring the warm recesses of his mouth. His hand slipped from her breast to pull her closer, leaving her with an ache she couldn't ignore. Without a thought to how wanton it looked, she fondled her breast and caressed her nipple. He pulled back from the kiss and watched through those incredible long lashes.

"Sweet Jesus," he groaned before he pushed her hand out of the way and lowered his head.

The first touch of his mouth on her breast had Ellie almost jumping out of her heels. Then those perfect lips moved, and everything inside her melted. She started to slide down the wall of the elevator, but he caught her, hooking her leg around his waist before the delicious torture started again. The rhythmic flick of his tongue and the hot, wet pull of his lips turned her breast into an orb of tingling sensation that radiated out to every nerve in her body. Especially the ones between her legs. Before she knew what was happening, she stood on the brink. And she couldn't do anything to stop it. All she could do was hold on and catch the wave.

It washed over her in a swell that had her moaning out her release. It was the longest, most wonderful orgasm she had ever experienced. When it was over, all she wanted to do was snuggle up to the warm body next to her and sleep.

His deep voice interrupted.

"Did you just...?"

Ellie tucked her face in his neck and smiled.

Yep, she sure had.

Chapter Four

There were very few times in Matthew's life when he'd been surprised by a woman.

This was one of them.

And he wasn't quite sure where to go from here. He knew where he wanted to go. He wanted to jerk up the skirt of her black dress and sink deep inside of her. But it was all wrong. This was all wrong. He didn't have sex with strange women in elevators—okay, there had been that one time, but he'd been young and drunk—and he certainly didn't seduce women over a silly bet. What had he been thinking? When he got back to Denver, he was going to make sure he kept in touch with Uncle Rudy. Boredom could really screw up your mind.

His gaze traveled down to the most beautiful breasts he'd ever seen. Okay, so maybe it wasn't all boredom. What woman could reach orgasm from just touching her breasts? Even with all his experience, he'd never seen anything like it. And the hardness of his dick attested to the fact. He couldn't remember the last time he'd been this turned on. Too bad his conscience wouldn't let him go any further. With a heavy sigh, he carefully adjusted her clothing and reverted back to the manners his mother had drilled into his head at an early age.

"Thank you."

A laugh pulled his gaze away from her sweet twins to a pair of pretty brown eyes that sparkled with humor.

"I think that's supposed to be my line," she said. "Especially when I was the one who got the most enjoyment out of it."

"I wouldn't say that."

She cocked her head. "Then why did you stop?"

Matthew reached down and picked up the room key, driver's license, and credit card that had fallen out of her bra and handed them to her. "Because you don't really want to have sex with some stranger in an elevator."

She took the items and slipped them back in her bra before crossing her arms, causing the sweet flesh to swell above the neckline of her dress. "And I suppose that besides being gorgeous, you can read women's minds? Because I don't remember saying anything about not wanting to have sex with you."

Great, the snooty, smart girl had finally arrived. Since he'd been wrong about everything else tonight, Matthew had hoped he'd been wrong about that, too. Unfortunately, the calculating intelligence in her eyes and the stubborn tilt of her chin said otherwise.

"And if you weren't interested in sex, then why did you

stop the elevator?" she said. "I might be naïve, but I'm not stupid. I know that you paid the bouncer to hold the elevator so we could have all the time we needed." She chewed on her bottom lip as she studied him. The gesture made him grow even harder. "So I guess you're pretty much an expert on women." Before he could figure out how to reply to that, she continued to theorize. "It makes perfect sense given your looks. Women probably fall all over themselves to get into bed with you. So why me? Out of all the women in the club, why did you choose me?"

"Why wouldn't I choose you?"

"Because of the contrast effect." She spread her hands out as if making sure he got a good look. "When average-looking women are surrounded by beautiful women, they appear uglier to men. And I'm an average-looking woman."

Obviously, she was more than a couple steps above smart. Which made Matthew stumble around for his next words. She spoke before he could find them.

"Be honest. Do you think I'm beautiful?"

Normally, he would've lied and punctuated it with a few kisses to take her mind off the subject. But for some reason—Mitch's stupid theory or the sincere brown eyes that stared back at him—he told the truth. "No. I chose you because of your breasts. I wanted to see if they were real."

He braced for a resounding slap, but instead the stubbornness melted from her chin, and she smiled. "They are."

His eyes shifted down to the bountiful beauty. "I know." It was a struggle to pull his gaze away, but he did.

"So while we're being honest, why did you say yes when I asked if I could touch them? Is it something you let a lot of men—and women—do?"

She laughed. It was a husky sound that didn't go with her innocent brown eyes. "What happened in the bar with that woman was a freak incident." She waved a hand around. "Like this. Believe it or not, I didn't even hear what you asked."

"So why did you nod?"

"Let's just say that I was stunned by your godlike good looks."

He smiled. "Godlike?"

She rolled her eyes. "As if you didn't know."

Her reply had him smiling again. Genuinely smiling. He studied her only for a second before he took his room key out of his wallet. "I've changed my mind."

"About what?"

"About letting you go."

When they reached his suite, Matthew paused at the door, wondering if they shouldn't have gone back to her room. The suite was more of a joke than a place to bring a woman—especially a smart woman. But figuring that there was no help for it now, he unlocked the door and pushed it open. She stepped into the foyer, and her gaze swept over a room that was decorated entirely in various shades of red. From the sectional couch to the marble bar and leather barstools. From the picture frames and vases to the plush carpeting and textured walls. Even the Christmas tree in the corner was a deep burgundy red with bright cherry-red ornaments.

After only a second, she spoke, "Very feng shui."

He laughed. "I've heard The Heat Suite called many things, but never that."

"I took a college course on colors and their effect on moods." She moved down the steps and ran a hand along the bar. "Red increases energy, passion, and hunger."

"Well, it's working," he said as he closed the door. "Suddenly, I feel very hungry." He turned the lock. The click had her gaze snapping back to him, and it was easy to read the apprehension in her big brown eyes. "If you're worried I'm going to serve you up with fava beans and a nice Chianti," he teased, "why did you agree to come to my room?"

She smiled, and just that quickly, her face was transformed from average to well above. "You can't blame me. I feel like I just stepped into Dante's Inferno."

Matthew unlocked the dead bolt and moved down the steps, slipping his arms around her waist and pressing his lips to the spot behind her ear. "Worried about getting burned?"

Her words came out in a breathy puff. "Not if it feels like it did in the elevator."

He took a nip of her sweet skin. "I think we can improve on that." Releasing her, he took her hand and led her into the bedroom. The king-size, circular bed with its red satin sheets and dozens of throw pillows stopped her in her tracks. Or maybe it was the shiny brass pole that went from ceiling to floor.

"Holy smokes," she breathed.

"Relax." He stroked his thumb over the back of her hand. "We're not going to do anything that you don't want to do."

Her gaze was transfixed by the stripper pole as if she expected a fireman to come sliding down it at any moment. "And what if I want to try everything?"

His cock grew another inch, and if he didn't want to completely humiliate himself, he needed to slow things down. "How about a shower?"

"With you?"

He bit back his grin. "I was hoping with me, but if you'd rather take one—"

"No. I'd like to take one with you, but could I call my friend first? If I don't, she'll have the entire Las Vegas police department looking for me."

Matthew brushed a kiss over her lips. "The phone is on the nightstand." He had only taken two steps before she stopped him.

"Do you have any sexually transmitted diseases?"

The woman's mind moved so quickly that it was hard to keep up.

He turned back around. "No. Do you?"

She shook her head. "Are you married?"

"No."

"Fiancée?"

Hmm, interesting question.

"No," he said. "Now I have a question. What's your name?"

She shook her head. "No. No names. Let's just be two strangers who met in Vegas for one night of..."

"Mind-blowing sex." He didn't even wait for her mouth to close before he walked into the bathroom. Once there, he turned on the shower and stripped. As he pulled a condom out of his wallet and put it on a shelf in the shower stall, he called himself all kinds of crazy. He didn't do things like this. In fact, he had always been extremely selective about the women he took to bed. He didn't have a set timeline before sex, but he knew the woman's background thoroughly before he peeled off the first article of clothing. He knew nothing about this woman except that he wanted her. Wanted her like he had never wanted a woman before.

The soft click of high heels on marble drew his attention, and he turned to find her standing in the doorway. When she caught sight of him naked, her eyes widened and her pale flawless complexion turned the same color of the red tile. Still, she didn't look away. Instead, she studied his erection like a specimen slide beneath a microscope. It was this combination of innocence and lack of inhibition that excited and intrigued him. He reached for the zipper on her dress.

"So are you rich?" she asked as the dress pooled at her feet, revealing the black strapless bra and plain white underwear beneath. Matthew couldn't remember the last time he'd seen a woman in mismatched lingerie. Or a pair of panties that were bigger than a postage stamp. He liked those postage stamps, but, at the moment, he liked plain white cotton better. Especially on such an amazing body. "I can't imagine that The Heat Suite comes cheap," she said.

"Actually, my friend owns the hotel so he always gives it to me as a kind of a joke." He flicked open her bra, releasing a purseful of items and one hundred percent genuine breasts. They weren't as large as he had first thought—probably no more than a generous D-cup. It was the contrast between them and her petite body that had thrown him. On a taller woman, they would be noticeable but not eye-popping. On this woman, they stood out like sweet, ripe melons on the vine.

"And I guess I'm not the first woman you've brought here," she said.

"No." Damn, the honesty thing had gotten completely out of control.

Fortunately, the truth didn't stop her from slipping off her underwear to reveal a light brown patch of hair. Hair that hadn't been hot waxed to a skinny runway strip, a weird goatee, or complete nothingness.

He liked it.

A lot.

But before he could reach for her and show her how much, he noticed the beige bandage on the inside of her wrist.

"What's that?"

She followed his gaze, and she blushed hot red. Matthew felt just the opposite. His heart froze solid as his erection wilted. *Shit*. Well, that explained a lot. She wasn't intriguing, just crazy.

He reached for a towel, trying to keep his voice from betraying the anger he felt at his own stupidity. "Look, I think we should call it a night. I have an early flight in the—"

"That's it?" Her eyebrows lowered. "You're kicking me out because I slipped in the shower and got one stitch?"

He blinked. "One stitch?"

"Yes, and I probably didn't even need that, but Sidney refused to listen to me when I tried to tell her—"

Matthew tipped back his head and burst out laughing. It felt good. Damned good. He couldn't remember the last time he laughed so hard.

"Well, I'm glad you find it so amusing." She reached down to pick up her clothes.

That sobered him.

"Oh, no you don't." He dropped the towel and grabbed her around the waist, lifting her off her feet. He liked the fact that she didn't weigh more than a good-size law book and was much easier to read. "I'm sorry I laughed at you, but you've got to admit it's funny. Who gets one stitch?"

The knot eased out of her forehead as a smile tipped up her lips. She had a nice smile. Friendly and sincere. "A woman who is willing to appease her friend, even if it hurts like the dickens."

"Aww, poor baby." Matthew gave her a brief kiss before he opened the shower door and carried her inside. "Let's see if I can't make it up to you."

After setting her down, he turned off all the nozzles but one. He picked up the small bottle of body wash and lathered his hands before kneeling on one knee and lifting her foot. It was a dainty foot with pretty pink-painted toes that begged for a good sucking. Instead, he ran his fingers between each one before massaging the arch of her foot with his thumb. He repeated the process with her other foot, then washed his way up her trim calves and firm thighs. When his hands skated toward her hip bones, her hands tightened on his shoulders and her breath hitched. But remembering what happened when he'd kissed her breasts, he steered clear of the pretty patch of hair and instead caressed her sweet butt cheeks. This time, he didn't want her reaching orgasm without him. Once finished with her lower half, he stood and turned her toward the shower spray, massaging the tight cords of muscle along her shoulders.

For a woman who seemed so spontaneous, she had plenty of tension in her neck. He kneaded the knots until her head lolled back against his chest, and she offered up her ear to his lips. It hadn't taken him long to figure out that she was an ear girl. And just a few strokes of his tongue had her hips twitching and her breath coming out in irregular puffs. He sipped his way to her mouth and kissed her as he slid his hands over her breasts.

He skated over the slick, supple mounds, circling the large nipples before teasing the distended tips. She moaned, and the sound reverberated deep inside him, jarring his heart up against his rib cage. Her hands hooked around his neck as her hips did a sensual bump and grind against his thighs.

Then she pulled back from the kiss and reached for the bottle of body wash. There wasn't a lot of finesse to her strokes, but it didn't seem to make a difference. Skilled or unskilled, her soapy hands almost brought him to his knees. Unlike him, she didn't waste time on foot or shoulder massages. Instead, she went straight to the heart of things. She firmly gripped his erection, and his breath hissed out, and heat poured through his veins. Her gaze lifted and locked with his as she stroked and squeezed— squeezed and stroked—in a hurried, inexperienced way.

But there was nothing inexperienced about the way she made him react. He was on fire, each slide of her fist bringing him closer and closer to orgasm.

Deciding that it was time to adjourn to the bedroom, he stopped her sweet torture and turned all the nozzles back on so he could rinse off. Unfortunately, she wasn't willing to wait for her satisfaction. Positioning one of the lower nozzles, she leaned back against him and allowed the strong, pulsing jet to give her what he hadn't.

Her orgasm was long and loud. And the feel of her tight bottom as it undulated in ecstasy sapped the last of his self-control, and he only allowed her a second of recovering time before he spun her around and pressed her back against the shower wall. Gone was the relaxed, indifferent playboy, and in his place was a desire-driven man who wanted one thing.

Inside.

After slipping on the condom, he hooked her leg around his waist and entered her in one thrust. She was warm and wet and wonderfully tight. And it took an embarrassing ten strokes to reach climax. But it was one of the best he'd ever had. The intense orgasm gripped him and refused to let go until his knees gave out and he slipped down to the shower floor, pulling her along with him.

For a few moments, they sat in the swirling steam without moving. Then her head shifted on his shoulder, and he looked down into her upturned face. Her dark eyes stared back at him as water trickled down her flushed cheeks and over lips plumped from his kisses.

She smiled.

And suddenly, Matthew realized he *had* told a lie that night after all.

She *was* beautiful.

Chapter Five

A stripper pole?" Stretched out on her stomach with her chin in her hands, Ellie stared at the brass pole that ran from ceiling to floor.

"The idea came from a room at The Palms," her Vegas Lover said as he nibbled on her foot. "The Boom Boom Room."

She rolled her eyes. "Obviously, men read way too many Dr. Seuss books as children. The Heat Suite. The Boom Boom Room. What's next, The Fox Box? The Dildo Condo?"

"For a guy?"

She giggled and glanced over her shoulder at the man who sat back against the crushed velvet headboard and pile of red satin pillows. "I guess not. But women might like it."

He kissed the arch of her foot. "So you're a dildo girl?"

"No." She closed her eyes and savored the feel of his

warm lips on her sole. "I prefer vibrators." The words just popped out. It was weird how comfortable she felt with the man when she didn't even know his name. Maybe that was why. Anonymity led to candor.

"Really?" He sucked her pinkie toe into his mouth, and a tingle tiptoed up her spine.

"Really," she said rather breathlessly. "I have little doubt that the first dildo was thought up by a man not a woman."

His tongue slipped between her third and fourth toe. "And why would you think that?"

"Because sixty-eight percent of women don't reach orgasm during penetration. So why would we waste our time inventing something that doesn't work in the first place?"

Her foot plopped down to his chest. "Are you kidding?"

"No." She brushed her foot back and forth over the silky hair on his chest. "But that was only one survey. Actually, I think the number is probably higher." She slid a hand over the slick, cool satin of the sheet. Maybe when she got home, she'd buy herself a set. In red. Bright, sexy red.

"Higher?" He snorted. "Well, either I've only had sex with the other thirty percent or that's bullshit."

Rolling to her side, Ellie rested her head in one hand and looked back at him. He no longer looked all sated and happy. In fact, his body language said the exact opposite. His facial features were tight, and his jaw held more than a little tension. He was still drop-dead gorgeous.

Ellie smiled.

If someone had told her that she would be lying naked

on red satin sheets with a drop-dead gorgeous man in Vegas on New Year's, she would've had them come in for an evaluation.

"What's so funny?" he asked. "You don't think I can tell when a woman's reached orgasm?"

"Can you?"

"Of course I can."

"How?"

He jerked a pillow from behind his back and fluffed it with a rather violent punch. "Let's just say it comes with experience."

"Really? How experienced? More than twenty?"

His cocked eyebrow had her recalculating. With his looks, he could have a different woman every night if he wanted to. Given that he looked to be in his late twenties and there were three hundred and sixty-five days in a year, the number could be astronomical.

"So you're a sex addict," she stated.

"What?" Those green eyes widened, and he sat straight up, dumping her leg to the side.

"A sex addict," she said. "You know, someone who lacks the ability to control or postpone their sexual feelings and actions, often confusing their sexual needs with the need for intimacy."

The shocked look on his face was comical. The sexy mouth, which had brought her to climax more than once that night, hung open in disbelief.

"It's nothing to be ashamed of," she said. "Lots of men are sex addicts. My father included." She didn't know why she added that. "But recognizing that you have no control in this area is the first step to overcoming your problem."

His mouth snapped closed. "I am not a sex addict," he said between clenched teeth.

She shrugged. "If you say so."

"I say so." He almost growled the words.

She went back to smoothing out the sheet. "Just something to think about. And while you're at it, you might want to rethink the whole female-orgasm-penetration thing."

This time he did growl. "There's nothing to rethink. There's not a doubt in my mind that women have reached orgasm when I've been inside them." She lifted her brows, and he actually blushed. "Maybe not you, but plenty of others."

"By their *When Harry Met Sally* screams and pants, or do you have something a little more concrete?"

"Concrete? What the hell does that mean?"

She sent him her practiced, clinical stare. "It means, did you have any tangible evidence that they reached it."

He glared back at her. "You already know the answer to that."

"Exactly. Which means that there is no way to tell if a woman reached orgasm or not while you were inside her."

"So you think they were faking it?"

She shrugged, feeling very proud of herself for winning this particular battle. "Probably. Over eighty percent of the women polled say they've faked it at one time or another." She sent him the same smug smile he had worn not more than a moment ago. "Even with players like you."

Now he didn't look shocked as much as pissed. "What are you? Some kind of statistical sex computer?" He jumped up from the bed. "Wasn't it Mark Twain who said, 'Facts are stubborn things, but statistics are more pliable'? Which translates to—you don't know shit about what you're talking about." He turned and stomped off to the bathroom, tossing a last retort over his shoulder before he disappeared. "And your hair is ugly."

Ellie's hand flew to the short strands before she realized that his insult was just a ploy to distract her from the topic. It didn't take a therapist to figure out how mad he was and why. There was probably not a woman alive who had ever questioned his ability in bed.

Ellie wasn't, either. The man could write a book on what made women sizzle. But he was also a little too full of himself, and she found a certain amount of satisfaction in ruffling his perfect feathers. Besides, she'd only given him the facts. A lot of women didn't reach orgasm during penetration, and if he thought he was some kind of sexual guru who could topple that statistic, he needed a reality check. As for being a sex addict, well, she might've overstepped her bounds a little on that one. After all, just because he'd been with a lot of women, that didn't make him an addict. Her father was a true addict, jeopardizing family, career, and personal health for his addiction. This man could just be enjoying what life had handed him, the gift of melting women into butter with just a glance from those field-of-dreamy eyes.

At least, that's what he'd done to her.

Releasing a long sigh, Ellie rolled to her back and stretched her arms over her head. In the mirror above the bed, a satisfied woman looked back. It was an image she hadn't seen all that much in her life. And certainly not in

RING IN THE HOLIDAYS

43

the last few years. Suddenly, she realized that instead of
doing her an injustice, Riley had done her a favor. Something had been missing from their relationship. While
they had been compatible in many areas, he'd never made
her feel this satisfied. This happy.

She laughed and pulled one edge of the sheet over her
breasts, striking a pose like Marilyn Monroe's famous
Playboy centerfold. Monroe had posed on red sheets,
too, but that's where the physical resemblance ended.
Monroe had perky breasts and beautiful hair, while Ellie
had huge breasts and—she tipped her head to one side
and studied her reflection—ugly hair. At one time, she'd
thought the short haircut had gone with her personality,
neat and professional. But not now. Now she felt sexy and
daring.

Getting up from the bed, she moved over to the stripper pole. She knew what women did with the pole. She
just didn't know how to go about doing it. Maybe it was
like the rope in gym class. Maybe all you had to do was
grab on and hoist yourself up. It sounded like a good
idea, until she was wrapped around the pole with the bot-
toms of her feet scrambling for leverage. Panties probably would've been a good idea. The cold brass took her
breath away.

"What the hell are you doing?"

She glanced over her shoulder. Her Vegas Lover stood
in the doorway of the bathroom, tying the belt of a terry
towel robe. She should feel embarrassed, but she didn't. It
seemed nothing she did in front of this man was embarrassing. Which was just plain weird. Especially for a
newly initiated virgin.

"What does it look like I'm doing?" She inched higher. "I'm pole dancing."

He walked over, and for the first time that night, they were eye level. "You're not supposed to climb it."

"I'm trying to learn." She lost her footing and slipped down, but before her butt could hit the plush carpeting, he caught her and set her on her feet.

"The only thing you're going to learn is how painful thigh burns can be. It takes years of practice, sweetheart. You're not ready for the Pole-ympics just yet."

"How do you know? I've always been a fast learner."

"Maybe later." He handed her another robe. "But for now, I've got some questions for you."

"Questions?" She dropped the robe and stretched out on the bed. She was really starting to like this naked thing. "I thought we agreed no personal information."

"We did." He picked the robe back up. "These aren't personal. At least, not that kind of personal." When she continued to ignore him and stroke the slick satin sheets, he got angry again. "Damn it!" He tossed the robe over her. "Would you cover up, woman? I can't think clearly when you're naked. Which is exactly what happened to my brain cells a few minutes ago."

"You can't think when I'm naked? Really?" She inched the robe down until her breasts popped into view.

"Enough." He pulled her to a sitting position and proceeded to put the robe on her. It was a struggle. Of course, she wasn't giving him a whole lot of help. She felt too giddy over his comment. He might not like her hair, but he liked her body.

By the time he had the robe on and tied, he was slightly

out of breath. "Okay. I'm going to ask you some questions, and I want the truth."

Ellie didn't know where he was going with this, but she played along. "Cross my heart, hope to die, stick a needle in my eye."

A frown marred his forehead. "I'm being serious here."

She shrugged. "Fine. You want me to swear on a Bible?"

The frown disappeared. "As a matter of fact..." He took her hand and lifted it. "Do you swear to tell the truth, the whole truth, and nothing but the truth?"

She tried to keep a straight face. "I do."

He ran a hand through his hair as he started to pace. "So let's start at the beginning. Did you, or did you not, reach orgasm?"

"What?"

He stopped. "Orgasm. Don't tell me you forgot what we'd been talking about?"

Between the pole and his compliment about her body and the weird oath thing, she had. But she found it amusing that he hadn't. She smiled. "Oh, yeah, orgasms. And the fact that a majority of women fake them."

He frowned. "Just stick to yes or no answers, please. Did you reach orgasm?"

"Yes."

He released a long breath. "Good." He cleared his throat and went back to pacing, but with far less tension. "Did you reach orgasm four times?"

"Yes."

"Did you reach orgasm with me inside you?"

"No."

"Would you like to?"

She smiled. "Yes, but I don't—"

He sat down next to her and placed a finger on her lips. "Just yes or no answers please." When she nodded, his finger slid over her bottom lip, trailing a line of fire with it. "Do you swear to tell the truth about what feels good and what doesn't?"

The sincerity in those green eyes finally registered, and she realized that he wasn't kidding. And hadn't been kidding since he'd stepped from the bathroom. What she had viewed as sexy foreplay had been much more to him. He had been wounded by her careless words. And a person was only wounded by words when those words threatened the perception of self. Obviously, pleasuring women was important to him. Almost too important. It had become something he used to define his worth.

The therapist side of her wanted to jump up from the bed and grab the hotel notepad so she could write down her thoughts to all the questions she wanted to ask him. But the woman side of her was trapped by those green sparkling pools and wanted nothing more than to soothe his fears and insecurities.

She lifted a hand and caressed the length of his stubbled jaw. "I promise to tell the truth."

He turned his head and kissed the palm of her hand. "Especially if you don't like it?"

"Yes."

Her robe was untied and pulled from her body much easier than it had been put on, and he laid her back down on those cool satin sheets.

"So let's talk about penetration," he whispered against

her lips as his fingers wandered over her hot, growing-hotter-by-the-minute body. "Let's talk about deep, satisfying penetration."

But they didn't talk about it.

They had it.

Chapter Six

It took a while for Ellie to wake up. Her eyes fluttered open, taking in the pale light that sifted in through the open curtains, then fluttered closed again. If it hadn't been for all the aches and pains throbbing through her body, she probably would've gone back to sleep. But it was hard to sleep when everything hurt. And since she usually woke up feeling rested and refreshed, her mind struggled to figure out her present dilemma. It didn't take long.

Her eyes flashed open.

A woman looked back at her from the mirrored ceiling. A woman with wild hair and even wilder eyes. A woman with kiss-swollen lips and razor-burned bare breasts. Or not entirely bare. One breast was partially covered by a man's hand. A hand with long fingers and a hot palm that caused her nipple to harden without moving an inch.

Her eyes slammed shut as her breath rushed in and out of her chest. Good Lord, what had she done? The answer was swift and brief. She'd had a night of debauchery with a complete stranger.

Ellie groaned, and his hand tightened, causing her heart to almost jump out of her throat. If she thought she was freaked out now, it would be nothing compared to how she would feel if she had to come face-to-face with the man who had contributed to her debauchery.

She held her breath and peeked up at the mirror. Thankfully, nothing moved in the reflection except a slight twitching of her eye. Carefully, she inched away from the hand. It slipped over her shoulder and softly thumped down to the mattress, but not before trailing a line of fire in its wake. The loss of heat was immediate, and she fought the urge to replace the hand on her breast.

Instead, she sat up, cringing when her feet hit the floor.

Ellie ached in almost every part of her body. And it all had to do with the man sprawled out next to her. Or maybe not all. The headache could be accredited to the Cape Cods, and the sore thigh muscles to the stripper pole she had tried to master but failed. The only thing her Vegas Lover was responsible for was the soreness between her legs, the whisker-burn on her neck and breasts, and the dull ache in the region of her chest. It was the ache that bothered her the most. The ache that prompted her to get the heck out of there before it became worse. But as she stood, she couldn't help taking one last look.

He didn't look quite as perfect in the light of day. He had bad bed head, a crease along one cheek, and his mouth was open against the pillow in a drooling kind of way. But his body . . . his body was as close to heaven as a mere mortal could get.

One leg was bent while the other stretched across half the bed, a large pale-soled foot dangling off the edge of the round mattress. His legs weren't overly muscular, just long and lean with a sprinkling of black hair. Much like the arm that reached out to the spot Ellie had so recently vacated. His back was smooth and rippled with muscles. His hips slim with zero fat. And his butt . . .

Ellie cringed.

It had happened by accident. Or so she tried to convince herself. One minute, she was teasingly pointing out his erogenous zones with the pen she'd found on the nightstand, and the next, she had tattooed him. He hadn't commented on it, probably because she was touching one of his main erogenous zones the entire time she'd been writing. That, and the fact that she'd placed the small heart in an inconspicuous spot under one cheek. Looking at it now, it didn't look so inconspicuous. The ink tattoo sort of glared back at her, confronting her with the reason she'd put it there in the first place.

Regardless of how cavalier she'd acted, she wanted him to remember her. Not just some nameless woman, but her. And did she really believe that it would make a difference? With a little soap and water, it would easily be erased, along with the entire night.

Pulling her gaze away, she went in search of her clothes. Once she was dressed, she started to feel more like herself. And by the time she was heading for the door, she was able to rationalize the confusing emotions that swirled around inside her.

Last night hadn't been anything special. It was merely Newton's third law—to every action there is an equal and opposite reaction. Last night had merely been her reaction to the news of Riley's infidelities. No more and no less.

Fortunately, there would be no dire consequences from her lapse of good judgment. Once she walked out the door, she would pretend it never happened. Pretend she'd never met a man with seductive green eyes. Never kissed a pair of sweet, firm lips. Never melted into strong, muscled arms. Once she walked out the door, she would go back to being Sweet Virginal Ellie Simpson from Kansas.

Her fingers froze on the cold metal of the door handle as the feelings she had tried so hard to ignore swelled up like a huge tidal wave, completely obliterating every logical thought in her brain. With tears blurring her vision, she glanced back at the man stretched out on the bed.

Except she didn't want to go back to being Sweet Virginal Ellie Simpson.

She wanted him.

Matthew woke up hungry. No, more like famished. Except it wasn't his stomach begging for substance, but his rock-hard penis drilling a hole in the mattress. He reached out across the sheets to grab what he was hungering for. Unfortunately, his hand came up empty. He opened one eyelid and stared at the vacant side of the bed, then rolled onto his back and looked around the room.

When he didn't see her, he stretched his arms over his head and listened for the shower, picturing her petite, but very shapely, body slick with soap. He grew harder. Swinging his legs over the side of the bed, he got up and made his way to the bathroom. When the shower turned up empty, he knocked three times on the door to the toilet before opening it.

No shapely body.

On the way through the bedroom, he glanced at the stripper pole. Who would've thought that an inept amateur would turn him on more than a seasoned professional? Obviously inexperience had its rewards. He'd sure felt rewarded watching her awkwardly slide around on the pole.

But he wasn't rewarded when he arrived in the front room of the suite. There was no cute little ass waiting for him on the red couch, no sweet breasts resting on the granite bar. His disappointment surprised him. As well as the hurt that quickly turned to anger. Stomping around the suite, he looked in every possible nook and cranny.

After jerking open the mini-fridge and examining the bottles of water and beer as if she might be hiding there, he realized his state of agitation. What the hell was the matter with him, anyway? He wasn't some green kid who'd just lost his virginity and confused sexual desire with love. He was Matthew McPherson, an experienced man who had hundreds of women at his beck and call.

Maybe that was it? He'd beckoned, but she didn't answer. And that rubbed him wrong. He was the one who set the time limit on one-nighters. In fact, he usually didn't invite women to his place. He usually went to theirs and slipped out sometime during the night or, at least, before the sun came up. He'd learned early on that the sun had a sobering effect on women. It changed them from sexually uninhibited creatures of the night to somber, introspective females of the light who wanted nothing more than to discuss their deepest feelings over croissants and cappuccino. Which in turn made them start thinking about permanent relationships—the feelings, not the croissants and cappuccino. Although Matthew was convinced that those food items had something to do with it. If a man could avoid the morning after, it made things a lot easier.

So what was his problem?

Instead of standing nude in an empty suite staring angrily at bottles of water and beer, he should be thanking his lucky stars that she was gone. She had done him a huge favor. Now there would be no awkward moments or uncomfortable good-byes. In fact, she'd given him exactly what every guy dreamed about: no-strings-attached sex.

He slammed the refrigerator door, then jerked up the phone that sat on the bar. He dialed the front desk, but replaced the receiver when it started to ring. What was he going to ask them? He didn't have a name, a room number, or any other information. All he had was a description. And, somehow, he didn't think the front desk would be able to locate her with just that.

He should've checked out her driver's license when he'd noticed it lying on the floor during a bathroom break. Instead, he'd ignored it out of some kind of misplaced integrity. Now he was shit out of luck.

Out the window, the Vegas sun rose high enough to reflect off the hotels that lined The Strip. His hard-on was gone. Unfortunately, the hunger wasn't. And the thing that really pissed him off was that it wasn't just the sex he was hungering for. He wanted to look at her. Laugh with her. Discuss her crazy views on sex.

Hell, he even wanted to talk about her feelings over croissants and cappuccino!

With a frustrated groan, he headed for the bathroom.

This was all Mitch's fault. It was all the honesty bullshit last night that had done him in. Truth was a bad bedfellow. It screwed with a guy's emotions. Dicked up their common sense. When a man stopped telling lies to women, they became friends. And friendship and sex just didn't mix.

At least, not in Matthew's book.

What he needed was a long hot shower and room service with no croissants and no cappuccino. Well, maybe coffee. And he'd have steak and eggs and pancakes. Manly food.

A loud knock caused his hand to freeze on the handle of the shower door. All his anger dissolved beneath a feeling that could only be described as elation. Without a thought to his undressed state, he turned and strode through the bedroom to the door.

Dumbass, he thought. Obviously, she had left to let her friend know she hadn't been served up with fava beans and Chianti. But his smile wilted when he jerked open the door and found Tubs standing there with a questioning look on his face.

"So?"

Disappointment left Matthew speechless and surly again. He turned and walked back to the bathroom.

Tubs followed him. "We were right, weren't we? All you had to do was ask her. So are they real or fake?" When Matthew ignored him and turned on the shower, he laughed. "They were real, weren't they? I knew it. That's why you're so pissed. Man, Mattie, you're losing your mojo."

Without a word, Matthew stepped into the shower and jerked up the bottle of body wash. Just that quickly, the memory of her hands running over his body flooded his mind, and he set the bottle back down on the shelf and turned up the cold. He let the frigid water pound him for a few seconds before he shut it off and stepped from the shower.

"I guess she stayed the night," Tubs said from behind him. "Was she good?"

Good didn't come close to describing it.

Matthew remained mute and reached for the robe that hung from the hook, realizing too late that it was the same one she had worn. He paused and stared at the soft, white terry cloth.

"What's up with you, Mattie?" Tubs asked. "Did this Ellie broad screw you over?"

It took a moment for the words to sink in. Slowly, Matthew turned and stared at his friend. "Ellie? How did you know her name was Ellie?"

Tubs looked confused for a few seconds before he took Matthew by the shoulders and turned him so his back was facing the large mirror over the double sinks.

Before he could ask Tubs what he was doing, a flash of red caught his attention. Matthew froze and stared down at the bright red heart on his left butt cheek. A heart with one word written inside.

Ellie.

Damn, the woman had branded him.

Chapter Seven

So, Dr. Simpson, let me see if I understand correctly. You're saying that celibacy is crucial for a happy, healthy relationship?"

Ellie cleared her throat, something she felt like she'd done at least a hundred times in the last two minutes of the interview. She could feel sweat collecting beneath her feathery bangs. And her armpits had long since given up the battle. So much for her deodorant's claims of keeping her dry in pressure situations. Of course, the scientists who developed the formula probably never considered being interviewed on national television as something the normal population would need to worry about.

Ellie wished she didn't have to.

"No, I'm not saying that at all," she said. "I'm just saying that—"

Another one of the four women who sat on the couch

leaned in. "But your book, *Virginal Love*, portrays sex as an evil that lurks around every corner waiting to distort genuine feelings."

"Yes, well"—she cleared her throat again—"when taken out of context, it could sound that way. But the point I'm trying to make is—"

"Sex is bad?" the youngest woman asked with a bright smile on her wide-eyed face.

"No. Sex is fine."

"Just fine, Dr. Simpson?" The brunette raised her brows at the cameras. "Obviously, you haven't been with the right man."

The live audience laughed.

Ellie could feel her face heat up as the redhead closest to her took her hand and squeezed it.

"Don't worry, honey. There's nothing wrong with still being a virgin. We've all been there." She paused for a moment and looked at the audience. "Some of us just have trouble remembering when."

After more laughter, a guy who stood at the side of a camera signaled to wrap things up. The older woman who had done most of the interview turned to Ellie. "Thank you for being on our show today and"—she lifted Ellie's book off the coffee table and held it up to one of the cameras—"everyone in the audience will receive a free copy of *Virginal Love: Separating Lust from True Emotions*."

There was a mad round of applause, and then a rush of people surrounded the group of women, touching up makeup and hair, adjusting microphones, and refilling coffee cups while a young woman came over and quickly ushered Ellie off the stage.

"That was great, Dr. Simpson." She led Ellie down a long hallway to a dressing room. "So you really think people shouldn't have sex until they're married?"

Finally, Ellie thought. *I get to answer a question.*

"No. I'm not trying to put a restriction on when a person should have sex. What I tried to point out in my book is that sex and love are separate things and should be treated that way. Abstinence is a way to create that separation. To see whether or not you're compatible outside the bedroom."

"So you don't condone one-night stands?"

She cleared her throat again. "No."

It wasn't a lie. She didn't condone them. The one she'd had still haunted her, which confirmed her belief that sex completely screwed with your emotions.

"But what if my boyfriend and I have already had sex?" the young woman asked. "You think I should cut him off?" She stood at the door of the dressing room, a clipboard clutched against her cardigan and a black headset hooked over one ear. She looked to be no more than nineteen, too young to be worried about serious relationships.

Ellie smiled. "I think you should read my book. It outlines the benefits of abstinence and how you can tell if your relationship is sexually driven or emotionally driven."

The young girl nodded thoughtfully before she turned and headed back down the hallway.

"Hey, you were great!" Sidney exploded out of the dressing room with a half-eaten muffin in her hand.

"Thanks." Ellie brushed by her on the way to retrieve her purse and coat. "But how could you tell? All I did was clear my throat and answer in half sentences."

"Pretty much." Sidney set the muffin down long enough to grab her coat off a hook. "But you looked great doing it. And you have me to thank for making that hair appointment for you when we were in LA. Your hair looks amazing—as does your wardrobe." She scrutinized Ellie's dress. "Although your fetish for red is getting old."

Ellie pulled on her coat before she wrapped her red scarf around her neck. She *had* bought a lot of red lately—for reasons she didn't want to examine too closely. "So what's next?"

"I thought we'd go shopping until your two-o'clock book signing." Sidney hooked her purse on her shoulder. "I was talking with one of the makeup artists, and she said that some of the street vendors have great knockoffs. So I canceled the limo back to the hotel and figured we'd walk around so I can get some of my Christmas shopping done."

"Christmas is still months away. Besides, I thought we did your Christmas shopping in Chicago?"

"That was for my friends and family," Sidney said as they moved down the hallway. "This is for me."

Ellie laughed and hooked her arm through Sidney's. If it hadn't been for her, Ellie wouldn't have made it through the last nine months after Vegas. She wouldn't have even made it through the first five hours after Vegas. It was Sidney who prevented her emotional breakdown when the airplane backed away from the Vegas Jetway. Sidney who convinced her that her attachment to the man had nothing to do with love and everything to do with her outdated beliefs in saving herself for the right one. Sidney who finally took her cell phone away when Ellie kept calling the hotel and harassing the front desk for the name of her Vegas Lover.

Thankfully, as time went on, Ellie's sanity returned.

She still thought about her night in Vegas, but just not every second of every day. And the fantasies that started out with him being upset to find her gone faded beneath more realistic images of him being in The Heat Suite with a multitude of women who were much more agile and experienced than the inept virgin he'd bopped on New Year's. Her crazy emotional reactions were just brought on by deeply embedded societal norms that suggest only a slut would go to bed with a man she hardly knew. Which only further supported her theories in her book.

It was still hard to believe that her dissertation had gotten published. Long before Vegas, she had signed a contract with the small publishing house her professor had recommended. She just didn't think her book would hit the *New York Times* bestseller's list only a few months after its release. Or that her theory would be discussed at book clubs and coffee shops around the country. Ellie was famous. Not movie star famous, but famous enough to go on a book-signing tour. Famous enough to hire her best friend as her assistant. Famous enough to be interviewed on national television. Famous enough to be too busy to think about him.

Except at night, when it was just her and her vibrator.

For the next couple hours, she and Sidney shopped the stores and vendors that lined Times Square. They bought souvenir t-shirts, snow globes, and a spoon for Ellie's collection. They even stumbled upon a man who gave them directions to a shop that sold knockoff purses. Since it was illegal, Ellie refused to go inside, but that didn't stop Sidney. She came out with a big shopping bag and an even bigger smile.

"You're going to love what I got you for Christmas," she said as she took Ellie's arm and steered her through the mob of tourists and New Yorkers. "Now let's grab some coffee."

Ellie sent her an exasperated look. "I thought you drank three cups back at the studio?"

"I did, but I can't help it if I've become addicted." She pointed to a coffee shop on one corner. "Call it jet lag."

Ellie sympathized. Ten cities in a little over two weeks had given them both a bad case of jet lag. Especially when they'd started in LA and ended with New York. She didn't think she would ever get back on a good sleep schedule.

Once inside the coffee shop, Ellie looked around for a table while Sidney ordered. Two men vacated a tiny table by the window, and she quickly slipped around them and took a chair. She jerked a napkin out of the holder and wiped the damp rings off the top, then watched as Sidney flirted with the young man behind the counter.

Ellie envied her friend. Being comfortable around men came so easily to Sidney. Of course, Sidney loved men while Ellie just tolerated them. No, *tolerate* was too gentle a term. Since Riley, she was barely able to have a normal conversation with a man without becoming hostile and bitter. She knew it was wrong, not all men were cheating jerks, but it was hard to trust them when everyone she'd ever gotten close to had betrayed her.

Everyone, except her Vegas Lover.

He was the only male who had ever been totally honest

with her, not once pretending to be anything but what he was—a player out for a good time. He had never professed undying love or plans for the future. All he wanted was one night of raunchy sex.

And she had more than given him that.

"I got you Chai." Sidney slipped two cups onto the table.

"Thanks," Ellie said, not at all surprised Sidney had gotten her exactly what she wanted. It was the reason she had convinced Sidney to become her assistant. Sidney always seemed to know what she needed, even when Ellie didn't. Whether it was buying Chai, a trip to Vegas, or escorting her on a book signing tour, Sidney never let her down.

"So I guess this is as good a time as any to ask you for a raise," Sidney said.

Ellie laughed. "You've only worked for me for the last two months."

"Oh, yeah. I guess I'll wait until our six-month anniversary." An attractive man in a business suit walked by their table, and Sidney's eyes followed him. "Although you should give me a raise just because of the damage you've done to my sex life."

Ellie tried to take a sip of tea, but it was too hot. So she just held it and let it warm her hands. "What about the surfer dude you met at the mall in LA?"

Sidney shrugged. "When he found out I was with you, he dumped me flat. It seems that men hate your guts." Ellie cringed as she continued. "They think The Virgin Queen is the number one reason they're not getting any."

"The Virgin Queen?"

"That's what everyone's calling you."

Ellie glanced around to see if anyone was listening before whispering, "But I'm not a virgin."

"I know. But the rest of the world doesn't. Especially after reading your book."

"But why would it cause them to think that?"

Sidney looked at her as if she'd lost her mind. "Maybe because you're promoting abstinence."

Ellie's eyes narrowed. "You've read my book and should know that abstinence is just one path to achieving an emotionally driven relationship."

Sidney shrugged. "True, but men don't see it that way. Thank God most men don't watch daytime television or spend a lot of time reading self-help books, so they don't know what you look like. Therefore, it shouldn't be too hard to get you laid again. We'll just lie about what you do for a living." Ellie started to speak, but Sidney cut her off. "And don't give me that abstinence crap. You can use it to sell books, but no one actually believes going without sex is good for anyone. Look how screwed up it's made you."

"I'm not screwed up."

"Everyone is screwed up, Elle. But most people are willing to admit it. You're just a perfectionist who finds it hard to admit you're wrong. Even when the facts are staring you straight in the face."

"What facts?"

"The fact that you loved getting your brains screwed out in Vegas."

"I didn't get my brains screwed out!" The couple next to them looked over, and Ellie gave them a weak smile.

"One time or fifty," Sidney said, "you loved it and you want more."   •

Ellie kept her voice low. "I do not want more."

"Of course you do. Everyone does. Especially if the sex is good. And with the way you spend your days daydreaming, it must've been phenomenal." She took a deep drink of her coffee. "But that was then and this is now. It's time to quit dreaming and step back into reality. A reality filled with guys who will be just as good, if not better."

It seemed doubtful. No one could be that good. And definitely not better.

"I am over it." Ellie snapped off the lid of her Chai and blew on the dark tea, the spicy steam warming her cheeks. "I'm just not going to rush out and find another bed partner. At least, not when I have a book to promote."

"The book tour is almost over, Elle. Besides, that's why we hired a publicist. You have nothing but free time all through the holidays."

"I wouldn't call it free. Not when my editor keeps dropping hints about a new book, and when I need to find a place to live. And not when my holidays will be spent attending functions with grumbling relatives who can't understand why I didn't mention them in the acknowledgments."

Sidney laughed. "Fine. But I think you'll still have time to stumble into some guy's bed. It only took you a few hours in Vegas."

"We don't live in Vegas." *Thank God.*

"No, we live in a small town with few opportunities." Sidney cradled her cup in her hands and looked out at the busy street. "What you need is a bigger playing field. A field with more men and less gossip. Maybe we should move here."

"No," Ellie said. "All these tall buildings freak me out."

Sidney arched her brows. "It's called claustrophobia, Elle."

"I'm not claustrophobic. I just don't like to be crowded."

"Right." Sidney rolled her eyes. "Which is why you start sweating in elevators."

She did sweat in elevators. All except one. But that was an avenue she refused to go down.

"Okay, so you don't like New York," Sidney continued. "What about LA?"

"Too smoggy."

"Chicago?"

"Too windy."

"Phoenix?"

"Too hot."

"Denver?"

Ellie stopped with her cup inches from her mouth. "Denver was nice."

Chapter Eight

"Mattie, are you listening to me?"

Matthew pulled his gaze away from the computer screen and looked at his sister Cassie, who sat in a chair across from his desk. In the black-and-white maternity shirt, she looked a little like the main attraction at Sea World. The woman had been pregnant three times in the last five years, and with each pregnancy, she'd gotten bigger and bigger. At the rate she was going, if she had another kid, she would be the size of a small motor home. "Yes, I'm listening," he lied.

Cassie tipped her head to the side. "So what did I say?"

"You were talking about renting out your condo."

Her green eyes narrowed with annoyance. "I was talking about that fifteen minutes ago. Just now I was asking you if you thought Case was a good name for the baby."

"No. We already have a nephew named Chase. And

your son is named Jace. If you have another kid, what are you going to name them? Ace?"

"There might not be a next one," she muttered, before going completely off subject. "Do you think James's new clerical assistant is pretty?"

"James got a new assistant?" He went back to scanning the legal document one of their contractors had sent over.

"Where have you been, Mattie? Sierra went off to med school so he hired Celia who has been working here for three months."

"Oh, yeah, Celia." He kept reading. "I guess she's pretty enough. Why? Don't tell me you want me to fix her up with Patrick. Wheezie has already been on me about getting him dates. And believe me, Patrick isn't going for it."

"I wasn't thinking about hooking Patrick up with Celia." She paused. "I'm worried about James hooking up with her."

Matthew stopped reading and looked at his sister's sad-sack face. "James? Are you kidding?" He glanced down at her stomach. "I think James has been much too busy to hook up with anyone."

Cassie leaned forward, and the back legs of the chair lifted a good inch off the floor. "But that's just it. He hasn't been too busy—at least, not with me. He's been working late, and when he does get home, all he wants to do is sleep. Even if I'm waiting for him in bed stark-raving naked!"

Matthew held up his hands. "T.M.I., Cass!"

"Fine." She flopped back in the seat. "I just figured that if anyone knew what evil lurks in the hearts of men, it would be my playboy brother." A frown wrinkled her forehead. "Although, lately, you haven't been your normal, evil, playboy self. What happened? Did you finally wear yourself out?"

It was a good question, and the only logical explanation for his pitiful social life the last eleven months. Well, maybe not the only logical explanation. There was another one. One he didn't want to examine too closely. One that involved a night in Vegas and a certain petite blonde with extremely sensitive breasts.

Ellie.

Not that Ellie was her name. After getting the hotel guest list from his friend, Matthew had spent countless hours looking for an Ellie, Gabriella, Eleanor, or any other name that could use Ellie as a nickname. He hadn't found a one. Which really made him angry. Why would a woman write a bogus name on his ass? That was just plain sick.

"Mattie?"

He brought his attention back to his sister. But this time he remembered what they were discussing. "No, I do not think that James has evil lurking in his heart for his secretary. For reasons I can't comprehend, it's easy to see that his heart belongs to you."

"Aww, that's so sweet." She rested her elbows on the desk. He hoped the glass could withstand the stress. "That statement almost makes me feel guilty for letting it slip to Mom that you were experiencing a little dry spell."

Matthew sat straight up. "Tell me you're kidding."

She smiled sweetly—too sweetly. "I'm kidding."

"Cass, you're dead."

She studied her fingernails. "Tsk, tsk, little brother. You mean to tell me that you'd harm your pregnant sister? Besides, this is just payback for short-sheeting my bed, switching out my toothpaste for Preparation H, and all the other stunts you pulled on me when we were little."

He struggled for a reply, but all he could manage was a simple groan. Since Matthew had always had his fair share of women, the matchmaking females in the family left him alone. But if Cassie changed their minds, there was no telling what lengths they would go to.

Unless he quickly did some damage control.

He jerked up the phone receiver and rammed it at Cassie. "Call her and tell her you were wrong. Tell her... I'm having lunch with Stella."

Cassie didn't reach for the phone. "Are you having lunch with Stella?"

"No, but that's what you're going to tell her."

"Uh-uh."

He shook the phone at her. "Damn it, Cass."

"Watch your language, baby brother." She caressed her huge belly. "You know I don't like cussing in front of my children."

He would've exposed his nephew to even more foul language if a thought hadn't struck him. His smile was as sly as hers. "You either call her and tell her I'm dating Stella or I'll tell her all about the escorts you used to hire."

Cassie eyes widened. "You know I only did that to escape her matchmaking. And I never had sex with any of them."

"Never?"

Her face turned a bright red. "Fine, I'll call—"

As bad luck would have it, before she could finish, his mother walked in. Dressed in a beige pantsuit and designer heels, Mary Katherine McPherson fit the image of a multi-millionaire's wife to a tee. But beneath the styled hair and manicured nails was a woman who had no problems handling her hot-tempered Scottish husband and five hardheaded kids.

"You'll call whom, dear? And, Matthew, why are you glaring at your sister?" She gave Cassie a big hug and stroked a hand over her protruding stomach. "Is something going on?"

Since he couldn't bring up Stella now without his mother getting suspicious, Matthew lied like a rug. "Nothing's going on, Mom." He stepped around the desk and kissed her cheek. "We were just going to call you to see if you could go to lunch."

"Oh, I can't." She looked so disappointed that Matthew felt guilty for the lie. "Aunt Louise wants me to go Christmas shopping with her." She took the chair next to Cassie's.

"Is Wheezie my Secret Santa?" Cassie asked. "Because if she is, you need to steer her toward the power tools. James flat out refuses to let me buy any more, and there is a drill I have my heart set on."

"Wheezie is shopping for the children in the family, not the adults, Cassandra," his mother stated. "The adult Secret Santa exchange is not about material things. It's about doing something special for the person whose name you drew—something that they won't or can't do for themselves."

Matthew shot his sister a smile. "Like tying their shoes."

"Don't be mean to your sister, Matthew." His mother pinned him with her dark Italian eyes. "And I didn't come here to talk about the gift exchange. I came to talk to you about the Holiday Art Benefit next Saturday for the domestic violence women's shelter. I'd like you to be there, Matthew. In fact, there's someone I want you to meet."

Matthew's eyes narrowed on his sister who suddenly seemed preoccupied with pressing down her protruding belly button. "I'm sorry, Mom," he said, "but I have a date with Stella."

"Stella Connors?" When he nodded, his mother looked confused. "But didn't she just get engaged?"

Great. That's what he got for not keeping up with the dating world.

"Umm, we're just going as friends."

His mother shook her head. "You'll do no such thing. No man wants his future wife being friends with you." She got to her feet. "The benefit starts at seven, so try not to be late. Shirley Wilshire is always punctual so I'm assuming her niece will be, too."

Matthew groaned. "Pamela Wilshire?"

His mother lit up. "Oh, good. You already know her. That makes everything so much easier. I realize she's been divorced three times and is a little older than you, but I think an experienced woman is just what you need."

A snorted laugh came from Cassie, and when Matthew glared at her, she unsuccessfully turned it into a cough. "Excuse me," she said. "The baby must be giving me a little congestion."

His mother nodded at Cassie's feet. "Along with swelling ankles. You need to go home and put your feet up,

Cassandra. And while you're there, you might want to look this over." She rifled through her leather designer bag and pulled out a hardback book. From his vantage point, all Matthew could see were the reviews on the back cover. But the title must've been a doozy because it got his sister to stop looking at her swollen ankles and stare at the book in shock.

"What in the world am I going to do with this?" she asked when their mother handed her the book.

"Read it." She glanced down at Cassie's stomach. "I think you and James could use a breather." Her eyes settled on Matthew. "Don't forget Sunday dinner." Then in a subtle waft of expensive perfume, she walked out of the office.

"Great." Cassie stared at the book. "I thought marriage would end my family's meddling. Obviously, I was wrong."

"Meddling?" Matthew said. "Your meddling has gotten me a date with Pamela Wilshire who everyone knows won't be happy until she finds a man to spoil her just like her daddy."

Cassie held up a hand. "Don't look at me. I was just kidding around with you. I really didn't mention anything to Mom. She had to have heard it from someone else." She tossed the book down on Matthew's desk. "So are you my Secret Santa?"

He sat back down. "No. I drew Mom."

"Well, that should be easy. She's been wanting one of her boys to volunteer at the women's shelter."

He shook his head. "One time was enough. The way those women looked at me made me feel guilty as hell for being a man." He leaned back in the chair and stared up at the ceiling. "I wish I'd gotten Wheezie. If I pawned Pamela off on Patrick, I could've killed two birds with one stone."

"I wouldn't do that if I was you. If you think one night with Pamela is bad, it will be nothing compared to the holidays with Mom's anger. So I suggest sucking it up and living with it. Besides, Benjamin Franklin loved older women. He said they were extremely appreciative in bed." She waddled to the door. "I'm going home to soak my feet."

"Hey," he called after her, "don't forget your afternoon read."

Cassie turned. "Considering my fears about James's new assistant, the last thing I need is a book on abstinence written by a virgin."

Matthew glanced at the cover and laughed. "Maybe you better rethink that. At the rate you're going, you'll become the next octo-mom within six years."

She sent him a saucy smile. "If that happens, I promise to name my eighth after my youngest brother." She disappeared out the door.

Still smiling, Matthew picked up the book.

Virgin Love. He shook his head. More like Loser Love. Because who but a loser would go without sex for . . .

Eleven months.

Damn, he was a loser and he didn't even have the love to go along with it. Suddenly, a date with Pamela Wilshire didn't seem like such a bad idea. Maybe his mom and Cassie were right. Maybe what he needed after his night in Vegas was an older woman. Someone more appreciative of his skill. Or, at least, someone who had enough manners to stay around long enough to say thank you.

He looked down at the author's name. Dr. E. B. Simpson. He wondered what the E. B. stood for. More than likely Extraordinarily Boring. Only a boring guy who couldn't get any sex would think it was a good idea to go without it. The doctor was probably some nerd who spent all his time at a computer inputting data from his lame surveys.

Curious as to what the geek looked like, he flipped open the back cover. The small, color photo had him blinking and leaning closer. His heart thwacked against his ribs as all the memories he'd been trying to repress came flooding back.

Dr. E. B. Simpson wasn't a studious-looking man with thinning hair and wire glasses. In fact, he was a she. And not just any she, but a she with ugly hair and rich chocolate eyes that could stare straight into a man's soul.

Once the initial shock wore off, a slow smile slipped across Matthew's face.

"Virgin, my ass."

Chapter Nine

You have an appointment with the Realtor this afternoon." Sidney slid another book in front of Ellie.

"How is it that you found a place so fast and it's taking me forever?" Ellie asked as she watched the frazzled-looking woman who was next in line try to maneuver the huge stroller up to the signing table. The two children inside weren't making it any easier. The toddler tossed his sippy cup over the side and reached out to knock over a display of books, while his baby sister screamed bloody murder.

"Because I'm not as picky as you are," Sidney replied.

It was true. Sidney wasn't picky. With men or condos. She found a small starter home in a day while Ellie couldn't make up her mind after two weeks of looking. A house was too large for just one person, and the town houses and condos she'd seen so far had no personality.

The frazzled-looking woman finally reached the table

after sticking a pacifier in the screaming baby's mouth, haphazardly flipping the books back on the shelf, and handing the sippy cup back to the toddler who promptly took one sip and tossed it overboard again. But this time, the woman chose to ignore it.

"So you're Dr. Simpson?"

Ellie smiled and held out her hand. "It's nice to meet you."

The woman gave it a quick, sticky shake. "You look younger than the picture on the cover of your book."

It wasn't the first time Ellie had heard this. At first, she had felt defensive; now she only smiled and treated the statement as a compliment.

"Thank you." She lifted her pen. "Whom did you want me to make this out to?"

"Actually, I didn't come here for an autograph." The woman leaned in and whispered, "I have a question about Chapter Thirteen."

"Bringing Excitement Back into the Marriage Bed?"

The woman nodded. "But more specifically Step One—abstaining two weeks from sex."

"Ahh." Ellie smiled. "That can be a difficult task to undertake."

The woman rolled her eyes. "Especially when you're married to a man who has sex on the brain. A man who won't let one night go by without making me feel like the worst wife in the world because I don't want sex anymore." A look came over her pretty features that could only be described as pure frustration. "I mean, I like sex, too—at least, I used to before…" She glanced guiltily back at the stroller. "And I'm not complaining about my kids, mind you. I love them. It's just that after I've fed them, cleaned up after them, bathed them, read to them, and gotten them to sleep, I can barely stumble to bed, let alone set it on fire. And I don't think it's fair for my husband to expect me to be all excited about riding the wild bronco when he never goes out of his way to help me with the house or the kids. All I'm asking for is six hours of uninterrupted sleep a night. A few words of appreciation. And an occasional hug that doesn't lead to an invasive body search. Is that too much to ask for?"

"Of course not," Ellie said sympathetically. It seemed, as more and more people read her book, more and more book signings became therapy sessions. She really didn't mind, but Sidney did and had no problem saying so.

"Dr. Simpson would love to answer all of your questions." She pulled one of the new business cards she'd just had printed up off the table and handed it to the woman. "And you happen to be in luck because Dr. Simpson has started up a practice right here in Denver." She pointed at the card. "Just call this number, and we'll set you up with an appointment within the week."

The woman barely glanced at the card before she looked at Ellie for confirmation.

Ellie knew the purpose behind the book signing was to drum up business, but she couldn't help taking pity on the poor, overworked mother. "I'd love to meet with both you and your husband, but I think the first thing you need to do is sit down with him and have a talk. Let him know just how tired you are and how much you could use his help. Then allow him to state his feelings. A lot of men use sex as a stress reliever, so it's possible that your husband is feeling as stressed about work and the children as you are. Maybe all you need to do is find some middle ground—he helps with the kids at night and you work on being more sexual. Although I do think a few weeks off from sex would help you both put things into perspective. But that doesn't mean you get to fall into bed and not acknowledge your spouse. A warm kiss before you go to sleep can go a long way in mending fences."

At that point, the baby started to scream again as the toddler attempted to climb out of the stroller, possibly to retrieve the sippy cup so he could throw it. The mother gave Ellie one last weary look before pocketing the business card, grabbing up the sippy cup, restrapping the toddler, and popping the pacifier back in the baby's mouth.

As she rolled the stroller out of sight, Sidney leaned over and whispered, "Remind me not to have children."

For the next hour, Ellie continued to sign books, trying her best to briefly answer people's questions while Sidney continued to hand out cards. It had been Sidney's idea to promote her practice by having a book signing, and it seemed to be working. With any luck, she would start therapy sessions by the beginning of next week.

It didn't seem possible. In fact, it seemed like only yesterday that she and Sidney were in New York discussing a move to a new city. And heading back to Lawrence after the book tour had helped her make her decision. Her mother had invited her to a welcome home dinner, not telling her that she'd invited Riley as well. It seemed that the thrill of sex with Valerie had fizzled out, and Riley wanted her back.

As if.

Ellie spent the entire dinner ignoring Riley's attempt to get her alone. What she couldn't ignore were the three "business" phone calls her father received. Or the way her mother smiled and acted like it was perfectly normal for an accountant to be called on a Sunday. By the end of the night, Ellie was more than ready to live anywhere but Kansas.

Sidney slid another book to her, and Ellie flipped open the cover.

"Who can I make this out—?" She glanced up at the man who stood there, and the pen dropped from her suddenly numb fingers and thumped down to the book.

She would've thought that she was having another fantasy if the man didn't look better than her dreams. His dark hair looked richer. His eyes looked greener. And his body looked harder. He smiled, and Ellie forgot to breathe. All she could do was try to figure out why he was there. He didn't belong in a Denver shopping mall. He belonged back in The Heat Suite. Or locked inside her head where she could take him out at will. Certainly not here in the middle of her organized life.

Sidney's elbow in her ribs brought Ellie out of her thoughts. With nothing else to do, she tried to bluff her way through this awkward situation.

"So who can I make this out to?" She picked up the pen. The question caused his smile to wilt and both eyebrows to lift.

"Don't tell me you've forgotten me already."

She plastered on a smile and tipped her head to one side. "I'm afraid I'm at a loss. Do I know you?" She snapped her fingers for dramatic effect. "Of course, you were that man in New York who wanted me to sign a book for his partner, Phillip. Did Phillip enjoy it?"

His laser green eyes pinned her to the chair. "Try Vegas."

Sidney sucked in her breath, then groaned when Ellie kicked her beneath the table.

"Ahh, Vegas." Ellie nodded. "Of course. How are you?"

"Fine. And you?"

"I'm doing well, thank you." She lowered her gaze to the book. "A name?" There was a slight quaver in her voice, but hopefully not enough for him to notice.

"Just make it out to me, Ellie."

For a brief second, she'd thought he'd said, "Just make out with me, Ellie." Her gaze snapped up to his amused eyes, and she realized that he was laughing at her. His amusement at her expense caused her to stop acting like a flustered teen at the *American Idol* finals. The man was such a jerk. He knew she didn't have a clue what his name was. And while she didn't know his, he knew hers. Of course, she only had herself to blame for that. She quickly signed her name on the title page and shoved the book at him.

He opened it and looked at her signature. "That's it? I was hoping for something a little more personal. Something like . . . I'll always cherish the night we had in Vegas. Love, Ellie the Virgin." He flashed her a smile. "With a heart around Ellie, of course."

She jumped up from the chair and spoke through clenched teeth. "Could I speak with you in private for a moment?" Without waiting for a reply, she swiveled on her heel and headed through the rows of shelves to the deserted children's section in the back. She didn't look to see if he followed her, but somehow she knew he did. When she reached the secluded back corner, she whipped around, intending to give him a piece of her mind.

Unfortunately, in order to give someone a piece of your mind you have to be able to breathe, and all the air left her lungs in a painful whoosh when she turned to find a solid chest inches away from her nose. It was like getting too close to the sun. His brilliance and heat surrounded her, dissolving all her angry words beneath the subtle scent of musky cologne and virile man.

Slowly, she lifted her gaze. Up past the striped tie, the square chin with the small dent in the middle, the full lower lip and thinner top, over the twin nostrils that flared with his rapid breathing, to the hungry green of his eyes. Her tongue flicked out to wet her suddenly parched lips. But before she could achieve her goal, his warm hands cradled her jaw and his mouth descended.

While her mind had tried to explain her uncharacteristic behavior in Vegas on Riley's betrayal and alcohol, her body hadn't been listening. At the first touch of his lips, she melted. Her lips melted into his lips. Her breasts melted into his pecs. And the spot between her legs melted against the hardness of his thigh. And not one part of her wanted to stop kissing him.

In fact, she might've gone on kissing him forever if he hadn't stepped away, replacing heat with cold emptiness. She opened her eyes to twin pools of green that looked as unfocused and confused as she felt. He blinked, and the confusion was replaced with annoying arrogance.

"So what did you want to talk about?" He leaned a shoulder against the wall and crossed his arms.

Her anger came back in full force, and she jabbed a finger at her chest. "Me? I'm not the one who showed up and embarrassed you in public by talking about what happened in Vegas!"

"Oh, so suddenly you remember the night in Vegas."

"Vaguely."

"Cut the crap, Ellie. Nobody forgets six orgasms." He grinned. "Or was it seven?"

How could she have gone to bed with such an annoying man? She had to stifle the urge to grab up Harry Potter and beat him over the head with *The Deathly Hallows*. Instead, she latched on to the one thing she knew would make him as angry as she was. "Are you sure I didn't fake them?"

That pretty much did it. He unfolded his arms and came away from the wall. "You swore."

She shrugged. "It was in The Heat Suite, so it didn't count."

"But nobody can fake orgasms like that."

"If you say so." She tossed him a smug smile. "Now, if you'll excuse me, I need to get back to my book signing."

He blocked her way. "Do these people know you're a fraud? No virgin would've done what you did on a stripper pole. Funny, but I didn't see a chapter on that in your book."

"You read my book?"

"All three hundred and sixty-three pages of crap."

"If it was crap, why did you keep reading it?"

He shrugged. "Curiosity, I guess. I was looking for one shred of valuable information."

"Which you couldn't find because nothing in my book pertains to you. The only thing you're interested in is getting women into bed, not out of it. And what are you doing at a shopping mall in Denver?"

The amused smile was back. "Fate."

Ellie didn't believe in fate. She believed that people made their own fate and freaky things that happened were mere coincidence. This was all just a freaky coincidence. A very, very freaky coincidence. One she needed to get through without doing anything to embarrass herself—like having sex with him on the Little Tikes table in the corner.

"Sorry to interrupt, Ellie." Sidney peeked around a bookshelf and stared at them like they were two of her favorite reality television stars. "But there's a woman waiting to speak with you"—she glanced at her watch—"and you meet with the Realtor in thirty minutes."

"Realtor?" Her Vegas Lover shot her a surprised look. "Are you moving here? Your bio said that you lived in Kansas."

Without replying, Ellie pushed past him. On the way back to the front of the store, she tried to calm her nerves with a little internal dialogue.

Okay, this is no big deal. So you ran into the only man you've ever had sex with. So what? Other women run into their one-night stands all the time and deal with it. You can, too. Of course, other women probably don't wrap themselves around their one-night stand like shrink-wrap.

She took a deep breath and slowly released it. Well, it wouldn't happen again. Denver was a big city. Even if he lived here, that didn't mean she had to see him. And even if she did, it would be a cold day in hell before she let him touch her again.

When she arrived at the signing table, a woman was waiting. A nervous woman who couldn't seem to stop fiddling with her necklace. Ellie knew how she felt. She almost jumped out of her skin when her Vegas Lover came up behind her.

"I wouldn't want to forget this." He picked up the book she'd signed and walked away. Even as angry as she was, Ellie couldn't take her eyes off the way his charcoal pants hugged his rear. Or the way his black belt encased his trim waist. Or the way his pale blue shirt wrinkled in the middle of his back.

Get a grip, Ellie!

She turned to the woman and held out a hand. "Hello. I'm Dr. Simpson."

The woman briefly shook her hand before she went back to sliding the silver cross back and forth along the chain that hung around her neck. "It's so nice to meet you, Dr. Simpson. I got your book at the library, and when I found out you were going to be here, I thought that maybe I'd...that maybe you could help me."

Sidney went to reach for a business card, but Ellie stopped her. The woman didn't look like she could afford to buy her book, much less a therapy session.

"Of course, what can I help you with?" she asked.

"It's that chapter you wrote on connecting emotionally. While I just love Anson to death and"—her eyes skittered away—"he loves me, there are times when I don't think we're connecting. And I think if we could connect on that emotional level that you were talking about, well, I think it would help him to use words instead of..."

"Sex to express his emotions?" Ellie filled in.

The woman paused for only a moment before she nodded. "Umm, yeah, sex."

Having just dealt with a sex fiend, Ellie didn't mince words. "All I can say is that you need to be brutally honest with your husband. If you are not feeling emotionally satisfied, then you need to let him know. Silence will only intensify the problem and let your husband continue his behavior, which will ultimately destroy your marriage. A healthy relationship starts with friendship. Sex is the product of that friendship, not the cause."

The woman looked a little confused, but she nodded. "I need to be strong and talk with Anson."

"Exactly." Ellie picked up a book. "I'd love to give you a copy of my book—free of charge."

Once Ellie had signed the book and the woman had left with it, Sidney pounced.

"OMG!" she breathed. "That was your Vegas Lover?" Ellie only nodded as she got up and slipped on her coat. She desperatcly wanted to leave and get out into the cool air where she could breathe. "No wonder you thought you were in love," Sidney continued. "I'm in love, and I don't even know him. So what did he want?"

"I don't know."

It was the truth. Ellie didn't know why he'd read her book, or why he was in the store, or why he'd kissed her senseless in the children's section. All she knew was that it couldn't be good.

Not good at all.

Chapter Ten

Louise McPherson Douglas, or Wheezie to her family and friends, was tired. Her bones hurt. Her muscles ached. And it was becoming harder and harder to get out of bed in the mornings. The only thing that kept her going was the desire to see her great-nephews happily married. As happily married as she'd been with her husband Neill. Some people would call it matchmaking, but she liked to think of it as more of soul-mating. Anyone could match-make, but it took a keen eye to find the perfect mate for the soul. Wheezie had that keen eye, but so far it hadn't helped with Patrick. Being a loner through and through, Paddy kept to himself so much that she'd been unable to get him with a female long enough to see how they matched up.

Which was why she'd enlisted Matthew's help. Although, lately, he'd fallen down on the job. Something she intended to take care of.

Just as soon as she took a nap.

Unfortunately, she had just gotten comfortable on the leather couch in Albert's study when the door opened. Since the couch faced the fireplace, she was completely hidden. She had just started to sit up when Big Al's booming voice rebounded off the walls.

"I don't know why your mother got it in her head to do some crazy Secret Santa exchange this year," Albert McPherson said. His desk chair squeaked in protest as he sat down. "Just what does an act of kindness mean? It would've been an act of kindness if she just let us go to the mall and buy a gift like everyone else."

His oldest son Jacob laughed. "You know Mom. She's always looking for a way to give back."

Albert snorted. "She should try giving back to her husband. Since she started working at that battered women's shelter, I'm lucky if I get a cold ham sandwich for dinner—make that turkey. Ever since my heart attack, pork hasn't entered this domain."

"Speaking of which, are you supposed to be lighting up that cigar?"

"Damned right, I am! Since your mother is always gone, it's the one enjoyment I get."

A waft of smoke drifted over the back of the couch, and Wheezie had to stifle the strong urge to jump up and box her nephew's ears. The only thing that stopped her was her love of eavesdropping—something she had picked up while working at the bar she'd owned with her late husband.

"So what's going on with your brother?" Albert said. "What's this I hear about him losing the McPherson charm?"

"I don't know about losing his charm," Jacob said, "but he has been burning the midnight oil. Something I never thought Matthew would do."

Matthew? Losing his charm? It was the first Wheezie had heard of it. Of course, lately the only things the family had talked to her about were walkers and nurses. It was hell getting old.

"Maybe he's burned himself out on women," Albert continued. "He certainly has spent the majority of his life surrounded by them." Another puff of smoke came over the couch. "Even as a kid, he had more little girls ringing the doorbell to play than he did little boys. If he hadn't loved sports and roughhousing so much, I might've been worried." He chuckled. "He was a competitive little squirt."

Wheezie wanted to snort. Of course, Matthew was competitive. What choice did he have growing up with a domineering father and three brothers who loved to tease him about being the youngest and a mama's boy?

"Well, whatever is going on with him," Jacob said, "the extra work he's put in has been good for the company. And speaking of the company, what's James working on? Cassie said he's not going to get here until later because he's working on a new bid."

"There's no new bid that I know of, but I'll talk to him about it on Monday. For now, we better get back to the tree decorating. You know how your mother hates for us to discuss business during family time." The chair squeaked as he got to his feet. "So who did you draw for the Secret Santa?"

"Rory," Jacob said. "And Melanie got Amy so she

thinks we should take the kids for a weekend so they can have some alone time. Who did you get?"

"Wheezie. And I don't have a clue what act of kindness I can do for my ornery aunt."

"What about a walker or a nurse?"

"Hmm? Those aren't bad ideas—"

The door closed, and Wheezie popped her head up and scowled. "Over my dead body, Albert McPherson." Of course, with the way she was feeling lately that might be the case.

Which meant that she needed to hurry and find Patrick a wife. In fact, since Wheezie's nap had been interrupted, she might as well talk to Matthew about finding some more women for his brother to choose from. And while she was at it, she planned to ask him about this nonsense of losing his charm. It wasn't likely. Matthew had more charm than the leprechaun on that cereal box.

She started to push to her feet when the door opened again. Since she learned more about the family in the last few minutes than she had all year, she laid back down. After a few minutes of silence, she peeked over the edge of the couch and saw just the person she wanted to talk to.

Matthew was standing at the window right next to one of the many Christmas trees Mary Katherine had spread around the house. His back faced her as he looked out on the night, and the stiffness of his shoulders had her reconsidering his father's words. She was about to make her presence known when the door opened again. She rolled her eyes as she ducked back down.

"Okay, so you want to tell me what's going on, little brother?" Patrick said.

Matthew released an exasperated groan. "Would everyone just give it a rest? So I've been working late. So what? Everyone used to be pissed because I didn't work enough."

"I'm not talking about your late hours," Patrick said. "As far as I'm concerned, it's about time you quit chasing tail and took your job seriously. I'm talking about you being wound as tight as a tennis ball and almost snapping Cassie's head off when she asked if you planned on bringing someone to the company Christmas party."

"I didn't snap her head off."

"Bullshit. Now explain yourself before I kick your ass for hurting her feelings."

"I really doubt that I hurt Cassie's feelings." Matthew moved closer to the couch. "But you're right. I was out of line. It's just that…" He paused. "Look, if I talk to you about something, I don't want it spread around, okay?"

"It depends on what it is. If it's something about the business, it needs to be shared with the entire family."

Wheezie smiled. She had always loved Patrick's loyalty.

"It's not about business." Matthew moved away. "It's about a woman." The desk chair squeaked before he continued. "And the thing is that she's not my usual type of woman. I mean, she doesn't have legs—well, not long legs. She's got nice legs, but she's not tall. And she's got short hair. It's longer now and doesn't look half-bad, but it's not the length I normally go for. And she doesn't wear much makeup or spend a lot of time on clothes. Although she looked pretty good in the skirt and sweater she had on when I ran into her at the bookstore. And she's a brain. A doctor of psychology who wrote some bestseller about sex—"

Patrick jumped in. "Please tell me it's not *Virgin Love*."

"That's it!"

Wheezie's eyes widened. She had heard of the book. In fact, she'd seen the author on one of her daytime talk shows. Although she thought the young woman's theories were as crazy as they come, she got more than a little annoyed when the yammering hosts hadn't even let the poor girl talk. And now here was her Mattie talking about the same girl. Interesting. Very interesting.

"So that's why you're so ticked off," Patrick said. "Well, join the club. From what I've heard, the woman has ticked off most of the men in the country. But I didn't realize that she lived here."

"She just moved to Denver."

There was a long stretch of silence that had Wheezie wanting to throw a shoe at them to hurry things along. Finally Patrick spoke.

"So I think I'm starting to get the picture. You met this woman and you find yourself attracted to her, but she doesn't want anything to do with you."

"Wrong," Matthew said. "I wasn't attracted to her. At least, not at first. But then we had sex and—"

Wheezie's ears perked up, and thankfully Patrick asked the exact same questions she wanted to. Bless his heart.

"Wait a minute, you're telling me you had sex with the Virgin Queen? When?"

"New Year's Eve in Vegas."

"So she's not a virgin," Patrick said. "Was she?"

"Of course not. What kind of a virgin would have sex with some guy she didn't even know?" The chair squeaked as Matthew got up. "I mean a woman wouldn't do that, right?"

"How the hell would I know?" Patrick said. "You're the expert on women. So now you're thinking she was a virgin?"

Matthew came over by the couch, but was so preoccupied that he didn't even notice Wheezie before he turned and walked back to the desk. "I guess it's possible. She didn't act experienced, and she was—" He stopped. "It doesn't make any difference now. She wants nothing to do with me."

Patrick laughed. "Damn, Mattie. Sex has come way too easily to you."

"What does that mean?"

"It means you've never had to work for it. All you do is crook your little finger and women come running."

"And your point is?"

"My point is that if you're not over the woman, what are you doing sitting here? Why aren't you using that great charm of yours and getting her back in bed?"

There was another long stretch of silence before Matthew spoke. "You're right. What am I worried about? Dr. E. B. Simpson might have a doctorate in sex psychology, but I have a doctorate in making women happy. And regardless of what she tried to make me believe in the bookstore, she was plenty happy on New Year's Eve. All I need to do is get her back in bed and remind her." He paused. "Which could prove to be a problem. How do I get her to go out with me?"

"Who says you have to get her on a date?" Patrick said. "She's a sex therapist, right?"

Matthew laughed. "Ahh, I feel a real sexual problem coming on."

Patrick moved toward the door. "I thought you might, little brother. And if that doesn't work, you can always get Cassie to rent her the condo."

"Not likely." Matthew followed his brother. "That last thing I need is an aggravating sex therapist living next door." There was a muffled thump like he had just patted his brother on the back. "Thanks, Bro."

"Anytime," Patrick said. "And now you can do me a favor. Help me figure out what to get James for Christmas. I'm his Secret—"

The door clicked closed behind them, and Wheezie sat up and smiled. She didn't know what James wanted for Christmas, but she knew what she wanted. And it wasn't a walker or a nurse. It was the same thing that she'd wanted a year ago.

But now Wheezie had her eye on a different groom.

Chapter Eleven

The view from the second-floor office building wasn't as spectacular as a high-rise, but Ellie loved it. There was just something about the neighborhood of sturdy, redbrick homes that made her feel like she was in a fairy tale. Each tiny, single-story house had a cute gabled front porch and a yard with evergreens that still clung to last week's snow.

A recess bell rang, and Ellie looked up the street to the elementary school on the corner. Children flooded out of the doors with their coats and jackets unzipped and flapping in the cold December breeze as they raced for their favorite equipment. A little girl in a bright pink coat caught her eye, and Ellie watched as the girl quickly scaled a dome-shaped climbing structure with a little boy in hot pursuit. When they got to the top of the jungle gym, the boy reached out and tugged a ponytail before he scrambled back down as the little girl gave chase.

Ellie laughed. These were forms of early mating rituals, rituals that would become less innocent and more serious as time went on. But to these children, it was still just a carefree game that would end as soon as the recess bell rang.

She turned from the window. How did love become so much more complicated for adults? Or maybe just for her? Obviously other people, like Sidney, had no problem playing the mating game. Ellie was the only one who couldn't seem to figure it out.

And after coming face-to-face with her wild night in Vegas, things were even more confusing. Why would an obvious player show up at her book signing? If it weren't for the fact that her Vegas Lover was, at least, three levels above her on the dating scale, she might think he was courting her. Yanking her ponytail to get her attention before he ran away. But that made no sense. Men like him weren't interested in dating an average-looking psychologist from Kansas.

She glanced down at her watch. An average-looking psychologist who was due to meet her first patient in less than five minutes.

She smoothed out the skirt of her new yellow suit, her gaze running over the room. The furniture had arrived on Friday, and she and Sidney had spent Saturday and Sunday putting on the finishing touches. A comfortable cream-and-green-striped couch with numerous throw pillows sat in front of the window, along with a coffee table with green wicker coasters and a few magazines. A small, cherrywood desk with her laptop and phone were on the opposite side of the room, framed by matching bookcases that held her psychology books, a potted jade plant, and her fax/copier/printer.

But her favorite piece of furniture in the entire room was the hickory rocker. A rocker her grandfather had made for her grandmother when she was expecting Ellie's mother. The wood was scarred and worn thin in the seat, but that only added to its comfort. Or maybe its comfort had more to do with the love her grandfather had sanded into each slate, or Ellie's own memories of time spent in her grandmother's arms on the front porch of their farmhouse. The time spent at her grandparents' farm was the only genuine family memory Ellie had. Her grandfather had been the type of husband every woman wanted. The type who took the time to build a rocker for the only woman he would ever love.

Is that too much to ask for? A man who will love me, and only me, for the rest of his life?

Obviously, it was. Today, men purchased multi-carat diamonds to demonstrate a love that might last a year or only as long as it took for the ink to dry on the marriage license. Why should Ellie expect more?

Pulling herself away from her morose thoughts, she bent down to straighten the stack of magazines and pull two green wicker coasters out of the stack. She should be thankful for what she did have. Few people could boast a bestseller and a brand-new practice all in the same year.

Wondering if her first patient had arrived, Ellie walked to the door and opened it. She expected to see Sidney sitting behind the desk. But the small receptionist area was empty. No one sat behind the desk; no one stood beside the coffee machine waiting to offer coffee to Ellie's first appointment.

Great. She glanced at her watch. Sidney was probably down the hall chatting with the dentist they'd met on Saturday. Hopefully, chatting was all they were doing. After meeting him, Sidney had been unable to stop talking about the fantasy she had about having sex in his dentist's chair.

Not about to walk down the hall and find out, Ellie poured herself a cup of coffee and stirred in three packets of imitation sweetener before taking it back to her office. Leaving the door open, she sank down in the rocker and held the hot mug in her hands, allowing the heat to warm her chilled fingers. Along with the jade plant, the mug had been an office-warming gift from Sidney. The mug was large and red with the words *Let's Talk About Sex!* written across it in big, bold letters. Hopefully, her clients would find it amusing rather than offensive.

Ellie released a long satisfied sigh, then leaned up to take a sip of coffee. The warm liquid had barely passed her lips when someone rapped on the open door. She turned, and coffee spewed from her mouth in a sputtered choke, spraying all over her brand-new suit. She jumped up from the chair, gasping for breath and juggling her mug.

"Now that's more like it." Her Vegas Lover strolled into the room as if he had done it every day of his life. She continued to cough, and he reached for the mug and pulled it out of her hands. "You're going to scald yourself if you're not careful." Those sparkling green eyes read the cup, and an eyebrow arched. "I'd love to."

Ignoring him, she walked out into the reception area where she grabbed some napkins and brushed at her skirt. It was useless. The stains weren't coming out. She tossed the napkins in the trash and glared at him.

It didn't seem fair that a man could look so sexy in every article of clothing he wore, or didn't wear. Dressed in a dark, expensive business suit, he exuded a sexual energy that left her feeling completely inadequate and clumsy. Thankfully, the office building had security. Security she had every intention of calling. Just as soon as she found out why he was there.

"What are you doing here?"

"I have an appointment." He glanced down at his watch. "Ten o'clock on the nose."

It didn't take long for the pieces to fall into place. "You're Matthew McPherson?" she said.

He pushed away from the doorjamb and reached out a hand. "In the flesh."

Ignoring the hand, she strode back into her office. "Well, I'm canceling." She sat behind her desk and picked up a pencil, furiously erasing his name off the desk calendar and blowing off the eraser remains.

"Hey, wait a minute." He looked a lot less cocky. "You can't just cancel."

"Of course I can." She pointed to the empty space. "See, I just did. Gone."

His eyes darkened, and there was a tightening around his jaw. "I think it's only fair to mention that I'm a lawyer."

"Am I supposed to be scared?"

He shrugged and looked around the office. "Not unless you're worried about a little something called discrimination."

"Discrimination? How do you figure?"

He moved over to one of the bookcases and browsed the titles of her books before he looked back at her. "You are discriminating against me because I had sex with you and know all your dirty little secrets." While she tried to keep steam from seeping out her ears, he pulled a copy of her book out and thumbed through it. "Not that I would ever say anything about elevators or stripper poles. That kind of gossip wouldn't be good for book sales." He looked up and closed the book with a snap.

Apprehension mixed with a whole lot of dislike for the evil man in front of her. "So what do you want?"

"Help." He put the book back and glanced down at the faxes she'd received from her Realtor. "Having trouble finding a place to live?"

She ignored the question. "Help with what?"

"Maybe you should rent first. Find out what neighborhood you like best."

"I have a Realtor, thank you." She got back to the original question. "Why are you here?"

He shrugged and strolled over to the couch, slipping out of his jacket on the way. The muscles beneath the expensive silk rippled just enough to make Ellie's mouth go dry.

"You see," he said as he neatly folded the jacket and laid it across the arm of the couch before he sat down and slipped out of his black loafers, "someone I recently—or not so recently—had sex with brought something to my attention." He flashed her a knowing look before he laid back and rested his feet on the arm of the couch, then tucked his hands beneath his head and stared up at the ceiling. "Something I've started to worry about."

Ellie moved out from around the desk, but came no closer. With his totally hot body dwarfing her couch, she didn't trust herself. So instead of taking her chair, she leaned against her desk and crossed her arms, trying to look as nonchalant and professional as possible. "And what would that be?"

He pulled his gaze away from the ceiling and looked at her. "I think I'm a sex addict."

Her eyes widened. "You've got to be kiddin' me."

"Not at all. Don't tell me you forgot our conversation about women's orgasms and me being a sex addict?"

Ellie remembered their conversations, had spent countless hours going over them in her head. She was just surprised he did. He seemed like the kind of guy who would forget everything about a woman once she was out of his sight. And Ellie had been out of his sight for eleven long months. Yet, he remembered her name, read her book, took the time to come to one of her book signings, and now stood in her office recalling one of their conversations. Things were getting more and more confusing by the second.

He sat up, his elbows resting on his knees and his gaze intent. "Do you think you can help me?"

The way he said the words made her heart thump madly against her blouse. It was much easier to deal with fantasies of him in the darkness of her very own bedroom. The mind could be controlled and fantasies easily dispelled by turning on the television or reading a good book. Or giving in to the fantasies and having a really good orgasm so she could then watch TV or read a good book. But when her fantasy was sitting across from her in the flesh, it became a lot more difficult.

She cleared her throat. "Forgive me if I don't believe

you. But after what happened in the bookstore, I think you're just here to yank my chain."

He shrugged. "Okay, so I got a little out of hand at the bookstore. The real reason I stopped by your signing was to talk to you. After reading your book, I'm starting to wonder if abstinence might help me find the right one."

"The right one?"

"You know, the one I want to marry."

It was hard to believe. The man was a player. He wasn't the type of man who was looking to get married. And he certainly wasn't the type to go without sex.

"And just how did you get my book?" she asked.

"My mother."

It made sense. Mothers were known for meddling. Just the other day, her mother had called and talked for a good hour about how wonderful Riley was. Since Ellie had yet to tell her about Riley's infidelities, her mother still had hopes for a grand golf course wedding on the eighteenth green. Which meant that maybe Matthew McPherson was telling the truth.

Especially since he'd never lied to her before.

She moved over to her chair and sat down. "Okay, you have"—she looked at her watch—"forty minutes, Mr. McPher—"

"Matthew." He laid back down on the couch and raised his arms over his head. The fabric of his dress shirt settled across his chest, defining muscles she remembered all too well. She swallowed hard.

"Okay, Matthew, when do you feel your compulsion for sex started?"

"What makes you think I have a compulsion for sex?

Just because I've been with hundreds of women, doesn't mean I'm the one who has—"

"Hundreds?"

Unconcerned with her shock, Matthew looked up at the ceiling in thought. "Maybe not hundreds. I think it might be closer to just one."

"One hundred?" Ellie's voice hit a shrill note, and for a second, she thought she might pass out. She had assumed the number was high, but hearing it straight from the horse's mouth made it so much worse. She had been one of a hundred women who'd had sex with him? One of a hundred? She tried to take a deep breath through her nose, but something was stuck in her chest. Like a big wadded-up ball of self-loathing. How could she have given her virginity to a man who went through women like Sidney went through coffee?

"I guess you're right," he said. "A hundred is a pretty high number. So what would be an average number?" He glanced over at her. "What about you? How many men have you been with?"

Did this man actually believe sex was something someone kept score of? Her nails sank into the wood of the chair. "None of your business."

"Ten?"

She glanced at the window behind the couch and wondered if a two-story fall would kill someone or just maim them badly. Either way, the thought was appealing.

"No." He shook his head. "That would be way too many for someone who supports your theories on abstinence. No, I think the number must be lower. Five? Four? Three?"

Ellie jumped up from the chair. "I want you to leave. Now." She knew she was being very unprofessional, but she didn't care. There was no way in Hades that this man was going to be her patient. She didn't care if he printed the sordid details of their night together in the front page of the *Denver Post*.

He sat up. "But you didn't tell me what an average amount of sexual partners would be."

She glared down at him. "Is it so hard to believe that people can control their sexual urges and wait until they find the right one before they go to bed with them?"

His brow knotted. "Then how do you explain what you did in Vegas? Are you telling me you thought I was the right one?"

"Of course not!"

"Then what would you call it... exactly?"

"Practice!"

The light left those sparkling green eyes, but the smile slipped for no more than a second. "Which is exactly what sex is for me. I'm just more of a perfectionist, so therefore I need to practice more."

Ellie pointed a finger. "It's different, and you know it. You view sex as some kind of recreational sport. Something to keep score of. A tally to have on your BlackBerry. And I think you should listen to your mother and get your brains out of your pants and back into your head. But do it with another therapist!" She strode to the door and waited for him to follow.

He took his time. Slowly, he unfolded from the couch and stretched like a cat waking up from a long restful nap. Then he slipped on his shoes and picked up his jacket, slinging it over one shoulder as he walked to the door. He stopped inches from her, so close her entire view was filled with pale blue shirt and solid male chest. Her gaze lifted, and his eyes pinned her to the new Berber carpeting.

"But I don't want another therapist, Ellie. I want you." Anger still coursed through her veins, which was probably why it took a second to identify the desire that pooled in the pit of her stomach. "How many, Ellie?" he asked. "How many men have you been with?" He brushed a strand of hair from her lips. "Two?" He paused a heartbeat. "Or maybe just one... me."

Everything inside Ellie stilled.

He knew.

It was all there in his eyes, the hard stamp of knowledge mixed with a slight tinge of possessiveness. It was that slight tinge that made her swallow hard and want to lie through her teeth. She couldn't stand the thought of a man who had gone to bed with a hundred women being the one man who had gone to bed with her.

"Are you crazy?" She tried to step around him, but he stopped her, the heat of his hand on her arm causing her knees to feel weak.

"I guess that's what we need to find out."

"But not with me."

He ran a finger down the side of her cheek. "But who better to cure me from sex addiction than someone who knows how to abstain from sex?" His finger slid over her chin and caressed the sensitive skin beneath. "Someone who"—his finger swept along the collar of her blouse, brushing her clavicle before it slipped over her sternum and stopped on the soft swell of one breast—"won't fall prey to the desires of the flesh."

Then before Ellie could even release her breath, he was gone, leaving behind a weak-kneed woman who had fallen prey to the desires of the flesh.

Chapter Twelve

Elle? Are you okay?"

Ellie jumped at Sidney's voice and bumped her hip against the doorknob. The pain got rid of the last of her desire, but her legs still trembled as she walked back into her office and slid down into the chair behind her desk.

Sidney followed her. "What's wrong?"

Ellie leaned her head against the chair and closed her eyes. "Everything."

"This wouldn't have to do with your Vegas Lover, would it?" Sidney asked. "I thought that was him I saw walking down the hall."

Ellie opened her eyes. "Was this before or after you deserted me for the dentist?"

"After. And I didn't desert you. I just wanted Keith to check one of my fillings."

"Is that all he checked?"

Sidney laughed as she walked over and flopped down on the couch. "For now. But I've got high hopes for that dentist's chair." She picked up a pillow and hugged it to her chest. "And he's got a single friend. Not a dentist, but some real estate investor. I thought we could double next Saturday night. That's if you don't have other plans with your hot Vegas Lover."

Ellie shot her an annoyed look before closing her eyes again. No, she didn't have other plans. Especially not with her hot Vegas Lover. She never wanted to see the man again. All she really wanted was to forget everything about him and hope he did the same for her. Unfortunately, it didn't look like that was going to happen.

Matthew McPherson seemed to be a man on a mission. A mission to start up another relationship with her. She just wasn't sure what kind of relationship he had in mind. His words said professional, but his body said something else entirely.

"So what did he want?" Sidney asked.

"He had an appointment."

"He's Matthew McPherson?"

"The same."

She could almost hear Sidney's brain ticking. "But why? You can't tell me that man has problems with relationships."

"That's what he says." She lifted her head and looked at Sidney who was sprawled out on the couch. "He wants me to help him abstain from sex. According to him, he's been with hundreds of women and—"

Sidney sat up. "Hundreds? Wow." She looked truly impressed. "The guy must be phenomenal in bed."

"I told you he was."

Her mouth tipped in an apologetic smile. "Sorry, Elle. But it's hard to take the word of a virgin." She rested an elbow on the pillow in her lap and placed her chin in her hand. "So this guy wants you—a woman he had wild sex with in Vegas—to help him not have sex? You're right. That doesn't make any sense. Maybe he's using it as an excuse to see you again. Because there's no way you are going to keep a man who looks like that out of women's beds. The guy just smiled at me, and I almost reached orgasm."

Try having him push you up against an office door, Ellie thought. Just the memory of his lips brushing her ear as he whispered about desires of the flesh made her knees tremble.

"I'm not going to try to keep him out of other women's beds," she said. "I refused to treat him."

"Why not?" Sidney stared at her. "If he is a sex addict, then he came to the right person. The whole thing with your father has made you an expert on the subject. And isn't sex addiction what you're thinking about writing your next book on? So while you're helping the poor guy out, you can pick his brain. What better research than a guy who has had sex with hundreds of women?"

The words were barely out of Sidney's mouth before her face lit up. "Better yet," she said as she jumped up, dropping the pillow to the floor, "why don't you write about something people really want to read about? Why don't you write about the players? You know, the guys who use women as sex objects." She paced in front of the couch. "It could be like a guide to the playboys of the world—a book about how they think and what they do to get women into bed. It would sell like hotcakes." She stopped and stared off into space. "*Men Who Are Unable to Make a Commitment*—no, how about *Men Who Are Unable to Stay Committed*?"

"How about *Jerks I Would Never Waste My Time Writing About*?" Ellie said.

But Sidney wasn't listening. Once she got an idea in her head, she became a steamroller: Everything in her way either moved or got squashed into nothingness. She hurried over to the desk and moved the chair, with Ellie in it, then took control of the laptop, typing information in at record speed.

Ellie leaned up. "What are you doing?"

"Googling Matthew McPherson."

Ellie groaned. "This is crazy, Sid. I'm not writing a book based on Matthew McPherson."

"Why not? It looks like you've been handed the poster boy of womanizers." She pointed at the screen that was filled with a picture of Matthew in a tuxedo kissing a stunning blonde.

Before Ellie's stomach stopped doing flip-flops at the sight of those lips attached to someone else, Sidney clicked and another picture came up. But this time, the woman was brunette in a low-cut top with perfect breasts. They weren't kissing, but the satisfied look on the woman's face said they'd done that and a lot more. Click. Another blonde. Click. A redhead. Click. Another blonde. Click. Two blondes. Click. Two raven-haired beauties. Click. A brunette with a white banner across her perky breasts that read *Miss Colorado*.

Unaware of Ellie's discomfort, Sidney clicked through the pictures and read the subtitles with growing excitement. "An executive lawyer whose father owns a multi-million-dollar construction company. Wow, look at that flashy car. Great, here's a blog page devoted to him. Just look at all these posts."

Ellie listened to all of it with growing concern for the throbbing pain in her head and the swelling emotion that felt a lot like anger. Of course, she wasn't angry about the multitude of women—okay, so she was angry about the multitude of women—but she was also angry about the fact that, at a time when she thought Matthew was being totally honest, he had lied through his teeth. When she'd asked him in Vegas if he was rich, he'd acted like his friend had given him The Heat Suite as a joke. But after seeing all the pictures on the Internet, there was little doubt that he had rented the room himself for one purpose and one purpose only...to seduce stupid women. Ellie wasn't a violent person by nature, but she really wanted to hit something. Like the image of the smiling playboy on the screen of her laptop.

"Wow," Sidney said as she scanned the blog page. "This guy is one hell of a player. Every woman on here adores him. Except for this one, Demi, who sounds a little like a crybaby to me. It seems her orgasm was cut short because his sister went into labor. The guy can't be all bad if he puts his sister before sex." She hit the print button, and the printer started up.

A good ten pages had printed out before Ellie finally spoke. "I won't do a book on Matthew McPherson."

Sidney stopped typing and turned to stare at her. "You're not doing a book on him. With all the legalities, that would be insane. No, you're going to do a book on players. And since most men are players, the book will actually be about the male psyche. And you're going to use this guy as research."

"No, Sid." She moved her chair up and closed the Internet window. "I'm not kidding. First of all, he doesn't seem like the kind of guy who would agree to it. And, secondly, I don't want to do it."

Sidney leaned back against the desk and crossed her arms. "Who said he has to agree to it?"

"So we're going to lie about it?"

"No, we're just not going to tell the truth, which is completely different. Besides, he's not going to be the only guy we use for research. I've dated quite a few playboy types myself. True, they aren't even close to being in this guy's league, but their little minds all work the same. This guy just happens to be a perfect specimen. And he practically fell straight into our laps. So you treat him for sex addiction, and, while you're at it, you learn the secret to his success. Then you come up with all your psychological bullshit for why he does what he does and how damaging it is for him and the women he takes to bed. Of course, we'll need a few chapters thrown in on how to avoid getting stuck in bed with these types of men." She paused, and a dreamy look came over her face. "Or how they can get into bed with men like this—and voilà! You've got a bestseller."

Sidney held out her cell phone. "Now, all you need to do is call him and tell him you changed your mind and decided to take him on as a patient after all—no, wait! It might be best if he isn't your patient. You'll help him out as a friend. It will be a friendship thing."

"Except I can't be friends with the man."

"Why not?"

"Because I'm sexually attracted to him and don't want to risk falling back in bed with him."

Sidney tipped her head to one side and studied her. "So you can tell other women to cut off their boyfriends from sex so they can build a healthy friendship-slash-emotional relationship, but you can't do it yourself? Somehow that doesn't sound very fair, Elle. Maybe you should try practicing what you preach. Besides, this will give you the perfect opportunity to study a player and figure out all the reasons behind the screwed-up childhood you keep whining about. Hell, it might even mend your relationship with your father."

"Doubtful," Ellie grumbled. "Hey, where are you going?"

Sidney glanced over her shoulder as she headed for the door. "Keith has a fifteen-minute break between appointments, and I told him I'd bring him a pastry from that little shop down the street."

"I thought you were going to be my receptionist?"

"You don't need a receptionist. Look how well things turned out with the last appointment." She stopped at the door. "Besides, you need some time to think about this new idea for your book. It's a good one, Elle. I can feel it."

As quickly as she breezed in, Sidney breezed back out.

"Bring me a bagel!" Ellie yelled after her. "No, a cheese Danish! No, a blueberry scone! You choose!"

Laughter echoed down the hallway.

Ellie fell back down in her chair and released an

exhausted sigh as she glared at the dark brown coffee stains on her skirt. Sidney was always exhausting and hard to keep up with, but today Ellie never stood a chance. Not after her unexpected encounter with Matthew McPherson had left all her brain cells frying on the back burner while her body sizzled on the front. She could barely repeat her name, let alone brainstorm on possible subjects for her new book. Especially when the brainstorming had to do with the same womanizer who caused her body to sizzle.

Her gaze lifted from the coffee stains to the screen of her laptop, and she only hesitated a second before reaching over and clicking on one of the recent websites. It was the picture of Matthew with Miss Colorado. The fingers of his right hand curled around her waist and her bare shoulder rested in the space beneath his arm. The woman looked up at him with appreciation and awe.

Ellie understood the awe. In a tuxedo with a crisp white shirt and black bow tie, Matthew McPherson was awe-inspiring. He didn't look as good as he did resting back against red satin pillows with his hair all messy and his chest all naked, but he looked darned close.

As for the appreciation, Ellie had a pretty good idea what the woman was so appreciative about. Ellie felt the same way after her seventh orgasm, and if someone had taken a picture of them together in The Heat Suite she would've been giving him the same dopey you-are-the-center-of-my-universe look. Sex did that to people. Or sex with really experienced players did that to people.

Turned them into breathless, coffee-spewing fools.

Unless they were smarter than that. Unless they could

detach themselves from the physical and look at things logically.

Sidney was right. Ellie needed to grow up and practice what she preached. So what if the guy made her and every other woman on the planet burn? She was a strong, intelligent therapist who had control over her body. If she couldn't trust herself to be in the same room with the man without giving in to her physical side, then she had no business writing books that told other people to do it.

She clicked open the blog page and read through a few excerpts. It was mind-boggling. It seemed that Matthew was the Don Juan of Denver. He knew how to play the game so well that the women he used and abused were grateful for the experience.

After reading all the adoring posts, Ellie no longer felt appreciative. Instead, she felt like she did after being on the South Beach Diet—angry that something that tasted as good as refined sugar could be so detrimental to your body. It didn't seem fair. But then life wasn't fair. Matthew wasn't some kind of a sex god. He was only an arrogant man who viewed women as sexual objects rather than human beings and life as a game rather than an opportunity for growth.

Suddenly, she felt absolutely no remorse whatsoever in enlightening the women of the world about men like him. Quickly, she typed in her own little story for the blog page. Leaving no pertinent information, of course. She published it, then grabbed a pen and started jotting down some notes on her yellow notepad.

It seemed Matthew McPherson was about to become her next case study. She had an appointment open on

Thursday. She would call him today—no, tomorrow was soon enough to let him know. An hour should do to start with, not only for him but also to help her keep things in perspective. She was a strong and intelligent woman, but she had formed an attachment to refined sugar and had been without it for eleven long months. It was best to limit temptation.

She wouldn't become his friend, not even for research. But she would give him free therapy in exchange for picking his brain. After all, she was a professional and, Lord knows, he needed help. She would look at him as a charity case, someone who was drowning in his own sexual quagmire and didn't have a clue how to get out. She didn't believe she could help him. Not with his history. But stranger things had happened. And if she did help him out of his self-centered sexual haze, she deserved the Nobel Prize along with a bestselling novel.

A title popped into her head.

The Players: Emotionally Challenged Men.

Now that had a nice ring to it.

Chapter Thirteen

So tell me a little bit more about your relationship with your mother."

Matthew looked over at the serious woman in the somber brown suit and wondered for the fiftieth time why he was making such an effort with someone who was as uptight as Ellie. Probably because he remembered a night when she wasn't uptight. A night when she'd been a seductress who wore nothing but a sexy smile, rather than a pain-in-the-butt therapist who was all buttoned-up, prim, and proper with a pair of black-framed glasses perched on her pert little nose. The same nose she kept looking down. The way she kept looking down at him in that superior, know-it-all way was really starting to piss him off. And the more pissed off he became, the more he wanted to rip the buttons off that maidenly blouse and touch her sensitive breasts, like he'd been fantasizing about for the last forty-five minutes.

Or eleven months.

Instead, he was stuck on the couch answering dumb-ass questions. It was getting old fast.

"For the last time," he said, "I have a great relationship with my mother. She's one of the most brilliant women you'd ever want to meet. She's beautiful and smart and funny and caring."

Ellie scribbled on her yellow pad and mumbled something that sounded a lot like "Oedipus complex." But before he could warn her to watch where her over-developed brain was going, she changed the subject. "And your father? Is he a lady's man like you?"

Matthew laughed. "He thinks so, but I'd say he's more of a fighter than a lover. Which brings us back to me and why I'm here. I'm here to figure out a way to control the lover part of me, not to waste time discussing my family."

She stopped writing. "I can't help you abstain if I don't understand where you're coming from."

"Sure you can. What happened to coping skills? I just need some good, sound advice on how to cope with my libido when it goes a little crazy."

She heaved a long sigh and looked at her watch, just one more thing she'd repeatedly done to annoy him. "Fine." She flipped a page over. "What makes your libido go crazy?"

It was weird, but at the moment, the thing that was making his libido go crazy was that little indention at the base of her throat. He wanted to kiss the spot and slide his tongue over it. Then he wanted to suck the soft skin into his mouth. While he was doing that, it wouldn't be any trouble at all to unbutton those buttons on her blouse until he reached the dark shadow of cleavage he could see through the crème-colored material.

"Mr. McPherson?"

He lifted his gaze to the brown eyes that were studying him over the rim of her glasses. "Matthew. We're old friends, remember?"

She gritted her teeth. "Matthew. You were going to tell me what makes you want to have sex."

If her tight jaw was any indication, she wasn't ready to hear his fantasies.

At least, not about her.

"Women," he said.

Those brown eyes darkened. "All women or just certain ones?"

In the last eleven months, it had been a certain one. And it annoyed the hell out of him.

"Just certain ones," he said as he allowed his gaze to rake over her body. "Tall, long-legged women in dresses. I'm definitely turned on by dresses." His gaze settled on her chest. "And nice, average-size breasts. Not too big and not too small." He cupped his hands to demonstrate. "And fluffy, long hair—at least down to their perfect-size breasts." He studied her hardening features. "And no glasses. I don't get turned on by glasses."

"Is that all?" she asked sarcastically. "Is there a hair color that works better for you? Or a certain age you prefer?"

"Nope." He tipped his head. "I pretty much like any hair color. Except for really weird ones, like blue or green. As for age, it's all a matter of mind. If you don't mind, it doesn't matter. And as long as they meet my criteria and are old enough to drink, I don't mind." The latter was pretty much a lie. After going out with a twenty-two-year-old who talked nonstop about Justin Bieber, Matthew had made a strict no-younger-than-twenty-eight-year-olds rule.

Ellie's lips pressed into a firm line. "And these women turn you on so much that you can't control yourself?"

He thought for a moment. "I guess it's not really me I have to control. It's them. Women have a tendency to get pretty upset if I don't give them sex."

Ellie pulled her glasses off and stared at him. "You've got to be kidding. You're now blaming the women you date for your problem?"

"I'm not blaming them. I'm just saying that I'm usually not the one to make the first move—Vegas being the exception." He squinted his eyes. "Although if I remember correctly, you did become very aggress—"

"We're not talking about me," she snapped. "And if you can't forget about that night in Vegas, then our session is over."

He held up his hands. "Fine. No Vegas. So what do I do when women start coming onto me?"

Ellie rolled her eyes, completely unconcerned with how insensitive she was being. "Why don't you start by saying no?"

"I tried that, but they never seem to listen. Although there was this one time that this woman wanted to tie me up and whip me and I said a firm no to her, but only because she had one wicked-looking whip. I don't mind a little spanking, but—"

Ellie started writing again. "So you like being punished?"

"Not really. I prefer to do the spanking."

She stopped writing and looked at him. "So you think women need to be punished?"

He didn't, but since she looked as happy as a preacher on Sunday to discover another deviant side to his behavior, he played along.

"Yes." He tried to give her his most serious look. "Sometimes that's exactly what they need. So I give it to them. It's sort of like the little moans you make every time I touch your ears. I knew you liked ear lovin'."

Her soft lips dropped open as she looked up. "I don't like ear loving."

"Of course you do." He pointed a finger at her. "But remember—we're not supposed to talk about that night."

She made a sound that was a cross between a disbelieving snort and an agitated cough before asking, "So you just make a guess that certain women need punishing and start spanking them?"

He really wanted to laugh, but he knew if he did, their time would be over. He shot a quick glance down at his watch. As it was, they were well over his hour. But Little Miss Therapist was too interested now in spankings to pay attention to her watch. Finally, he was enjoying himself.

"No, I don't guess. They say something about being a naughty little girl, and I usually answer them by saying"—he paused and waited until she stopped writing before he continued—"'just how naughty are you?' If they say, 'very naughty,' I say, 'You know what happens to naughty little girls, don't you?' That's about the time I pull them over my lap."

"And punish them?"

"Sort of. It's more like a slow, sweet torture," he said. She looked so naïve and confused that he did laugh. "I can see that you've never been a naughty little girl. So you'll have to use your imagination. Say it was you who was naughty—"

"I don't think—"

"Shhh, humor me. After all, it's my psyche that you're trying to fix." She clamped her mouth shut, and he continued, pulling a throw pillow onto his lap. "So I have you over my lap, all sweet and naked—"

"Mr. Mc—"

"Hush, I'm just getting to the good stuff. Besides, how can you be a good sex therapist if you're fidgety about sex talk?" He adjusted the pillow on his lap, then leaned back and closed his eyes. "I wouldn't touch you right away. Instead, I'd look at all the sweet perfection spread out in front of me and watch as anticipatory chill bumps rise up on the satiny smoothness of your naked flesh."

He cracked his eyes open and shot a quick glance at Ellie. She had stopped writing, her pen poised over her pad, but other than that she looked less affected by his words than he was. The pillow was hiding a major hard-on. Annoyed by her non-reaction, he kicked it up a notch.

"When I couldn't take it anymore, I'd have to touch— to trace a finger over each curve and chill bump. To fondle and shape your warming flesh to the perfect fit of my hand. To dip deep into the snug crevice and stroke and tease—"

A soft thump brought Matthew's eyes back open, and he couldn't help grinning at the sight that greeted him.

Ellie was no longer studying him like a bug under a microscope. Nor was she taking notes. In fact, the tablet had slipped off her lap completely and lay on the floor at her tightly crossed feet. Her hands clutched the arms of the rocking chair in a death grip, and her eyes were as tightly closed as her legs. But those soft lips were open, and through them, he could hear each uneven breath she took.

It appeared Ellie was a very naughty girl, after all.

He smiled wickedly, but not too wickedly, considering he was just as turned on as she was. God, how he wanted her. Now all he needed to do was go in for the kill.

"But I couldn't let all the naked sweetness make me forget that you are a very naughty girl. And that very naughty girls need very naughty treatment, so now that I have you helpless and whimpering with need..."

He smacked the pillow hard.

Ellie jumped, and her legs tightened, but her eyes remained closed.

Slowly, he slid off the couch. "I wouldn't hit you hard, just enough to sting. Just enough to leave the heated imprint of my hand. But I'd feel real bad about that mark." Carefully, he moved around the table. "So bad that I'd have to lean down and kiss it better. I'd use my entire mouth to make it feel better. To lick... and suck... and kiss the sting away." He slipped around the back of her chair. "Then just in case you had a change of heart, I'd have to ask you again."

He leaned down, his lips inches from her ear. "Are you still naughty, Ellie?"

Startled, she jumped, and her head cracked him in the chin, forcing him to bite his tongue.

"Shit." He held a hand to his mouth and tasted blood.

Ellie looked up at him. Her brown eyes were still slightly glazed over with desire, but it was nothing compared to the anger that swirled in their chocolaty depths.

"Your time is up." She pointed at the door.

Matthew frowned. Things weren't going as well as he thought they would. It seemed Little Miss Abstinence was a harder nut to crack than he'd first thought. He'd wasted an hour of his time, and all he had to show for it was a penis as hard as a diamond drill bit and a severed tongue. Of course, he hadn't really wasted the entire hour. The last twenty minutes had been pretty fun. So much fun that he wasn't ready to give up.

At least, not yet.

He moved over to collect his jacket and shoes. "So I guess I'll see you tomorrow."

"No, you won't," she said. "My schedule is full for the rest of the week."

He turned. "But what about my problem? I have a date on Saturday night." Not really a date, more of a meeting with Pamela Wilshire, but Ellie didn't need to know that. "And you haven't given me one good suggestion on how to remain celibate." If he had a real problem, this woman would've found her ass fired in a heartbeat.

She glared at him from the doorway, the glazed look of desire long gone. "Cancel."

"I can't cancel. The poor woman would be devastated." He slipped into his jacket. "How would you feel if I broke a date with you?"

"Relieved."

"Funny." He liked her a lot better when she was horny.

He moved over and stood in front of her. "So that's it? That's the best you can come up with? You want me to never go out on a date again? I can't believe that's the only idea you have in that overactive mind of yours."

She released a long-suffering sigh. "Fine. Why don't you try double dating?"

He shook his head. "Sorry, I don't do that. It cramps my style." When she lifted an eyebrow, he finally got it. Obviously, he couldn't think clearly with those phenomenal breasts inches from his body. As he studied those sweet mounds, he had to admit the whole double-dating thing was a good idea. Not that he would ever use it. But it would give him something to talk about on his next visit.

His brain cells fired with the possibilities of how he could end up having sex without the other couple knowing. A quickie in the bathroom. A hand job in the front seat. Or maybe he could include the couple in the back. No, that was too disturbing. Even for him. Unless...the couple in the back were two lesbians. Now that would be a great fantasy.

"Okay, I'll try it." He held out his hand. "Good job, Doc." Ellie looked at his hand as if it were a cobra ready to strike; still, she took it and gave it a brief shake just as her friend came waltzing into the office with two Starbucks cups.

"Hey, we meet again." She handed a cup to Ellie. "Sidney Lindstrom."

"Matthew McPherson."

"Nice to meet you. Although I feel like we're old friends." Her blue eyes twinkled with more than a little knowledge. Obviously, Ellie had told her all about The

Heat Suite. He wasn't surprised. If he learned anything over the years, it was that women were ten times more likely to kiss and tell than a man was.

She tipped the cup at him. "You want some? It's the coffee of the day, Maple Spice something-or-other with lots of whipped cream."

"No, thanks." He glanced over at Ellie who was holding the cup in both hands and glaring at him. "I need to get going."

He had just turned when Sidney stopped him.

"So do you know of any good entertainment here in Denver? Ellie and I are double dating on Saturday night, and I want to make sure we're not taken to some lame club."

A smile spread across Matthew's face, but he hid it before he turned to her.

"Double dating?" He shot an innocent look over at Ellie. "What a coincidence. We were just talking about double dating. In fact, Dr. Simpson suggested double dating as part of my therapy. And if double dating works, triple dating should really work. I could get us tickets for the Holiday Art Benefit."

"No!" Ellie said. When both he and Sidney looked at her, she quickly explained. "When I mentioned double dating, I meant with someone besides the therapist who is treating you."

He studied her with confusion. "But when you called me, you acted like we were friends, not doctor and patient."

"Exactly," Sidney jumped in. "Oh, come on, Elle. I've heard about the art benefit, and it's the hottest ticket in town."

Matthew could have kissed her. Instead, he sent her one of his trademark smiles. She didn't melt. Instead she threw him a wink that said she knew exactly what he was up to and had decided, at least for the moment, to be on his side. Smart woman. He would need to be very careful if he wanted to keep up his charade. "So how about if we meet here around seven," he said. "I'll rent a limo to fit all six of us, and I'll take care of the dinner reservations."

"Great." Sidney's enthusiasm was in complete contrast to Ellie's grumpy acceptance. "Should we dress up or down?"

"Up." He gave Ellie the once-over. "Dresses would be nice. Short dresses."

As he walked away, he heard Sidney trying to pacify her friend. "Cheer up, Elle. How bad could it be?"

Matthew smiled to himself.

Oh, he planned on being bad.

Very, very bad.

Chapter Fourteen

Whoever thought that harp music was soothing didn't have one foot in the grave.

Wheezie had more than one foot. There were times that she felt like only a toe stuck up out of the dirt. One arthritic toe that cramped every time it rained. And she certainly didn't need to hear harp music before she entered the pearly gates.

If that was where she was headed.

She shuffled away from the harpist who was playing a weepy rendition of "Greensleeves" and looked around for the bar. There wasn't one in the entire art gallery. Just a bunch of waiters carrying silver trays of fluted champagne glasses as they weaved through the crowd of peacock-dressed socialites. And Wheezie hated champagne almost as much as she hated harp music. She actually considered walking out of the art gallery and looking for a neighborhood bar so she could order a glass of scotch whiskey, but then Mary Katherine zeroed in on her and she figured the drink would have to wait.

Mary swept toward her in a floor-length formal gown that looked like it weighed more than Wheezie. "Where's the walker Albert got for you, Aunt Louise? You know the doctor told you to use it when you're in large crowds."

"And that doctor needs to have his head examined. Once you start using a walker, it's downhill from there."

"You'll think downhill if you fall and break a hip."

There was probably some truth to that, but Wheezie wasn't willing to admit it. Instead, she changed the subject.

"So who did you draw for the Secret Santa exchange?"

"Believe it or not, I got my own husband." She smiled and waved at Shirley Wilshire, who Wheezie thought was a horse's ass if ever she'd seen one. "Since he just bought that hunting cabin, I thought I'd get the boys to go up with him for the weekend."

"I'm not sure it's the boys' attention he's wanting right now," Wheezie said. "I get the feeling he is a little upset about the time you're spending at the shelter."

Mary pulled her gaze away from the crowd, and her eyes snapped with anger. "Well, that's just too bad. It's a worthy cause, Louise, and Christmas is the best time to get people to donate. So I can't just drop everything because Albert wants a little attention and an artery-clogging steak dinner." She flashed a smile at the mayor before continuing a rant that sounded to Wheezie like it had been bottled up for way too long. "Do you know how many times in my life I could've used a little attention from my husband? And I can count on my fingers how many times he pulled himself away from his precious company to be with me. Does he love me? Yes, I believe he loves me, but I also believe that he wouldn't know an emotionally driven relationship if it bit him in the butt."

She whirled away in a swish of taffeta, leaving Wheezie with the opened can of worms. So it looked like Matthew wasn't the only one who needed help with his love life. And speaking of Matthew . . . Wheezie looked around, but her youngest nephew had yet to show up. Although she did see Patrick standing against one wall, looking as out of place as a hooker in church in his faded jeans and flannel shirt.

Wheezie grinned. She had always loved a man who marched to his own drummer.

"Hey, there, Wheeze," he said when she shuffled up. "You're looking beautiful tonight." He kissed her on the cheek.

"And you're looking awfully rugged. Did you miss the memo on formal dress?"

"Yep." He grinned, something he did much too rarely. If he did it more often, he'd probably have as many women as his brother. Which moved her toward the next topic of conversation.

"So tell me about Matthew. I heard through the grapevine that he's spending a lot of time at work. Should I be worried?"

Patrick took a drink of his beer. Where he'd gotten it, Wheezie didn't have a clue, but she planned on talking to the waiters first chance she got to see if she could get some scotch. "Nothing to worry about. In fact, I think his long work hours are about to change."

She tried to look surprised. "You don't say. Why's that?"

"Why else? A woman." He shot a glance over at her. "But don't be getting any ideas, Wheeze. Mattie has no plans to get married."

"Of course I'm not thinking about Matthew getting married. He's still too young for that. And has way too many women to choose from." She tipped her head. "Besides, he told me that you're the one who is lonely. The one who needs a wife in a bad way."

Patrick choked on his swallow of beer. "What? Mattie told you that?"

Wheezie smiled and nodded. "He even agreed to help me out in matchmaking by parading women over to your condo."

His eyes narrowed. "Why that low-down, backstabbing brat."

"Now don't be angry with your brother. He just wants you to be happy." She sighed. "And he knows I have my heart set on wedding bells for Christmas." She sent him her most depressed, old-woman look. "In fact, it's the only thing that keeps me hanging on." She glanced across the room. "Oh, there's your sister. I need to talk with her."

Wheezie shuffled away and smiled. One seed planted. One more to go.

Cassie seemed to be hiding in the corner behind a white Christmas tree. When Wheezie touched her on the shoulder, she jumped and dropped one of the annoying cell phones that should be banned at any and all functions.

"Geez, Wheeze! You scared me to death." Cassie tried

to squat down to retrieve the phone, but her huge stomach wouldn't let her and she bumped into the tree, causing the gold balls to wobble.

Wheezie bent over to pick it up, but she wasn't much better. Her bones creaked like a leather sofa as she grabbed the phone. She glanced at the picture on the screen of Cassie and the kids. A picture James had shown her before.

"Isn't this Jimmy's phone?" Wheezie asked as she handed it back to Cassie.

"Umm, yes," Cassie said. "I forgot my phone and needed to make a call to the babysitters." Her face flushed the shade of red that had always indicated a lie.

"Which is why you were hiding behind the tree." Wheezie lifted her brows. "Looking up porn on the web?"

"No!" She glanced around. "If you must know, I was looking at James's text messages." Her face fell. "He's cheating on me, Wheeze."

Good Lord. The entire McPherson family is falling apart.

"Now what makes you think that?" Wheezie said. "Was he sexting?"

Cassie blinked. "How do you know about sexting?"

"I'm old, not dead. So was he texting with another woman or not?"

"Not. But that doesn't mean anything. He could've erased them all." She glanced over at her husband who was talking with her mother and the mayor. "And all the other signs point to it. The late nights at work. The pretty new secretary. His lack of interest in sex. Not to mention, reaching the five-year-itch mark."

"I believe it's seven-year itch. And even that is phooey." Wheezie flapped a hand. "If people get an itch, it has nothing to do with how long they've been married. It has to do with keeping the fun and sex in their marriage."

Cassie stroked her huge stomach. "It's hard to be fun and sexy when you're as big as a house."

"I disagree. Most men I know think pregnant women are beautiful."

"Then why doesn't James want to have sex with me?"

"Maybe he's worried about hurting the baby?"

"But that didn't stop us the other two pregnancies."

Cassie did have a point. Wheezie glanced over at James. Was it possible? James was good looking and virile. His eyes scanned the crowd as if looking for someone. When they landed on Cassie, the look that entered them could only be described as adoring. Nope, the man was crazy about her. But if she knew Cassie, she wouldn't let it go until she had proof.

"Let me do a little detective work," Wheezie said. "An old woman can be nosy without anyone getting suspicious. In the meantime, you need to relax and not worry. You don't want that child turning out high-strung like your cousin Lenny."

"Thank you, Wheezie." She hugged her. Or tried to. Her arms barely outreached her stomach. "You're the first person who hasn't thought I was just a hormonal nut." She tugged down the stretchy material of her dress to reveal more cleavage. "And now I'm going to take my husband home and try to seduce him. If Mohammed doesn't come to the mountain, I'll take the mountain to him."

After a quick good-bye kiss on the cheek, Cassie waddled over to James, and within minutes they were heading for the coat check. Wheezie had just commandeered a waiter and offered him a twenty to get her a glass of scotch, when a group of people walked in the door. She recognized her nephew immediately. In his tailored tuxedo, Matthew stood out like Frank Sinatra in the Rat Pack. The other two men didn't compare. But Wheezie wasn't concerned with the other two men. Or the tall woman in the tight, too-short dress. She was concerned with the petite blonde who Matthew couldn't seem to take his eyes off.

She was a tiny, little thing. About the same height as Wheezie before her bones had started to deflate. She went to remove her coat and the man next to her reached out to help, his gaze roaming over the neckline of her demure, black dress. Wheezie looked back at Matthew and couldn't help grinning. For a man who normally had a smile on his face, he looked like he'd just eaten an entire lemon tree. His mouth puckered, and his eyes squinted. Yes, nothing like a little competition to make things interesting. But while a little competition was nice, too much could spoil good plans. Which is why Wheezie turned back to the waiter.

"Better make that a bottle."

Chapter Fifteen

Sidney had been right. Matthew McPherson was a world-class womanizer and the perfect subject for her book. Ellie just didn't know if she could be the one to write it. Not when every time a woman hooked her arm through Matthew's or leaned up to whisper in his ear, Ellie wanted to clock them in the head with her Louis Vuitton knock-off. Which was absolutely ridiculous. Especially when the man seemed to be thoroughly enjoying himself. No wonder he didn't look upset when he'd informed her that his date had canceled. He wasn't a man who could be satisfied with just one woman. It was very obvious by the smile on his face that he thrived on being mauled by many.

He stood in the center of the art gallery like a statue of Adonis while hordes of females circled and admired him more than the paintings that hung on the walls. And Ellie was no better. She couldn't seem to keep her eyes off him.

She blamed it on the tuxedo. She had always loved a man in a tux. But if that was true, then why didn't she have a problem keeping her eyes off her date for the evening?

As it turned out, that worked out just fine because her date had no problem keeping his eyes off her.

Keith's friend Jeff was more into networking for his real estate company than he was into entertaining Ellie. Of course, it didn't help that Matthew had mentioned her book at dinner. It seemed that Jeff's ex-girlfriend had read it, and the book's catchphrase "emotionally driven relationship" had come up a lot during their last fight.

The Virgin Queen strikes again.

Ellie took a sip of her champagne and scanned the crowd for Sidney and Keith. They were nowhere to be seen. And after the heated looks they were exchanging during the limo ride over, Ellie didn't doubt for a second that they had slipped into the bathroom for a quickie.

Which left Ellie sitting there like a wallflower. She had just decided to call a cab—and the night a disaster—when she noticed the man standing not more than a few feet away from her. While everyone else in the gallery was dressed to the nines, he wore a faded pair of jeans and a flannel shirt that had been washed so many times it conformed to his broad shoulders and wide chest like a well-tailored shirt. The sleeves were rolled up to his elbows, displaying muscular forearms that spoke of the type of strength you got from chopping down trees.

Although the clothes and lumberjack good looks didn't surprise her as much as the fact that he was walking straight toward her.

"You look like you're enjoying this about as much as I

am." He held out his hand. "Patrick." She started to introduce herself, but he stopped her. "I know who you are, Dr. E. B. Simpson."

"Great." Ellie glanced around for another waiter. "But before you start yelling at me for ruining your last relationship, I need another drink." She set down her empty flute on a passing tray and picked up a full one.

Patrick laughed. "That bad, huh?"

"You don't know the half of it." She took a sip. "Believe it or not, I wrote the book to help relationships, not hurt them."

"Oh, I believe you. But you have to understand that men view you as the candy store owner that just flipped over the closed sign."

She laughed. "I guess that's one way to look at it. Although men should blame their own gluttony on the store being closed."

Patrick shook his head. "It will never happen. We're much too selfish."

She laughed again, but this time it came out as more of a giggle. Obviously, she'd had too much to drink. But she didn't care. For the first time that night, she was actually enjoying herself.

"Are you one of those selfish men?" she asked.

"Pretty much. Right now, I'm thinking how nice it would be if I got to spend the rest of the evening in your company." He held out his arm, a gesture that was in complete opposition to the way he was dressed. "Would you care to join me at a little art viewing, Dr. Simpson?"

Even if Jeff had made it as plain as the muscles on this man's arm that he wasn't interested in dating her, she started to decline, when she glanced up and saw Matthew watching her. That was all it took for her to accept Patrick's arm and allow him to lead her from the room. They spent the next hour talking about her book, his love of building things, and her condo search while they admired the art that hung on the walls.

"What do you think about this painting?" he asked as he stopped in front of a huge abstract with brilliant splashes of red.

"I love it."

"Me too." He picked up the pen that sat on the podium next to the painting and wrote a number on the bid sheet.

"I hope you didn't skimp on that bid, Patrick." An attractive, middle-aged woman came up. "That painting was done by one of the residents at the shelter, and I'm hoping it will raise enough to get the artist and her mother out of their current situation." A frown marred her forehead. "Although I fear her mother will change her mind and return to her abusive husband. Many do." She held out a bejeweled hand. "I'm Mary McPherson. As usual, my son failed to mention that he was bringing a date."

"McPherson?" Ellie looked back at Patrick and finally noticed his green eyes. And that wasn't the only similarity. He had the same lips as Matthew and a smile almost as charming.

"This is Dr. E. B. Simpson, Mother," he said.

Mrs. McPherson's eyes widened. "*The* E. B. Simpson? The one who wrote *Virgin Love*?"

Ellie swallowed. "The same."

Mrs. McPherson engulfed her in a hug. "Well, it's a pleasure, Dr. Simpson. I read your book, and while I don't agree with everything, I do agree with women needing to stand up for their own emotional needs." She lifted a fist. "It's time to stop being doormats and start being proactive. Start living our lives for ourselves instead of our men."

It was strange, but Mrs. McPherson wasn't the first woman who had read something in Ellie's book that wasn't there. It was like people only saw what they wanted to see. Men saw a prudish woman who hated men and wanted to punish them through sex. And women saw her as the sage who understood exactly what they needed. Ellie was more scared by the women's perception than the men's. The men didn't expect anything from her except an apology and retraction. The women expected a guru.

"I would love to have lunch with you sometime and discuss your views," Mrs. McPherson said. "Maybe get some pointers on my marriage." She turned to her son. "Or better yet, Patrick can bring you to the house for dinner during the holidays."

"Patrick is not bringing her to the house."

Ellie turned to find Matthew standing there without one woman clinging to his arm. And speaking of clinging, Patrick settled a hand on her waist and pulled her closer.

"Oh, I don't know about that," he said. "I guess that depends on Dr. Simpson."

Matthew tipped his head like a confused dog. "What are you doing, Paddy?"

"I'm entertaining Dr. Simpson." He shrugged. "Can you blame me for seeing an opening to be with a beautiful woman and taking it? Especially when you seemed to be preoccupied."

The "beautiful woman" part had Ellie blushing and Matthew sending his brother a hard glare. He held out his hand. "Come on, Ellie. I think it's time we left."

Ellie was about to tell the insufferable man to take a hike when his mother jumped in.

"What in the world is going on? I thought Dr. Simpson came with Patrick."

"She didn't come with me, Mother," Patrick said as he winked at Ellie, "but I hope she's leaving with me."

"Like hell." Matthew grabbed Ellie's hand and tried to pull her away, but Patrick refused to relinquish his hold on her waist. Something of a tug-of-war ensued, and since Ellie had never been fought over by two men—especially two extremely attractive men—she was struck speechless.

"That is enough!" Mrs. McPherson hissed.

Patrick listened. Matthew did not. Which resulted in Ellie flying into his arms so hard that she knocked him back into the painting. It fell off the hook and crashed to the floor just as Matthew regained his balance.

"You dumbass!"

A young girl came out of nowhere. A teenager with so many piercings she looked like an office bulletin board. She had five or six earrings in each ear, two studs in her nose, and a knob hanging out of her bottom lip that was the exact size of the one on Ellie's jewelry box. She did what Ellie had been wanting to do for a long time: She slugged Matthew hard in the shoulder.

"Hey!" He caught her wrist before she could do it again. Her reaction to the physical touch told Ellie more than words ever could. As the girl tried to tug away and couldn't, her eyes betrayed her fear. Even if her words didn't.

"Let me go, you butt wipe!"

"Not a chance," Matthew said as he looked at his mother. "Call security."

"I'll do no such a thing, Matthew," Mrs. McPherson said. "Let Joey go this instant."

"Joey?" Matthew released the girl who immediately stepped out of his reach. "You know this kid?"

"This is the artist who painted the picture you and Patrick knocked off the wall by your brutish behavior." Mrs. McPherson knelt down to examine the painting, completely unconcerned with her gown. "It's fine, Joey. I don't think anything was damaged in the fall." She glanced up at her sons. "Both of you get this painting back up and apologize to Miss Hastings and Dr. Simpson."

"No!" the girl snapped. "I don't want them touching it." She grabbed the huge canvas, struggling with the awkward size. "In fact, I'm taking it with me. I should've never let you talk me into selling it to some snobby freaks who don't know how to appreciate art." She carried the painting like a battering ram, using it to force people out of the way as she headed for the exit sign.

"You want me go after her?" Patrick asked, but his mother shook her head.

"It won't do any good. The damage has already been done." She looked at Matthew. "You do realize you might've cost that young lady a new home? A home away from her abusive father. And that's all I have to say on the subject." She took Ellie's arm and led her away from both men. "Please excuse my sons, Dr. Simpson. They weren't raised in a barn, just with a hot-tempered Scot who thinks roughhousing is the best way to handle a dispute." She waved at a group of people. "I should get back to my guests, but I hope you'll stop by Hope House. I'm very proud of what we do there."

"I'd love to," Ellie said. "And it was very nice meeting you."

"Believe me, the pleasure was mine."

Once Mrs. McPherson had left, Ellie headed for the coat check. She had had more than enough excitement for one night. Unfortunately on the way, she ran into her date for the evening. Or more like he ran into her. The man was completely wasted. And had the gall to be leaning on a little old woman.

"You be-her watch out, you be-her not cry, you be-her not pout." He waved a hand and almost took out a waiter's tray of empty glasses and continued, "I'm tellin' you why. San-na Claus is comin' to town." He finally noticed Ellie, and his eyes narrowed. "Thas-s-s her. Thas-s-s the one I was tellin' you about. The Virgin Queen that ruined my life."

The little old woman smiled sweetly. "I think your young man has had too much to drink. In fact, I was just getting ready to call him a cab."

The last thing that Ellie wanted to do was deal with a drunk, but she couldn't see any way around it. Jeff might've ignored her the entire night, but he was her date, and she couldn't leave him for this sweet old woman to have to deal with.

She looked around for Sidney and Keith.

"If you're looking for your friends," the woman said, "I'm afraid they already left. I think the woman was experiencing some kind of toothache because she mentioned something about a dentist chair."

Ellie rolled her eyes as she hooked her shoulder under Jeff's. "Thank you so much for watching out for my friend, but I'll take it from here."

The woman smiled. "It was no problem. No problem at all—Ellie is it?" When Ellie looked confused, she nodded at Jeff. "He mentioned it. I had a friend named Ellie. She was a good, trustworthy friend who bowled two-fifty right up until they laid her in her coffin. Buried her ball right next to her." She shook her head. "Although I thought that was weird as hell."

Jeff weaved and almost pulled Ellie down with him.

"You sure you got him?" the woman asked. "Maybe I better get my nephew to help you get him in the cab." She shuffled off, weaving a little herself and making Ellie wonder how she had managed to hold up a full-grown man.

"I think that woman got me d-drunk," Jeff slurred as Ellie pulled out her phone to call for a cab. She shook her head. Leave it to a man to blame a woman for his own weaknesses. And a sweet, little old woman at that.

"So I guess Jeff can't handle women or liquor."

Ellie glanced over Jeff's shoulder to see Matthew walking up, the little old woman shuffling behind him. *Her nephew?* Were half the people in the room McPhersons? She might've ignored him if Jeff hadn't chosen that moment to lose all the strength in his legs. Matthew caught him before he hit the floor and effortlessly flipped him over a shoulder.

"The limo's waiting out front," he said as he headed for the door.

Ellie followed behind him. "I was just getting ready to call a cab."

"Why would you do that when it will be quicker to go in the limo?"

He did have a point. It would be stupid to wait another half hour for a cab when the limo was sitting there. While he and the chauffeur placed Jeff in the backseat, she walked around to the other side. She had just pulled open the door when she glanced across the street and noticed the beat-up Toyota truck. The young teenage girl and another woman were tying the painting down in the back. It was clear that Joey was still angry about what happened in the gallery. Her movements were sharp and jerky as she finished tying the nylon rope, then ran around to the other side to help the woman who seemed to be struggling with her end. More than likely because her right arm was in a sling. And that wasn't her only injury. Even from that distance, Ellie could see the bruises on her face. This must be the girl's mother. No wonder she had ended up at the shelter. It looked like someone had badly beaten her.

"Here, let me get that for you," the chauffeur said as he came up behind Ellie and held the door. It was hard to pull her gaze away from the woman. Not just because of the bruises, but because there was something so familiar about her. But before she could figure out what, Jeff leaned his head out the door.

"Has-s-s anyone ever told you that you've got great tits?"

Chapter Sixteen

Anger boiled in Matthew as he watched Jeff's hand inch toward Ellie's breast for the second time in less than five minutes. Matthew leaned up from the leather seat with every intention of breaking a few fingers. Unfortunately, Ellie pushed Jeff's hand away before he got the chance.

It was too bad. Since seeing her with Patrick, Matthew really needed an outlet for his anger. And Jeff was the logical target. He didn't like the guy. Didn't like the way he bragged about his achievements, the way he drank too much, or the way he'd covertly stared at Ellie's breasts all evening. The guy was an asshole who needed a few bones broken. And, for once in his life, Matthew had the strong desire to be the one to do it.

Of course, his brother deserved a few broken bones himself. He realized his siblings loved to piss him off, but Paddy had taken it a step too far. Brothers didn't mess with girlfriends. Not that Ellie was a girlfriend, but she was definitely a conquest, and Matthew considered that close enough. Especially when he had abstained from going to bed with Patrick's ex, Ashley, after she showed up at his condo wearing nothing but a fur coat and a smile. In fact, he hadn't even invited the woman in.

Patrick, on the other hand, had stepped in when Matthew had Ellie right where he wanted her—alone and needy. Of course, Patrick never could ignore anything that was lonely or needy. His condo was filled with stray dogs and cats. But that wasn't any reason to poach on Matthew's stray.

He glanced over at the woman who sat across from him. Ellie hadn't spoken a word to him since getting into the limo. Instead, she sat staring sullenly out the window. Of course, other than Vegas, she always looked sullen. Which was something else that pissed him off. When walking around the gallery with Patrick, she'd smiled and laughed. But with Matthew, she couldn't even conjure up a slight lip quiver. Still, he wasn't willing to give up. Somewhere beneath that sullen expression was the sexy siren he'd met in Vegas. And come hell or high water, he was going to get her back.

Thirty minutes later, after dumping Jeff off at his apartment, Matthew had his chance.

"Well, your plan worked, Doc." He inched closer to her. "I'm still celibate." *Hopefully, not for long.* He had a limo fantasy working that already had him hard as a stone. Too bad she wasn't cooperating. She was curled up in the corner with her arms crossed and eyes closed. Her posture said one thing: Back off. But Matthew had never been good at following directions.

"Barely," she said without opening her eyes. "A few women looked like they were seconds away from rape."

He laughed. "I think you're exaggerating. Most of those women are just friends."

She lifted her head and studied him in that therapist way he found so annoying. "If they're such good friends, tell me one thing you talked about tonight."

He tried to think of one thing, but he couldn't. Not one damned thing. Probably because his mind had been consumed with fantasies about this crazy woman.

"What did you and Patrick talk about?" he countered.

A smile played over her lips. "Everything. Unlike some people, your brother prefers stimulating conversation to sexual innuendos."

The woman knew exactly what buttons to push. "He doesn't get laid much, either."

"Commendable."

"Of course the Virgin Queen would think so."

"Most intelligent women would think so, Matthew." She closed her eyes and rested her head back against the seat. "But since it appears that you don't date intelligent women, you wouldn't understand."

The whole having-sex-in-the-back-of-a-limo thing went right out the window. "I date plenty of intelligent women who look at sex not as the plague but as an important part of a relationship."

"And what relationship would that be?"

"I've had plenty of relationships."

"Name one that lasted longer than a month of daily sex."

"Daily sex for a month is nothing to smirk at, lady!" he snapped.

She opened her eyes and looked at him. "It is when you compare it to a relationship of honesty, trust, and love."

"And you know a lot about those types of relationships, do you?"

The hurt that spread over her features was like a sucker punch to his esophagus. Which was weird. Why should he care if Ellie had an honest, trusting, loving relationship with some guy? Every woman he'd ever dated had been in relationships before and after him, and it had never made him feel this upset.

"Ahh," he said, "so now I get it. You fell for some guy who couldn't live up to the great Virgin Queen's standards. What, wasn't he satisfied with just a chaste kiss good night?"

"Shut up!"

"Struck too close to home, did I?" He smiled, even though he didn't feel like smiling. "Poor guy. It must've been hell following you around in hopes that you'd give in to your carnal side. How long did you hold the poor sap off? A year? Two?" Her eyes flickered. "You've got to be kidding. You made the poor guy wait for two entire years? What are you, some kind of sadist? No wonder he broke it off with you. He probably had the worst case of blue balls in history."

She came up out of the corner. "Well, you're wrong, Mr. Know-It-All McPherson! He didn't have blue balls. How can you have blue balls when you're screwing half the women in Kansas? All he had was a cheating heart and a lying mouth that convinced me he believed in all the things I believed in—convinced me that love was more important than sex." Once the words were out, she deflated like a punctured pool toy and wilted back against the seat, her attention returning to the city lights that slid past. "There," her voice quavered, "are you satisfied?"

Matthew wasn't. What was the matter with him? He didn't antagonize women. He loved women. All women. Except he was no longer concerned with all women.

Just this one.

He took a deep breath, then slowly released it. "Look, I'm sorry. I didn't realize you still had feelings for the guy."

"I don't," she grumbled. "My anger isn't about him as much as about his infidelity. About me abstaining when he didn't."

He leaned forward, resting his arms on his knees. "So if abstinence is so important to you, why were you willing to lose your closely guarded virginity to me?"

Even in the shadowy limo, he could tell that her face turned two shades darker. "Emotional trauma. One minute, Sidney was telling me about all the women Riley had gone to bed with, and the next, I was in The Heat Suite with you."

"Vegas? You found out about your boyfriend in Vegas?"

Her nod was like another sucker punch. This one aimed a little lower than his esophagus—more at the muscle that beat beneath his ribs. After weeks of trying to figure out why a virgin would let a complete stranger take her to bed, he finally had his answer.

And the truth hurt.

The thought of revenge had never entered his mind. In fact, he'd actually started to believe it had to do with some sweet naïve belief about love at first sight. And all the hate and anger she directed at him was nothing more than a smoke screen to hide her true feelings.

Except now he knew she wasn't hiding anything. The night in Vegas had nothing to do with him and everything to do with assuaging her broken heart. Matthew could've been anyone, and the results would've been the same. He just happened to be in the right place at the right time. Or, for him, the wrong place at the wrong time. No wonder Ellie acted like she wasn't happy to see him when he showed up at her book signing. She really wasn't happy to see him. To her, he was a fling easily forgotten. An experiment in the evils of unemotional sex.

Revenge on a man she did love.

Never in his life had Matthew felt so completely manipulated. He'd wasted the last eleven months of his life obsessing about Ellie, while she hadn't given him a thought. And why would she? She was a successful writer who had spent the time traveling around the country promoting her book and probably enjoying a few more one-night stands while she was at it. A successful writer who had been laughing herself silly over all his attempts to get her attention.

Well, it was time to set the record straight. He had done her a favor by initiating her into sex. A big favor. But he wasn't about to be as generous again. It would be a cold day in hell before Matthew McPherson gave Ellie Simpson seven orgasms. Or even one. And an even colder day in hell before he spent one more second trying to charm her.

"Be honest, do you actually blame the guy for screwing around on you?" he asked. "You can sell all the books you

want, but the truth is that men are wired for three things."
He counted off on his fingers. "Providing. Protecting.
And procreating. And since women are all into providing and protecting themselves these days, that leaves one.
Procreating." He glared at her. "And you ain't gonna stop
us from doing that. No matter how many stupid theories
you try to get us to swallow."

Her eyes widened. "I knew it!" She pointed a finger at
him. "You aren't interested in abstaining from anything."

He smiled as he leaned back in the seat and crossed his
arms. "Very perceptive."

Ellie looked like she struggled with a strong desire to
beat him over the head with the gigantic purse she held in
a stranglehold on her lap. "Then why did you show up at
my office saying you needed help for sex addiction?"

He shrugged. "Because I was trying to get in your
pants." Her mouth fell open, and she stared at him in
speechless shock. "What?" he said. "Did I shock the
Virgin Queen? I guess honesty isn't necessarily the best
policy."

It only took her a few seconds to regain her composure.
"The only time I've ever heard anything remotely honest
come out of your mouth was in Vegas. And even then, you
weren't completely honest."

He leaned up until he was inches from her face. "Oh, I
was honest that night. Completely. And did you like that,
Dr. Simpson? Because there's a lot more where that came
from." He pulled her onto his lap, knocking her purse to
the floor as he pressed her back into the seat. "Here's some
honesty for you. I don't like you, Dr. Simpson. I don't
like your height or your hair or the prudish clothes you

wear. And I especially don't like your screwed-up, narrow mind." He slipped his hand up her rib cage, encasing her breast with his thumb and forefinger. "In fact, the only thing I do like is the way you fill out a sweater." He knew he was being obnoxious and crass, but he didn't care. He needed his own revenge, and he lowered his mouth to hers and took it out on her sweet flesh.

Even with anger still simmering beneath the surface, the kiss consumed him. Each sip and slide of lips and tongues was like a perfectly synchronized dance. And it was more than just physical perfection. It was an emotional connection. Like two souls who were reunited after being away from each other for too long.

Reunited souls? Good Lord, he *had* lost his mind.

Matthew pulled back, wishing he could somehow start the entire evening over again. Or skip it entirely and go back to the day he'd seen her picture on the cover of that damned book. Or maybe before he met her in Vegas. No, he wasn't ready to give up the night they had in Vegas. He just couldn't survive a repeat.

A hard slap had his head ringing.

"You are such a jerk," she said.

"The biggest," he countered, and was more than relieved when the limo pulled up in front of the hotel and the doorman hurried to open the door. "Good-bye, Doc," he said as she climbed out of the limo. "I wish I could say it's been fun."

"Ha!" She tossed the word over her shoulder. "You wouldn't know fun if it bit you in the butt." Matthew watched as she marched through the open doors of the hotel.

"Aren't you getting out, sir?" the doorman asked.

"No. I'm over it," Matthew said more to himself than the doorman.

Which didn't explain why he felt so empty as the limo pulled away. No doubt because he never liked saying good-bye to a beautiful woman. And as much as he had said differently, Ellie was beautiful. She had a phenomenal body. Her hair wasn't that bad. And her legs were nice.

If she just hadn't talked, things might've worked out.

Chapter Seventeen

It took Ellie driving around the residential block several times before she found the address she was looking for. The house was a modest stucco with a high wall and enclosed courtyard. Ellie rang the bell and waited outside the secure metal gate until the person she spoke with through the intercom allowed her entry.

Since she had to get approval before she visited the shelter, she wasn't surprised that they knew she was coming. She *was* surprised, and flustered, to be greeted at the door by Mrs. McPherson. Ellie had assumed that the woman was only involved with the fund-raising. She hadn't thought that a wealthy socialite would actually work at the shelter. And the last thing she wanted was to see Matthew's mother. Not when just the thought of the man made her furious.

"So good to see you again, Dr. Simpson." Mrs. McPherson pulled her into her arms.

Never a hugger, Ellie just stood there with her face pressed against the cashmere sweater that smelled like vanilla and Elmer's glue.

"It's nice to see you, too," she said as she gave Mrs. McPherson an awkward pat on the back. "And please call me Ellie."

"And you must call me Mary or Mary Kay as the residents here get a kick out of saying." She finally pulled back. "I was worried that my sons' behavior the other night had run you off for good."

"I'm not easily run off."

Mary smiled one of those mother smiles. "Well, I was thrilled to hear that you were stopping by."

"I must admit that after the benefit I've been curious," she said. "Not just about the shelter, but about Joey's mother. I saw her with Joey outside the gallery on Saturday night, and I can't shake the feeling that I know her from somewhere. Where did they live before they moved to Denver?"

"I'm not sure," Mary said as she took Ellie's coat. "Joey acts like she's lived here all her life. But it's possible that I misunderstood." She hung the coat on a hook in the foyer. "Does the name Jennifer Hastings ring a bell?"

"No." Ellie shook her head. "I must've been mistaken. After all, it was dark, and Jennifer's face was badly bruised. I'm assuming her husband is responsible."

Mary nodded. "If you think she looks bad now, you should've seen her when she first arrived at the shelter. Her eyes were swollen shut, and her shoulder dislocated. The doctor on call had wanted to admit her to the hospital, but Joey was terrified that it was the first place her father would look."

"Are you worried that the husband will find them here?"

"No." Mary glanced down the hallway. "I'm more worried that Jennifer is going to go back to him. I've seen it too many times before. The women arrived battered and fearful, but within days they start making excuses for their men. And soon, they are right back in the abusive situation. I'd call it love, but in reality, it's more like a detrimental codependency."

Ellie nodded. In college, she had studied numerous domestic violence cases. Most had returned to their abusive husbands repeatedly before they finally left them. Unfortunately, one had been killed before she could escape the brutal cycle.

"Come on," Mary said, taking her arm. "Let me show you around Hope House and introduce you to some of our residents."

Although Hope House looked modest on the outside, it was large and roomy on the inside. There was a family room, a massive kitchen and dining area, a technology room, playroom, and six bedrooms and three baths. According to Mary, the stress of the holidays increased domestic violence. The house was filled to capacity, and the amount of people they ran into attested to the fact. Numerous children played in the playroom, four teenagers worked on the computers in the technology room, and eight women clustered around the dining room table. Ellie spotted Joey's mother immediately. She wore the same outfit she'd had on the night of the benefit, along with a pair of sunglasses that hid the bruises on her eyes but not the swelling of her jaw. Again, Ellie felt that nagging feeling that she knew the woman. Like the other women at the table, she was painting a glass ornament and listening to a professional woman in a business suit talk. At first, Ellie thought the woman in the expensive suit was the therapist for the group, but as she listened in, she soon realized her mistake.

"...I never knew what would set Robert off. One time, it was the dry cleaners I'd chosen. And the next time, it would be the way I handed him a glass of wine." The woman continued to paint as she talked. "You would think that being a lawyer, I would've been smart enough to figure out that it had nothing to do with my shortcomings and everything to do with his." She pressed her lips together. "But I didn't figure it out. I just kept thinking that if I was a better wife—a better person—he wouldn't hit me."

"That's how it works, sweetie," a large woman in an oversized shirt and tight leggings said. "It's all part of the brainwashing. The brutality followed by the guilty apology and declaration of love that always ends up putting the blame on you." She stopped painting and spoke in a sugary sweet voice. "'If you would only pay attention to what you do, Clarisse, I wouldn't get so angry at you, baby. But you know I love you. And you know I would never do anything to hurt you.'" She rolled her eyes. "This after he'd broken three ribs and my nose. Stupid asshole."

The gray-haired woman who sat at the head of the table glanced over at Joey's mother. "Would you like to add anything to the conversation, Jennifer?"

Jennifer refused to look up. "Anson's not like that. It was all just a misunderstanding."

The other women exchanged looks before Clarisse glanced up and noticed Mary and Ellie standing in the doorway. "We got us a new member of the family, Mary Kay?"

Mary smiled. It was so much like Matthew's that Ellie had trouble looking away. "Actually, Dr. Simpson is just visiting."

A shatter of glass had everyone looking at Jennifer, whose hand still curled around an ornament that was no longer there. A sinking feeling settled in the pit of Ellie's stomach. Not only did she know the woman, but the woman knew her too. Ellie desperately wanted to ask Jennifer where they'd met, but the fear she read in the woman's posture made her hold her tongue. Obviously, the woman didn't want to be recognized.

"No worries," Mary said as she started for the kitchen. "I'll get the hand vac, and we'll have that cleaned up in no time."

"It's not a big deal, Jenny," Clarisse added, and joined the other women who were helping to pick up the larger shards of glass. "It's hard to paint with two hands, let alone one. I'm surprised my big ol' meat hooks haven't broken more."

With so many helpers, Ellie decided that it was best to stay out of the way. Besides, it gave her a chance to observe. It was obvious that some of the women had been at the shelter longer than others by their actions and casual conversation. Jennifer was the only one who seemed hesitant and uncomfortable. When Clarisse patted her on the shoulder, she pulled back as if burned, then nervously reached for the open collar of her shirt. A memory flicked at the back of Ellie's mind, but before she could grasp it, Mary swept into the room with a handheld mini-vac.

Within minutes, she had all the glass cleaned up from the tile. It was surprising to see a woman of such social standing on her hands and knees vacuuming. Surprising, and also inspiring. It seems that Matthew hadn't lied about his mother. She was an intelligent, generous woman. Which didn't explain how she had ended up with such a manipulative, self-centered son.

"Dr. Simpson?"

Ellie turned to the woman who had been sitting at the head of the table. Her long gray hair hung in a braid down her back, and she wore a brightly colored tunic over black yoga pants. She held out her hand.

"I'm Dr. Beverly Stokes. I've been volunteering at Hope House for the last few years."

Ellie took her hand. "It's a pleasure to meet you, Dr. Stokes."

"The pleasure is mine. You certainly couldn't have come at a better time. My husband has recently retired and is ready to do some traveling. And I can't thank you enough for volunteering to help out when I can't."

Since Ellie had never been good at disappointing people, it was almost on the tip of her tongue to offer her help. But with looking for a place to live, starting a new practice, and writing her second book, she had little free time. Besides, her specialty was relationship counseling, not domestic violence. Which didn't explain what she was doing there. Just because Joey and Jennifer had struck a chord with her didn't mean that Ellie had a right to stick her nose where it didn't belong. She wasn't qualified to deal with this type of trauma. And any help she offered could do more harm than good.

"I'm sorry, Dr. Stokes," Ellie said, "but—"

"Dr. Simpson is only here because I invited her." Mary came up behind them. "She's a friend of the family's and wanted to see how I spend my days." She gave the woman a reassuring squeeze on the arm. "But don't you worry, Bev. I'll find someone to cover for you while you're traveling all over the countryside with that good-looking husband of yours."

Bev frowned. "But I planned on leaving next week to spend Christmas with my kids in Phoenix. How can you possibly find someone in that short of time?"

"It will all work out," Mary said. "It always—"

"There's a man in the courtyard!" A large woman in a polo shirt and jeans came hustling into the room. "While I was in the bathroom, the buzzer went off, and by the time I got back to the monitors to see who it was, I saw some guy climbing over the wall."

A pounding of fist against wood came from the front room, and more than a few fearful eyes turned toward the sound. The only person who didn't seem ruffled was Mary McPherson.

"Everyone get the children and get to your rooms and lock the doors. Bev, call nine-one-one." She tightened her grip on the mini-vac and, with a determined look, headed toward the front door as the women scrambled to follow her orders. All but Clarisse, who grabbed a baseball bat that was leaning by the sliding glass doors.

"I think I've had my fill of letting men bully me." She followed Mary out of the room, leaving Ellie all alone.

Since she hadn't been given an order, she stood there for a few seconds unsure of what she should do. She had just decided to follow Mary and Clarisse when she saw a stocking-capped head pass by the kitchen window. Before she could do more than gasp, the man opened the sliding glass door. Fortunately, he seemed to be preoccupied with something he carried, giving Ellie time to pick up the macaroni-art vase from the breakfast bar and bash him over the head.

With his thick stocking cap, it didn't break or knock him out. It just sent colored pasta flying in all directions. And before she could hit him again, he grabbed her wrist. Suddenly, she realized the type of fear the women in the house lived with every day. It would've been so easy for the man to snap her wrist in two. Instead, his grip was light. So light, she was able to jerk away and kick him hard in the shin.

"Sonofa—!"

The words caused Ellie's hand with the broken vase to halt in mid-swing. Or not the words as much as the voice.

"Matthew?"

Hopping around on one leg, he lifted his green gaze to hers. "Ellie?"

"What in the world?" Mary came flying back into the room with Clarisse close on her heels. She took one look around the room with colored pasta flung everywhere, and then her gaze zeroed in on her son. "Matthew, I would assume that you have an explanation for scaring us all half to death by jumping over the wall like some nefarious criminal."

Matthew stopped hopping and turned to his mother. If Ellie had thought he looked good in suits and tuxedos, it was nothing to the way he looked in a down vest, flannel shirt, and faded jeans. Clarisse must've been thinking the same thing.

"So I take it that you know this good-looking hunk of a man, Mary Kay," she said.

Mary made the introductions, and when she was finished, she added, "So what are you doing here, Matthew?"

"Not being a nefarious criminal." He reached out and pulled a Christmas tree through the open sliding glass door. "Merry Christmas, Mom, from your Secret Santa." He flashed a smile. Not the charming playboy smile, but a mischievous little boy smile that was twice as sexy. Clarisse actually sighed.

Mary looked at the tree and back at her son before a smile bloomed on her face. She walked over and planted a kiss on his cheek. "Thank you, dear. I couldn't have asked for a better gift."

"Good." Matthew pulled off his stocking cap and rubbed his head, casting a mean look over at Ellie. "Now, if you'll tell me where you want it, I need to get to work."

"Oh, no, you don't." Mary handed the mini-vac to Ellie. "You can't expect mere women to put up a tree that size by themselves." She looked back at Clarisse. "If you go get the tree stand and decorations out of the garage, Clarisse, I'll tell the ladies that everything is fine and have Bev inform the police about the mistake."

Just that quickly, Ellie found herself alone with Matthew. A scowling Matthew who seemed as annoyed as she was about the circumstances.

"So what are you doing here?" he asked. "I thought I made it clear that I didn't want to see you again."

"What an egomaniac," she said. "Do you actually think that I came here in hopes of running into you? I came at the invitation of your mother." She clicked on the vac and started cleaning up the pasta, cutting off whatever he was about to say. But that didn't mean she could keep her eyes off him. There was something about his casual clothes and messed hair that made Ellie slightly dizzy. Or maybe it was the way his biceps bulged beneath the flannel of his shirt when he hefted the trunk of the tree and pulled it into the next room.

Once he was gone, her equilibrium came back, along with her senses, and she shut off the vac and decided it was time to leave. She had just walked into the foyer to get her coat and purse, when her cell phone rang.

"I think I've found you a place to live," her Realtor's excited voice came through the receiver.

"You have a house for me?" Ellie asked.

"A condo, and it's not for sale. But this place is perfect for you to rent until you can decide on a home. So perfect that we'll have to move quickly if we don't want to lose it."

"When can I see it?" Ellie asked, now as excited as her agent. She was sick to death of living in a hotel—as was her wallet.

"Just as soon as you can meet me over there. It's in the downtown area."

She glanced at her watch. "I can be there in twenty minutes."

"Be where?" Mary walked up just as Ellie hung up the phone. "I was hoping you'd stay and help decorate the tree."

"I'm sorry," she said. "But I'm afraid I have to go. My Realtor has found me a condo, and she wants me to see it."

Mary looked thoroughly disappointed. "Well, of course, if you need to go, you need to go. But I hope you'll come back soon."

"I'll try," Ellie said, "but I'm afraid that with my new practice and book—"

"Oh, you're writing a new book? What's this one about?" Before Ellie could answer, Clarisse came in carrying a tall stack of plastic storage containers, and Mary hurried over to take the top one.

"A new book, huh?" Matthew stood in the archway of the living room, his arms crossed over his chest. "Let me guess. *Virgin Love Two: My Life as a Miserable Old Maid.*"

Just to wipe the smug look off his face Ellie started to tell him the actual title, when the women and children came out of the bedrooms and filed through the foyer on their way to the family room. Bringing up the rear was Jennifer. She still wore her sunglasses, but even with them on, Ellie knew Jennifer watched her. As she passed, she reached up and pulled a necklace out of her shirt and fidgeted with the pendant. A pendant of a thin silver cross.

Jennifer was the woman from the book signing.

Chapter Eighteen

I don't know, girls. What do you think? Should Matthew's balls be a little higher?"

Clarisse's double entendre had the other women giggling and Matthew laughing. Since arriving at the house, Clarisse had enjoyed making him the butt of her jokes, but her twinkling eyes and audacious winks let him know that it was all in fun.

And, surprisingly, Matthew was having fun.

The last time he'd been there, he'd only stayed long enough to feel uncomfortable and guilty. Now he realized his mistake. The residents of the house weren't man-haters who jumped whenever he entered the room. They were just women like any other women who liked to laugh and gossip and tease the heck out of him.

At least, most of them did. He glanced over at the woman who sat in the corner nervously fiddling with the chain of her necklace. Jennifer was the only one who seemed removed from the group. The dark glasses she hid behind explained the reason why. The purple and yellow bruises were just visible beneath the large frames of the Christian Dior sunglasses that had once belonged to his mother. Seeing them used to cover that kind of brutality made Matthew more than angry. It made him want to hunt down the bastard and give him an ass-kicking he wouldn't soon forget.

"I know it's hard to figure out."

The words had him looking down at Clarisse who stood next to the ladder he was perched on.

"People who don't live through it," she continued, "just don't understand how we can let someone do that to us. But the men we love don't start out as villains. They start out as knights in shining armor that we can't help falling in love with. Once the intricate web of love and punishment is spun, it's hard to distinguish between our dreams and reality."

"I'm sorry," he said. He didn't know why he apologized. Maybe for being part of the gender that could be so brutal. Or maybe he was apologizing for all the times he had spun a web—playing with women without any thought to their feelings. He would never hurt a woman physically, but he knew he had hurt some emotionally.

And maybe that was even worse.

Clarisse shook her head. "Don't feel sorry for us. We're the ones who climbed out of the web. It's the ones who are still caught that need our sympathy and help." She pointed to the ornaments he held in his hands, then up at the top of the tree. "It's a little bare up there."

Matthew climbed another rung on the ladder and hung the ornaments in bare spots. "What do you think?"

"I think that your balls look pretty good from here," Clarisse said.

Matthew quirked an eyebrow at her, but she only laughed and handed him more of the handmade ornaments. While Clarisse was helping him, the rest of the women and children were busy hanging ornaments on the bottom branches of the tree. Some sang along with the Christmas music his mother had put on, while others chatted about the holiday party that was planned for Christmas Eve.

It was the first Matthew had heard about it, and he wondered if his mother planned on attending. It was doubtful. His parents always had the entire McPherson family over on Christmas Eve, followed by midnight mass. He couldn't see his mother missing those two traditions. He planned on asking her about it when she breezed into the room a few minutes later, her apron dusted with flour and her hands sticky with cookie dough. She never gave him a chance before she started issuing orders.

"Matthew, when you're finished with the tree, I want you to take the ladder into the garage and get the outside decorations off the top shelf."

"So I'm assuming that I won't be going back to the office today," he said dryly.

"Now that's totally up to you." His mother sent him a smile before she sailed back into the kitchen.

Since there was nothing pressing at his office and this was his Secret Santa gift, he finished decorating the top branches before he got on his stocking cap and down vest and carried the ladder to the garage. It was a three-car with no cars. All the vehicles were parked in the long, enclosed driveway in front. In the garage were boxes and trash bags labeled with last names. As he stood in the open door of one stall, he couldn't help feeling sad that this was all the residents of the house had been able to take with them. But maybe that was a blessing. Maybe it was better to start fresh. And that was exactly what his mother was doing here at the shelter. She was helping to give these women a chance at a fresh start.

At that moment, Matthew couldn't have been prouder of his mom—or felt crappier for not coming to help her at the shelter sooner. But better late than never, Aunt Wheezie always said.

Matthew pushed the garage door the rest of the way up and carried the ladder in. It didn't take him long to find the boxes of outside decorations. They were mostly strings of lights. Once he plugged them into the sockets, he discovered that half of them didn't work. His father and brothers would've gone through each light, checking for broken bulbs or shorts. Matthew didn't have the patience. He'd rather buy new ones and be done with it. After plugging in each string, he collected the ones that didn't work and went in search of a trash bin. He found three wheeled containers on the side of the garage. He also found a small shed. When he peeked in one of the windows, he discovered the teenage girl from the gallery.

Joey sat cross-legged on the paint-splattered cement floor, her bare feet resting on her thighs in what looked like a yoga position. Her entire focus was on the canvas propped up against the wall. She leaned back and studied the painting before she went back to work. It was fascinating to watch. The brush moved as if by its own will—as if her hand was just along for the ride.

At the gallery, Matthew had barely noticed the girl's painting. But now he took the time to study her work. As much as he thought she was an out-of-control hooligan, he had to admit that she had talent.

He leaned closer to get a better look, and his head bumped the glass. She looked up, and her eyes registered shock before they turned belligerent and mean. Especially when she noticed the streak of acrylic paint across her canvas.

"You dumbass!" She yelled so loud that it was easy to hear her through the thick glass. But this time, Matthew wasn't taken by surprise. This time, he understood where the girl's anger came from.

He opened the door and stepped inside. "One dumbass at your service."

"You're not funny," she grumbled.

He shrugged. "I'm just warming up. I'm usually a lot funnier once you get to know me."

"Well, this isn't funny." She jabbed a finger at the streak. "You completely ruined it."

Matthew walked around behind her and examined the painting. It was an abstract of a woman with huge, empty eye sockets and no mouth. The streak of pink seemed to come out of the broken ribs of her chest. The pain communicated by the painting almost had him reaching for his wallet and offering the girl whatever she needed to get her out of her current situation. After all, he was responsible for her losing out on a sale the night of the benefit.

But somehow he knew that the feisty kid wouldn't go for charity. If he wanted to help her, he would need to take things slow.

"I wouldn't say that," he said. "Abstract is an artist's representation of their reality. All I did was alter yours. Now you have to decide if the change adds to the elements and principle of your design or detracts from it."

"And I guess that means I have to deal with your screwup."

He laughed. "Pretty much." He walked over to the table and picked up the tray of acrylic paints.

"Hey, get your filthy paws off my stuff!" she snapped.

He lifted an eyebrow at her. "Your stuff? Or the shelter's?" He nodded at the case of paintbrushes that sat open on the table. "In fact, if you look on the top of that box, I think you'll find the name Matthew McPherson—which is me."

"Whatever." She tossed the paintbrush down to the palette, splattering even more paint on the floor. "I don't want your stupid brushes." She went to get to her feet, but he walked back over and handed her the tray.

"Don't give up. Your reality is what you make it."

At the gallery, he had gotten the feeling that she didn't like being touched. She verified this by making sure not to touch his hand when she took the tray from him. Her fear had him using the same tone of voice he used when speaking to Patrick's skittish strays.

"I think it was Andy Warhol who said, 'They always say time changes things, but you actually have to change them yourself.' "

For long moments, she stared at the painting before she

selected a royal blue paint and poured a small amount on her palette. "So you paint?"

"I used to. Unfortunately, no matter how many lessons my mother paid for, I was always lacking one thing."

She looked up at him. "What?"

He flashed her a smile. "Talent" A tiny glimmer of a grin curved one side of her mouth before it was gone. "You, on the other hand"—he pointed at the painting—"seem to have it in spades. How long have you been working on this?"

"A few hours."

Matthew walked to the other side of the abstract painting and studied it from another angle. "It's good. Very good."

"If you don't have any talent," she said, "how would you know?"

"Because I've always had a good eye. How do you think I knew I didn't have any talent?"

This time, she did smile, and he was immediately reminded of Ellie. Both their smiles were rare and completely transformed their faces. Ellie hadn't smiled today. She looked as shocked to see him as he was to see her. And shocked wasn't the only thing he'd felt when he turned to find her standing there with the broken vase in her hand. But he refused to acknowledge the other emotion that had swelled up inside him. Joy and Ellie were an anomaly.

"So what are you going to do with this talent?" he asked.

Joey looked up at him, the knob in her bottom lip catching the sunlight. "I'm not selling it at that dumb gallery if that's what you mean."

"That's good." He moved a large painting resting

against the wall to look at the abstract behind. "Because these pieces aren't good enough for a gallery."

She quickly turned belligerent. "What do you mean by that?"

He replaced the canvas and turned to her. "I mean that you have talent, but it's not gallery quality... yet. It needs refinement. Something only a qualified teacher can give you."

She snorted. "Are you saying that you want to teach me? Because I'm not taking instruction from some untalented joker. I don't care how good his eye is."

It was hard to like the kid. Especially when she was like a cornered Rottweiler with a toothache. But there was something in her eyes that said she was much more bark than bite.

And most of Patrick's dogs responded better to tough love than to gentle.

"You're right. I probably don't have anything to teach you." He moved toward the door. "I'll let you get back to your finger painting." He slipped out before she had a chance to say anything, figuring he would give her some time before he made the offer again. Given the loud string of cuss words that came from the shed, it was a good decision. He grinned and shook his head as he walked away. The kid could sure rant and rave.

And speaking of ranting and raving, he came around the corner of the garage to find his mother standing in the courtyard talking on her cell phone. Or not talking as much as yelling. Since his mother rarely raised her voice, he became instantly concerned. Even more so when he realized who she was talking to.

"No, I'm not menopausal, Albert. Or taking too many hormones. Or frustrated because it's winter and I can't play tennis at the club. I'm just sick and tired of being treated like a spoiled housewife who has nothing better to do than get her nails done or fix dinner for you. And speaking of dinner, you can just fix your own!" She pressed the end button and whirled around to find Matthew standing there. She blushed guiltily before she collected herself and smoothed back her hair. "I'm sorry that you had to hear that, Matthew."

He tried to make light of it. "It's okay, Mom. I'm an adult and can handle my parents having a little argument."

A frown marred her brow. "You sound exactly like your father. He thinks that everything I say or do is little—your little reading club, your little college classes, your little volunteer work." She straightened her shoulders. "Well, I'm tired of everyone treating my interests and jobs as little things I do to fill my boring, trivial days."

"I wasn't—"

"What I do is important." She moved a step closer. Never having seen his mother this upset, he took a step back. "I raised five children practically by myself while your father wheeled and dealed in the business world. And yes, he is a wonderful provider and I've never wanted for anything, but a little respect would've been nice. Just some appreciation for all I do for him and you kids."

"I appreciate—"

"But no-o-o, he's too wrapped up in his own achievements to notice anyone else's." The wind picked up, and she rubbed her arms as she started to pace. "I thought he would get better after his heart attack—I thought we would spend more time together—but he's right back to working twelve-hour days."

Matthew took off his vest and hooked it over her shoulders. She barely noticed as she continued to talk. "So I decided to get my own interests"—she patted her chest—"my own life. And I'll be damned if he'll make me feel guilty about it!" Then just as Matthew was getting over his mother cussing, she did something really horrifying. She burst into tears.

Matthew had been around enough weeping women in his lifetime that the sight shouldn't have bothered him. Women wept during movies, commercials, and Josh Groban songs. And at any moment during their menstrual cycles. They cried if you gave them the perfect gift, or if you forgot to get them a gift. And they cried sometimes just because they needed "a good cry." Long ago, Matthew had given up trying to figure it out. But this was his mother. And his mother didn't cry unless someone died. Yet, here she stood sobbing as if her heart were broken.

"Aww, Mom," he said, and stepped closer and pulled her into his arms. "It will be okay. I'll have a talk with Dad."

She pulled back, her face streaked with tears and mascara. "You'll do no such thing, Matthew McPherson." She stepped away and wiped at her cheeks. "I had no business crying to you about my problems with your father. That's between us."

"But maybe Dad would listen to me."

Her eyes turned even sadder. "But that's just the point, Matthew. I don't want him to listen to you. I want him to listen to me." Handing him his vest, she turned and walked back in the house.

Matthew started to go after her, but then he realized he didn't know what to say to make things better. Especially when he wasn't having so much luck in his own relationships. Still, he couldn't let his mother be this miserable and not do something.

He reached for his cell phone. There was only one person in the family who could help.

Chapter Nineteen

Wheezie pulled the opera glasses away from her eyes and glanced down at the noise-making piece of technology Katherine had given her as an early Christmas present. The contraption didn't even have a normal telephone ring. It sounded like Rory and Amy's two-year-old son Douglas banging on his xylophone. And at least Douglas stopped when you clapped. She had yet to figure out how to shut this thing up.

"You want me to answer it?" Her chauffeur Barkley reached his big mitt of a hand toward the phone that sat in the console between them, but she waved it away.

"I got it! You just keep your eyes on the suspect."

Barkley shrugged and looked back at M&M Construction's office building. "I don't think Big Al is going to like us spying on his favorite son-in-law. A son-in-law who is a major shareholder in the company."

"Which is why I asked you to drive your car today. What Alby doesn't know, won't hurt him." Wheezie squinted at the phone. "Where the heck is the talk button?"

Barkley took the phone and briefly touched the screen with his big, calloused finger before handing it back. For an ex-boxer and construction worker, the man had a gentle touch. And was darn good at pinochle. Which was the only reason Wheezie kept him around. She knew how to drive. In fact, she drove a hell of a lot better than Barkley.

"Hello?" she said as she held it to her ear. "Hello?" Barkley reached out and flipped the phone to the other side. She sent him an exasperated look before trying again. "Hello?"

"Hey, Wheezie," Matthew's voice came through the receiver. "It sounds like you're getting used to the phone."

"When hell freezes over." She lifted the opera glasses back to her eyes. "Although with as cold as it's been the last few days, I wouldn't be surprised if it does." She waited for his laugh, and when it didn't come, she lowered the glasses. "So what's going on?"

"It's Mom."

"She didn't like you bringing over the tree? I thought she'd be jumping for joy to have one of her kids help at the shelter."

"No, she liked that. This has to do with the conversation I overheard her having with Dad. It seems she doesn't feel appreciated—mostly by Dad. Has she talked with you about it?"

Wheezie blew out a disgruntled gust of air. It was getting harder and harder to keep her family afloat. With the way things were going, she wouldn't be able to meet her maker until she was a hundred and ten. And fifteen more years with this wreck of a body was pushing it.

"She mentioned something about it," she said. "What did you overhear?"

"Just that she's upset about not being appreciated and wants Dad to make his own dinners from now on."

Wheezie laughed. "Well, I'd say it's about time. Your mother is the glue that holds this family together, and it's time your father realized that."

"And you think he will?" he said. "Dad is as hard-headed as they come. Remember how long it took him to warm up to James?"

Wheezie smiled. "But do you remember how quickly he changed his tune when he thought he might lose his daughter over it? His loved ones are the most important things in Big Al's life. Sometimes he just needs to be reminded of that."

"There he is." Barkley nodded at the Land Rover that had just pulled out of the parking garage.

Wheezie flapped a hand for him to follow, and Barkley put his Volkswagen Beetle in drive and pulled out after the Land Rover as she got back to Matthew. "So I was going to ask you about that pretty young lady you brought to the benefit the other night—Ellie, I believe her name is."

There was a long, telling stretch of silence before Matthew spoke. "What about her?"

"Oh, I was just wondering if you thought she would be a good match for Patrick. They seemed to be getting along pretty nicely."

"She's not getting with Patrick." Matthew's voice was hard. "In fact, you won't be seeing her again."

Wheezie smiled. *That's what you think.*

"Well, that's a shame." She tried to keep an eye on the Land Rover, but it was difficult given the fact that Barkley drove like Grandma Moses. "Hurry it up. We're losing him."

"Losing who?" Matthew asked.

She ignored the question. "Listen, handsome, I'll have to talk with you later. As we all know, Barkley has no sense of direction, and I'll need to navigate if we don't want to end up in Mexico. I promise I'll talk with your mother as soon as I get back to the house. This cell phone is like talking to a makeup compact."

By the time she finally figured out how to hang up the phone, Barkley was only a few cars behind the Land Rover. They followed it for a good twenty minutes before it pulled into a parking space in front of a coffee shop.

"Now why would he be stopping here?" Wheezie asked Barkley.

"Maybe he wants a cup of coffee."

She scrunched down in the seat as they cruised past. "In the middle of the afternoon when the office he just left has its own coffeemaker?"

"Maybe he likes flavored." Barkley made a U-turn at the end of the block and pulled into an empty space down the street from the coffee shop. "You want me to slip in and take a few pictures with your phone?"

She shot a glance over at his huge body that barely fit behind the wheel of the Volkswagen. "As if the Hulk snapping pictures would go unnoticed. No. I'm sure he's just meeting one of his clients for coffee." She sat back up. "I've done what I said I was going to do. So let's go home and play some cards. I want to get my quarters back after you beat—"

She stopped in mid-sentence when a Lexus pulled up behind the Land Rover. Within seconds, the door opened and a beautiful blonde in heels and a designer suit stepped out, her colored scarf and long hair blowing in the cold December breeze. Wheezie would've thought that her arrival within minutes of the Land Rover was a mere coincidence if the Land Rover's door hadn't opened and the suspect stepped out. He smiled a brilliant smile and greeted the woman, then escorted her around to the passenger side of the SUV and held the door while she climbed in.

The opera glasses slipped from Wheezie's fingers and thumped down to her lap. "Well, I'll be damned," she breathed. "James *is* fooling around on Cassandra."

Chapter Twenty

You're being ridiculous, Elle," Sidney said as they carried boxes up the stairs of Ellie's new condo. "Nothing you said in a thirty-second conversation got the woman beat up. While you are responsible for lots of men not getting any nookie, you aren't responsible for a reader who married a sick bastard who gets his kicks out of hitting women."

Ellie maneuvered her box through the living room to the stairs that led up to the third level. "But you should've seen the way she reacted when she saw me, Sid. If I'm not responsible, why didn't she acknowledge me?"

Sidney followed her up the stairs. "Maybe she was embarrassed. She probably didn't want the famous author she looks up to knowing that she let her husband use her as a punching bag."

It did make sense. Still, Ellie couldn't help feeling

guilty. She had no business handing out advice without knowing the circumstances. And she intended to make amends. Even if it meant going back to the shelter and volunteering.

"Well, she had no reason to feel embarrassed." Ellie placed the heavy box down on the dresser. "I realize how easy it is to become a victim. Just look at my mother."

"Your mother doesn't seem like much of a victim to me," Sidney said as she looked around for a place to set the box she carried. "She spends her days at the country club and her nights with a man who showers her with gifts and attention. What more can a woman ask for?"

"How about fidelity?"

"Please, no more bellyaching about your father being unable to keep his penis in his pants. Really, Elle, it's starting to get old." She set the box on the floor. "I was there when Mean Jean informed you that your father was bopping her mother. I was there when you discovered his car in front of the widow Murphy's house. And I was there when that floozy Cheryl Lines called and ratted him out thinking you were his wife. So I know how painful your father's infidelity has been for you. But don't you think that it's time to let it go?"

Ellie opened the box and pulled out some clean sheets. "You wouldn't be saying that if it was your father who had screwed around."

"No, my father didn't screw around. He just divorced my mother and left her to raise three kids on her own. A real world-class, great guy." Sidney picked out a box to start unpacking. "But you don't see me cutting off men because I had a bad dad—which you didn't have by the way. Despite his sex problem, your father was cool. He made you that tree house, brought home really nice presents from business trips, and was never too tired to play hide-and-seek at the park or Marco Polo in your swimming pool."

"All because he felt guilty."

Sidney sighed in exasperation. "Whatever." She opened the box. "Geez, Elle, how many vibrators does a woman need?"

Ellie stopped trying to hook the bottom sheet on the edge of the mattress and looked over to see Sidney unpacking a box she had no business unpacking. Releasing the sheet, she hurried over and took the box away from her friend. "These are for research. Besides, don't you read? This was marked personal."

"Which is exactly why I opened it," Sidney said. "I'm your 'personal' assistant. And this only reinforces my argument. It's time to get over your daddy issues and start dating so you can have orgasms with living, breathing men." She paused and added almost too nonchalantly, "Like Matthew McPherson."

Ellie gaped at her. "Have you lost your mind? Especially after I told you what happened in the limo."

"I've been thinking about that, and I think he's lying." Sidney clicked on a tiny vibrator that she had obviously removed from the box without Ellie knowing. She listened to the loud hum before she lifted an eyebrow at Ellie, who snatched the vibrator away and turned it off.

"What do you mean?" Ellie asked. "You think he lied about wanting to get in my pants?"

"No. He wants to get in your pants. But it's also as

obvious as the cute little dent in his chin that his attraction to you isn't just about sex."

It was annoying how badly Ellie wanted to believe her. "Then why would he say he doesn't find me attractive and never wants to see me again?"

Sidney shrugged. "Who knows? Men lie about everything. They lie to get women into bed—they lie to get them out. They lie to protect their fragile egos. And sometimes I think they lie just because they forget how to tell the truth. It's weird, but true. All I know is that Matthew couldn't seem to take his eyes off you the other night. And there were plenty of women there who would've gladly let him into their pants."

A giddy feeling swelled up in Ellie's stomach, but she pushed it down and finished putting on the sheets. But the entire time she smoothed and tucked, she couldn't help thinking about Sidney's words. Was it true? Was Matthew lying about his feelings? Did he care about her more than he was letting on?

"Well, it doesn't make a difference," she said as she reached for the new comforter set. "I won't be seeing him again."

"Of course you will." Sidney moved over to the other side of the bed and grabbed one end of the comforter. "Your relationship with Matthew isn't about him liking you or disliking you. It's about you doing research for your new book." She sent Ellie a dubious look. "Remember your new book?"

Ellie remembered her new book. After the benefit, in an attempt to work through her anger, she'd gotten on her laptop and written down copious notes. But instead of a cohesive, professional observation about a man who went through women like toilet paper, she ended up with twenty pages of diary-style ramblings that sounded like an angry teenage girl who had just discovered that her crush didn't like her.

It was pathetic.

With Sidney's help, it didn't take long to get the bed made, the boxes unpacked, and her bedroom set up. Once they finished, they both stood back to look at their handiwork.

"So what do you think?" Ellie asked. "Do you like the bed against the brick wall or do you think I should get a headboard?"

Sidney fell back on the bed, uncaring that Ellie had just finished smoothing it to perfection. "No, I like it the way it is. But a bunch of colored throw pillows would be nice. Do you want to go to Pier One?"

"No. I'm too tired. I'll get some tomorrow." She joined Sidney on the bed and stared up at the skylight.

"It's a great condo, Elle," Sidney said.

Ellie had to agree. According to her Realtor, the three-story brick building had been built in the late eighteen hundreds and had survived years of various uses and vacancy before being turned into commercial space and condos. The bottom floor had three small commercial shops facing the street and the condos' two-car garages facing the back parking lot. The living space was on the second level and consisted of a great room with high ceilings and multi-paned windows, a chef's kitchen, and a dining room. The two bedrooms and two bathrooms were on the third level. There was a balcony off the master bedroom and skylights throughout. The oak floors were original, and the master bath had a Jacuzzi tub. Conveniently located within walking distance of shopping and restaurants, it was in a perfect location. It would be even more perfect if she could buy it, but the Realtor said buying wasn't an option.

Ellie glanced over at Sidney. "So what are you doing for dinner? You want to order Chinese?"

"No, I'm going to dinner with Keith." She rolled to her feet. "But you could join us. Keith might have another single friend who isn't as big of a jerk as Jeff."

Ellie tried to hide her cringe. "No, thanks, I think I'll stay here and enjoy my new place."

Sidney headed for the door. "Okay, but call me later."

Once the door to the lower level closed, Ellie glanced around her apartment. It was the first time in her life that she had ever lived alone, and she had to admit that it was more than a little scary. But it was also liberating. This was her place. Not her parents'. Not Sidney's. Just hers. The thought gave her another burst of energy, and she tore down the boxes, then carried the collapsed cardboard through the garage to the outside trash bin.

A cold wind caught the cardboard, almost tugging it from her hands, but she held on and pushed toward the Dumpster where she proceeded to throw the flattened boxes over the side one at a time. While she was working, a calico cat came up and rubbed against her legs. She had just reached down to scratch its head when a sleek silver Porsche pulled into the parking lot and the garage door to the right of hers opened. Quickly, she threw in the last box and brushed cardboard remnants off the front of her old sweatshirt.

It would've been nice to meet her new neighbors when

she was dressed for work, not when she looked like a bum off the street in her faded jeans and straggly ponytail. Hopefully it was a woman who understood about moving day, a woman who was open to making new friends. Ellie might be a strong, successful woman who lived by herself, but that didn't mean it wouldn't be nice to have a friend living right next door.

She turned with a smile on her face.

It froze when she spotted the driver of the Porsche. She blinked. But the dark-haired male driver didn't change. The only indication that Matthew had seen her was the slight tightening of his mouth. After that, he completely ignored her, pulling the Porsche into the garage before closing it down.

Ellie's gaze remained transfixed on the garage door long after it closed. It took a good five minutes and a blast of icy wind before her mind started to unscramble. Then she muttered a very dirty cuss word under her breath and raced back to her condo. It didn't take long to get her real estate agent on the phone and even less to figure out how she happened to rent a condo right next door to Matthew McPherson.

The sun had slipped below the horizon, and the temperature had dropped considerably by the time she stood in front of Matthew's garage and pressed the buzzer for the intercom.

"Sorry, I don't need any cookies this year," his voice said through the speaker.

"Oh, I'm not here to sell you Thin Mints, you good-for-nothing piece of crap," she yelled. "How dare you tell me to stay out of your way when you had this planned—"

The intercom clicked off.

"Arrgh!" Ellie rammed her finger on the buzzer so hard she broke a nail, but Matthew refused to answer. So she pressed on the buzzer for a full minute, and when that didn't work, she tried a variety of different techniques. Rapid consecutive hits. Four short and two longs. And finally a rendition of "Jingle Bells."

Before she got to "oh, what fun," the garage door opened. It barely reached halfway when Matthew ducked under and grabbed her hand away from the buzzer.

"Fine! I get that you're pissed off. And believe me when I tell you that I'm not exactly thrilled with it, either. And as soon as I find out who in my family is responsible, there will be hell—"

"Your family! You're going to blame this on your family?" She poked him in the chest. When her cold fingertip came in contact with warm, hard muscle, she finally realized what he was wearing. Nothing. Or maybe not quite nothing. A towel was knotted at one hip bone, but it barely reached his knees.

Ellie's gaze settled on the pink puckered scar on one knee. A scar she remembered using her tongue on as she licked her way up his body on New Year's Eve. A gust of wind caught the edge of the towel, flashing her a tempting glimpse of man treat. While she sucked in her breath, Matthew released his.

"Look, I'm sorry about the condo." He placed a hand on one hip, further hiking the towel and her heart rate. "And that's not all I'm sorry about." Completely unaware of what a body like his did to a woman's libido, he lifted a hand and ran it through his hair, displaying one furred armpit and a ladder of ripped muscles that took all the moisture from her mouth. "I'm sorry about the way I've acted around you. Believe me when I tell you that I've never treated a woman like I've treated you in my life. And I can't explain it. I guess we just rub each other the wrong way."

Rub? Oh, Ellie wanted to rub him, all right. And in a very wrong way. Especially now that he had taken all the wind out of her anger by apologizing.

He lowered his hand from his hip, and the towel sagged even more. "I'll make the arrangements to find you another place to live and hire some movers first thing in the morning." He turned to head back into the garage. "In the meantime, I'd appreciate it if you would stay away from my intercom. Your rendition of 'Jingle Bells' sucked."

"Wait!" When he turned back around, she struggled to keep her eyes above his waist. "And what if I don't want another condo?"

Matthew's eyes narrowed. "What are you suggesting? Because I'm sure as hell not moving."

What was she suggesting? And why was she suggesting it? The book. It had to be the book. Sidney was right. It didn't matter if Matthew liked her or not; living right next to him would give her the perfect opportunity to study his behavior.

She cleared her throat. "No, I'm not suggesting that you move. Especially since your family owns this building. I'm suggesting that we act like two mature adults who find themselves in an awkward position—we make the best of it."

He studied her for only a second before he spoke. "No.

I won't live next door to a crazy therapist who thinks I'm a sex addict."

"Well, what would you call a man who's had sex with at least a hundred women?"

"Happy." When she rolled her eyes, he continued. "Look, I can't deny that I've been to bed with a lot of women. But I'm not an addict." He held up his hand and counted off on his fingers. "Firstly, I don't put sex before my family—ever. Secondly, while I might thoroughly enjoy sex, I can live without."

Ellie shot him a skeptical look. "For how long? A day?"

"Try eleven months."

She would've thought he was kidding around if, once the words were out, he hadn't looked so annoyed. Still, she couldn't bring herself to believe it.

"You mean to tell me that you've gone without sex for eleven months?"

"Something like that. Now if you'll excuse me, I'm freezing my butt off."

"Oh, no, you don't," she said. "You can't drop a bomb like that, then walk off without explaining why."

"I've been busy. Besides, aren't you the one who promotes abstinence as being the cure for all that ails you?"

"Yes, but I never thought for a second that you would agree with me."

"You're right," he said. "I don't agree with the idiotic notion that relationships are better off without sex. That doesn't make me a sex addict—just a man. Which is why it would be best if you lived elsewhere. M&M just finished building new condos a couple miles from here. And I can get you into one by the end of this week."

He turned to head back inside, but she refused to let him go. Not when it had taken her so long to find a condo she loved. And not when she was already moved in. And not when she wanted to know why he had gone without sex for eleven long months. She reached out and grabbed his arm, but the heat of naked flesh and hard muscle had her pulling back as if burned. Her hand accidentally bumped the knot in the towel, and in slow motion, it fell to his feet.

There was a moment when neither one of them moved. Matthew froze in place while Ellie more like melted—the sight of all his glorious naked flesh working like a blast from a blowtorch. Lust had such a tight hold on her that she barely even registered the rumbling of a truck pulling into the parking lot.

But Matthew did.

With a curse, he reached for his towel and secured it around his waist. It took a little longer for Ellie to come to her senses. By the time she looked over her shoulder, a white truck with M&M CONSTRUCTION stenciled on the driver's door was pulling into the first condo's garage. And in a matter of seconds, Patrick appeared.

"Welcome to Casa McPherson, Dr. Simpson," he said as he lifted up two pizza boxes. "Where men run around naked and pizza gets delivered straight to your door."

Chapter Twenty-one

Now, don't get your panties in a bunch, Matthew."
Wheezie cradled the phone to her ear and pushed back
the curtains in her front window, looking out at the driveway. So far, it was empty. But after the frantic call she'd
made earlier, she figured it wouldn't be empty for long.
"Yes, I talked Cassie into renting the condo to Dr. Simpson for Patrick's Secret Santa gift." She shook her head.
It was the last time she'd share information with Cassandra McPherson. The girl couldn't keep a secret to save her
soul. "But I don't see how that's skin off your nose. I was
just hoping to give Patrick a chance to get to know Ellie.
Since you haven't produced any marriage material for
your brother, I figured I'd have to take over."

"I thought I made it clear, Wheeze, that Ellie is not
good marriage material for Patrick," Matthew stated
with such finality that Wheezie smiled. "She's not good

marriage material for anyone. The woman is two cards short of a deck. Which is why you should've talked to me first before you rented her the condo. Ellie and I don't exactly get along. And her living next to me is going to make for a very uncomfortable situation."

Wheezie sure hoped so. Matthew's life was too comfortable. He needed someone to shake it up. And the little sex psychologist was just the one to do it. Most people might think that forcing them to live right next door to each other was a little extreme, but Wheezie figured it was the fastest way to see if they were compatible. And when you were in your nineties, the faster things moved along the better.

"Now I find it hard to believe that there's a woman on this planet you don't get along with," she said. "I thought you could charm a snake out of its skin."

"Ellie is a freak of nature. She doesn't go for charming."

Wheezie laughed. "Sounds like my kind of girl. Charming is nice for a dinner date. Honesty is much better for a . . . friendship." Since she didn't want to scare him off, it was the best word she could come up. And everyone knew that friendship was just a hop, skip, and a jump from love. Although it didn't sound like Matthew was up for either.

"Friendship," he snorted. "Not likely."

"Well, I wouldn't be so quick to pass judgment," she said. "Ellie sounds like the type of girl you'd want as a friend. Your mother called yesterday and said Ellie had volunteered at the shelter. In fact, I think I'll head on over this afternoon and thank her personally. Unlike some McPhersons, I don't have a problem making friends."

"I don't have a problem making friends," Matthew said. "I just don't want to be friends with her!"

"There you go getting your panties in a bunch again. Maybe Ellie can give you some free sessions for your anger management." Before Matthew could get out more than a frustrated grunt, a Land Rover pulled into the driveway and Wheezie dropped the curtain and ended the call. "Tea kettle's whistlin'. I'll talk with you later."

Wheezie had just hung up and placed the cordless phone back in its cradle when the door flew open and James came striding in. She almost felt guilty when she saw the look of concern on his face.

Almost.

But if anyone should feel guilty, it was James.

"Wheezie!" he yelled loud enough to shake the dust off the neon beer lights that covered one wall of the living room. Beer lights she just couldn't bring herself to get rid of when she and Neill closed down the bar. She had to admit that they gave a warm glow to the room.

"No need to yell," she said. "I'm right here."

When James glanced over and saw her, he looked confused. "I thought you fell and couldn't get up."

"I lied." She sent him a look filled with all the anger she'd been dealing with since catching him with the "other" woman. "Something, it seems, you've been doing a lot of lately."

A telling blush stained his cheeks. It was enough to break Wheezie's heart. After seeing him with the woman, she still held out hope that it was all a misunderstanding. James had never seemed like the type to cheat. He adored Cassie and the kids too much. But Wheezie also knew that the flesh was weak. And when presented with an offer from a beautiful woman, few men could resist the temptation. But that was no reason to give up on a good marriage. This was fixable. And Wheezie intended to fix it.

"Come on." She shuffled past him on her way to the kitchen. "I've got some muffins and coffee ready."

James followed without a word. When they were both seated at her kitchen table, she cupped her hands around her coffee mug and released her breath. "So how long has it been going on?"

"Six months." He refused to meet her eyes and, instead, looked down at the plate of muffins. "How did you find out?"

Since there was no need to go into details, she kept it simple. "I saw you come out of M-and-M the other day, and I wanted to talk with you so I had Barkley follow you."

He nodded. "I know you don't understand, Wheezie."

"Nope, I sure don't. Not with as much as you love Cassie."

He looked up. "But that's just it. I'm doing it for Cassandra. In her condition, it's just too much work."

Being a bar owner, Wheezie had heard every excuse under the sun for extramarital affairs: My wife doesn't give me enough attention. My husband refuses to really listen when I talk. It was only one night, and I was drunk. But this was the first time she'd heard this one.

"I don't think Cassie would agree," she said.

"Of course she wouldn't." He got up and started pacing. "She thinks she's some kind of a superwoman who can do it all: Work. The kids. Me. But she just can't do it, Wheeze. And I'm starting to worry that she's going to harm herself or the baby. The other night she put together this candlelight dinner, and before we even got to dessert, she fell asleep right there in her chair." A determined look came over his face. "No. Enough is enough. I don't care how pissed off Cassandra gets when she finds out, she'll just have to get over it."

Oh, her niece would be pissed all right. James would be lucky to come out of this with both balls intact. At the moment, Wheezie was actually considering picking up her coffee mug and throwing it right at his head. But before she could, James sat down and took her hand.

"Just two more weeks, Wheezie. That's all I need." He squeezed her hand, his expression as excited and thrilled as a kid who had just gotten a new bike for Christmas. "So what did you think of it? You think Cassandra will like it? It was built from the plans she drew up when we were first married. But with the kids and work, we just haven't had time to build it. Now with the new baby coming, we need more room, and I thought I'd surprise her with her dream home. Although meeting with the site manager every day and going over and checking on things at night hasn't been easy. I think Cassandra is starting to get suspicious."

Wheezie relaxed back in the chair.

A house. James was building Cassie a house. Wheezie didn't know if she wanted to jump up and do a jig or swat James upside the head for keeping the secret from her. The only thing that kept her from doing either was hurting James. He'd be devastated if he ever found out what his wife—and great-aunt—believed him capable of.

She squeezed his hand and smiled. "I think you're the best husband a wife could ask for. And a pretty darn good nephew, too. So when do you plan on springing this surprise on Cassandra?"

"I'm not sure. I guess as soon as it's finished. I don't like keeping secrets from her. I just hope she's not upset that I didn't include her in the building process."

"People don't need to be included in everything. And she has enough to worry about without building a new house." Wheezie looked out at the sparrows feeding at her bird feeder. "But it's too bad you're not her Secret Santa. She might take it better if you were."

"I thought about that. Instead, I got Matthew. And I don't have a clue what to get him."

Picking up the plate of muffins, Wheezie offered him one. "I'll see if I can't help you with that. You just worry about getting that house finished for your wife and kids."

"Then I'm afraid I can't stay, Wheezie." James helped himself to a muffin and got to his feet. "I want to meet with Samantha before I head back to work."

With a much lighter heart, Wheezie followed him to the front door. "I take it that Samantha is the pretty blonde you hired to manage the project."

"Yes, she's the best in the city."

"Just a word of advice," Wheezie said as he kissed her good-bye on the cheek. "It might be best if you kept that under your hat."

"I wouldn't worry about that. Cassie isn't the jealous type. After five years of marriage, she knows that I only have eyes for her." Completely ignoring Wheezie's grunt of exasperation, he pulled open the front door. "I wouldn't be going out tonight, Wheeze. According to the weather report, there's a bad snowstorm headed this way. And after the scare you gave me this morning, I don't want you slipping on the ice and breaking something." His eyes narrowed. "In fact, shouldn't you be using your walk—?"

"I'll call you later and check on your progress." She pushed him out the door. She had just shuffled back to the kitchen and started putting away the muffins when the front door opened again. Thinking that James had decided to hassle her some more about the walker, she headed back to the living room only to stop short when she saw her nephew. A nephew who looked like he'd spent the night in a trash bin.

Big Al hadn't shaved. His red hair was wild. And his shirt wrinkled.

"What in the world is going on?" Wheezie asked.

He stepped in and dropped a duffel bag to the floor, bellowing loud enough to send the sparrows on her bird feeder flying.

"The crazy woman kicked me out!"

Chapter Twenty-two

I can't believe we're supposed to have twelve inches of snow by morning," Mary said as she let Ellie in the front door of Hope House. "It feels like spring today." She flashed a smile. "Which might explain that bright sunny look on your face."

Not wanting to explain the reason behind her bright sunny look, Ellie tried to dim it. It was impossible. Especially when two words kept popping into her head.

Eleven months.

It was still hard to believe. Yet, somehow, Ellie did believe it. Matthew McPherson had gone eleven months without sex. And while she didn't delude herself that his celibacy had anything to do with some all-consuming love for her, she didn't believe that it was mere coincidence that his abstinence was so closely linked to their night in Vegas. Something had happened that night to change his way of thinking. And Ellie intended to find out what.

"I can't thank you enough for helping out while Bev is gone." Mary took her coat. "As much as I try to handle the support sessions on my own, I'm no professional."

"I'm sure you do just fine," Ellie said. "You are wonderful with the women. And they trust and respect you."

A deep sadness settled over Mary's face. "Too bad my husband doesn't feel the same way." She glanced back at the dining room where the chatter of women's voices competed with the Christmas music being played. "But this isn't the time or the place to talk about it. Although I would like to thank you for writing a book that opened my eyes to the lack of respect I was getting at home." She straightened her shoulders as if girding herself for battle. "And making me see that enough is enough." Without waiting for a reply, she turned and headed down the hallway, leaving Ellie to follow and wonder just what kind of trouble her book had caused this time.

Again she found the women of Hope House clustered around the dining room table. But this time, they were wrapping toys instead of making ornaments. They all looked up when she and Mary entered.

"You all remember Dr. Simpson, don't you?" Mary said. "She's going to be taking Bev's place for the holidays."

"Please call me Ellie," she said.

The women greeted her with friendly hellos before Clarisse spoke up.

"Well, don't just stand there, Ellie. We have to get these gifts the Elks Club donated wrapped before the kids get back from the movies. And we still need to come up with someone to play Santa. You wouldn't know any chubby, willing guys, would ya, honey?"

Ellie took a chair. "I'm afraid not."

"That's okay," Clarisse said. "If all else fails, I'll ask our cute mailman. I love a man who knows how to eat."

"I'm sure we'll figure something out." Mary headed back toward the front door. "For now, I better get to Costco and load up on toilet paper and paper towels before the storm gets here."

Once she was gone, Ellie might've felt a little intimidated if the women hadn't been so welcoming. Clarisse shoved a Barbie doll at her, and soon Ellie was wrapping right along with them. Not wanting to be too invasive during the first session, she decided to keep her questions to a minimum and listened instead. It didn't take long for her to figure out why Dr. Stokes set up activities for every session. With their hands occupied, the women seemed to speak more freely. And within an hour, Ellie had learned enough about each woman to draw a pretty good picture. The only woman she didn't get to know was Jennifer. Not because she didn't talk, but because she wasn't there.

"So where is Jennifer?" she asked. "I hope she's not sick."

"Just sick in the head," Clarisse said as she taped one end of the package in front of her. "She's going home today. Although I figure it won't be long until she's back. Not with the way she looked when she got here."

It was the last thing that Ellie wanted to hear. She had hoped to somehow make amends for what had happened to Jennifer. Now it looked as if she wouldn't get the chance.

Unless she took it now.

She got up from her chair. "Would you excuse me? I want to talk with Jennifer before she leaves. Where is she?"

"In her room packing." Clarisse tossed the package over to the corner with the growing stack. "But it won't do you any good to talk with her. She's still in the self-blame stage. She'll need to get to the pissed stage before she'll figure things out."

Ellie knew that Clarisse was probably right, but she still had to try to keep Jennifer from making a major mistake.

With only six rooms, it didn't take her long to find Jennifer's. Ellie peeked in the partially opened door and saw her standing next to a bed, placing neatly folded clothes in a trash bag. When Ellie tapped on the door, she jumped and turned around with a hand on her chest. Today, she wasn't wearing sunglasses, and Ellie could see the full extent of her injuries. The bruises were fading but still vibrant enough to tell the tale of the brutality she had endured.

"Hi," Ellie said. "Could I come in for a few minutes?"

Jennifer nodded before going back to packing, her shoulders tight and posture closed off. Not wanting to make her even tenser, Ellie moved over to the window and looked out. Dark clouds had rolled in, blocking out the sun and giving an ominous cloak of gray to the skies.

"I hope it doesn't start snowing before I get home," Ellie said. "I hate to drive on snow and ice. My father tried to teach me, but his efforts only resulted in a dented bumper and a higher insurance rate." She laughed, hoping Jennifer would join in.

Instead, she spoke defensively. "So I guess you remember me from the bookstore."

Ellie turned around. "Yes. And I need to apologize. I had no business counseling you without knowing the circumstances."

Jennifer shrugged. "It wasn't your fault. I knew better than to bring it up after Anson's job interview hadn't gone so well."

"You misunderstood me." She took a step closer. "I'm not apologizing for what happened to you. That wasn't my fault. Nor was it yours. The only person responsible is your husband."

Jennifer's expression became defensive and indignant. "So I guess you're like all the other women here. You're a man-hater who thinks that men are to blame for everything that happens to them. That women are perfect little angels who don't do anything to deserve what they get."

"I don't think that anyone deserves to be abused—men or women."

"Well, Anson doesn't abuse me," she snapped. "He loves me. This was all just a misunderstanding."

"A misunderstanding that's happened before?" Ellie asked.

Instead of answering, Jennifer walked over to the dresser to get more clothes. "You don't understand. He was abused by his father and doesn't know anything else."

"Then he needs to get professional help, Jennifer—before you and Joey go back to him. If you go back now, it's only going to start the cycle all over again. In order to help your husband, you have to break the cycle. You have to say that you're not willing to come back until he gets help. Help that might consist of months, even years, of therapy."

Jennifer whirled around. "I'm not going years without Anson! In fact, I'm not going a day more without him. I love him. And unlike the rest of these men-haters, I like being held and cared for. And I like sex." She pulled something out of the drawer and threw it at Ellie. "So you can just take your stupid book and shove it up your ass!"

The book whizzed by Ellie's head before it hit the opposite wall and slid beneath the bed. Jennifer looked more surprised by her behavior than Ellie. "I—" she started but couldn't seem to finish. She looked down at the floor and played with the cross around her neck, leaving Ellie to finish their conversation.

"I'll only ask for one thing. You know the signs, Jennifer. You know when things are escalating. If you see Anson reaching this point, you need to get out of there. I'm assuming that you have an exit plan—a plan to get you and Joey out safely." When Jennifer nodded, she hesitated for only a moment before adding, "I'll leave my card, along with my home number, on the counter in the kitchen. And if you should need me for anything, all you have to do is call." Ellie never gave her personal number out to patients, but regardless of what she'd said, she did feel partly responsible for what had happened.

At the door, she turned. "Where is Joey? If it's alright with you, I'd like to talk with her before you leave."

"She's out in the arts and crafts studio," Jennifer said in barely a whisper. She waited for Ellie to step out the door before she added, "I'm sorry."

"So am I." Ellie walked away.

Clarisse gave her directions to the art studio. When she tapped on the door and entered, she found Joey sitting cross-legged on the floor. Matthew sat right next to her.

A smile bloomed on Ellie's face at just the sight of his tousled hair and lawn-green eyes. "Hi." The word came out all breathy and way too giddy.

A frown tipped down the corners of his mouth. "Hi."

She moved farther into the room. "So is Joey teaching you how to paint?" she teased, but the joke fell short with her audience. Matthew continued to frown, and Joey more like scowled.

Ellie cleared her throat and looked at the painting on the floor. It wasn't an abstract done in bold, bright colors like the one at the gallery. This painting was of the studio window and done in soft pastels.

"This is very good, Joey," she said.

The young girl couldn't hide her blush. "Yeah, well, I didn't exactly do it all by myself. Matthew and Mr. Randall helped me."

"Mr. Randall?"

Matthew got to his feet. "The art teacher I hired for Joey."

Ellie didn't know what made her feel more lightheaded—Matthew in faded, paint-stained jeans that hugged his legs like a second skin or the fact that he had done something so nice. He must've read her dopey reaction because his eyes narrowed.

"So what are you doing out here? I thought you are supposed to be inside counseling the women."

"We already had our session, and I wanted to talk to Joey." She looked down at the teenage girl. "Your mother told me you were leaving."

The knob on her lip protruded. "And?"

"And... I was wondering how you feel about it."

Joey stared back at her for only a moment before she picked up a brush and dabbed it in paint. "Like shit. How would you feel if your mother was going back to a jackass who didn't know how to keep his fists to himself?" She slashed a streak of red across the painting of the window, making it appear to be bleeding. "Anything else you want to know?"

"You didn't tell me you were going home," Matthew said, seemingly unconcerned that she had just destroyed the painting.

Joey looked up at him. The belligerent scowl was gone, replaced with a vulnerable look that tore at Ellie's heart. "Will that make a difference in my lessons? The art teacher won't have to come to my house. Maybe I could go to his."

Matthew's eyebrow lifted. "So now you want lessons. What happened to the girl who said she didn't need any butt wipe teaching her?"

The knob bobbled as she pressed her lips in a firm line. "Well, maybe I could learn something. Mr. Randall did seem to know what he was talking about."

Matthew grinned. "No, you going back home won't change your lessons." He exchanged looks with Ellie. "But I don't see why you can't talk your mother into staying a little while longer. If you leave now, you'll miss the big Christmas Eve party."

Joey threw down her paintbrush. "She won't listen to me. He's brainwashed her."

"So why don't you stay here?" Matthew asked. "I'm sure my mother could get it worked out."

Joey looked appalled. "And leave my mom to that ass-hole? No way!"

"Of course you don't want to leave your mother," Ellie said. "But I hope you'll call me or Mary if anything starts to escalate at home."

"Yeah, sure." A cloud just as dark as the ones gathering out the window settled over Joey's features, and she quickly collected her brushes and took them to the sink. When her back was turned, Matthew nodded at the door, and Ellie took the hint and followed him outside. The temperature had dropped drastically, and as soon as they stepped out, Matthew leaned back inside and grabbed his leather coat. But instead of putting it on, he hung it over Ellie's shoulders.

"So you couldn't talk her mother out of it?" he asked.

She shook her head. "It's not unusual for women to go back to their abusive husbands. Now all we can do is pray that the next time won't be as bad as this one."

"Pray?" The wind whipped his hair away from his forehead.

"What?" She pulled the jacket tighter, enjoying the scent of leather and Matthew. "You thought I didn't believe in God?"

"The thought had crossed my mind. Especially after reading your book." He leaned on the side of the garage, his knee bent and booted foot resting against the wall. With his messed hair and hands stuffed in the front pockets of his jeans, he looked like James Dean waiting for his next rebellion. Suddenly she had the strongest urge to open up the leather jacket and invite him inside. Instead, she turned away and continued the conversation.

"The Bible teaches abstinence."

"Not quite the way you do," he said. "In the Bible, it's more of a moral issue. In your book, it's more of a weapon used to beat men into submission."

A month ago, Ellie would've defended her book and theories to the bitter end. But since moving to Denver, she'd started to have her doubts.

"Maybe you're right," she said. "Maybe I allowed my feelings about my father's infidelity to filter through to my writing."

Matthew came away from the wall. "What? The Virgin Queen is actually going to admit that she's wrong?"

"Not completely wrong. I still think that abstinence plays an important role in an emotionally driven relationship. But I concede the point that I may have gone a little overboard."

"A little?"

"Okay. A lot," she said. "But you have no room to talk. Not when you were at the other end of the sex spectrum." The word "were" hung there in the space between them, making Ellie say something she had no business saying. "I've been thinking."

"Great," he said sarcastically, but she ignored him and continued.

"It seems to me that the best way for you to overcome your problem of looking at women as sexual objects is to have one as a friend."

"That's what my sister is for," he said. "Although, since she's gotten married and started hatching kids like an overfed hen, Cassie hasn't been much of a friend. All she wants to talk about is potty training, breastfeeding, and stretch marks."

Ellie smiled at the thought of Matthew being forced to listen as his sister talked about poopy diapers. "But relatives don't prove anything. You need someone who isn't a relative to show you that friendship with a woman can be emotionally satisfying in ways beyond the physical."

"What are you getting at, Ellie?" he asked.

She cleared her throat. "I think we should be friends."

"No."

"Why not?"

"Because we've had sex."

"But don't you see?" She moved closer. "That's why we'd make perfect friends. We've already gotten the physical side of things out of our systems."

It was funny, but standing only inches away from Matthew, Ellie didn't feel like she had it out of her system. In fact, she felt just the opposite. She had the overwhelming desire to pull him close and taste his unsmiling lips.

He cocked his head like Patrick's stray basset hound when she had tried to get him to come inside her condo. "Besides your obvious need to try out some of your weird theories on a sex fiend, what's in it for you?"

Ellie shrugged. "A friend."

An inordinate amount of time passed before he spoke. "Fine, I'll be your friend. But on my terms. I don't like girlie flicks, salad bars, or hearing about what horrible thing your girlfriend said to you the other day. And don't expect me to open doors for you, pay for dinners, or pull out chairs. And no more psychoanalysis." He wheeled her around and proceeded to push her toward the back door. A door he pulled open for her. "Now get inside before you catch a cold."

Then before she knew what was happening, Matthew slipped the jacket off her shoulders and headed back the way they'd come. Halfway there, he stopped and turned around.

"Do you like basketball?"

She nodded.

"Good. I'll pick you up around seven." His eyes crinkled in thought. "Make that six; we'll grab a bite to eat before we go." He frowned. "And would you get inside? Damn, woman, it has to be twenty degrees out here."

Standing in the doorway, she watched until Matthew disappeared around the corner of the garage. Then she turned and almost ran into Mary.

"Was that Matthew I heard?" Mary asked, looking slightly confused. "And did you just agree to go out on a date with him?"

A smile bloomed on Ellie's face. "Yes. Yes, I did."

Chapter Twenty-three

The snowstorm that was forecast for that night fizzled out, but a week later another storm hit with a vengeance, dropping enough snow to close schools and highways and keep people home from work.

Ellie didn't realize the extent of the storm until she opened up her garage to go to work and saw the winter wonderland. After spending a few minutes taking in the snow-laden parking lot and the crystal flakes that still fell from the sky, she closed the steel door and proceeded to call her patients and cancel for the day. She had just started a load of laundry when Matthew called and invited her over. And since hanging out with a hunky guy was much more appealing than a pile of dirty underwear, she grabbed a book, her afghan, and a box of cocoa mix and tromped through the snow.

It didn't take long to get cuddled up on Matthew's

comfortable couch with her book. The condo felt warm and snug with the gas logs flickering in the fireplace and the snow swirling outside the multi-paned windows like a profusion of down feathers.

She tried to read, but her gaze kept drifting over the top edge of her book to the man who sat on the other end of the couch, working on his laptop in a pair of old jogging pants, mismatched socks, and a torn long-sleeve t-shirt. A man who looked nothing like the perfect playboy who had first enticed her on a Vegas nightclub's dance floor. This man had bad bed head, over a day's growth of dark whiskers, and a faint remnant of a milk-mustache in one corner of his mouth.

Which didn't explain why Ellie felt all breathless and light-headed. How was it possible that the messy man across from her was twice as appealing, and ten times more dangerous, than the charming Vegas stranger? Maybe that was it. Matthew was no longer a stranger. After the last week, he'd become a friend.

On Thursday night, they went to the Nuggets' basketball game at the Pepsi Center and Ellie yelled so much she couldn't talk for the rest of the night—which Matthew claimed was a blessing. On Friday, she begged him to go with her to a performance of *Nutcracker* at the Performing Arts Complex. He agreed, but fell asleep during the Dance of the Sugar Plum Fairy. And no matter how beautiful the ballet was, it didn't compare to the beauty of Matthew sleeping.

Saturday, Matthew went with her to Hope House and fixed a leaking faucet while she had her group session; then he gave the women legal advice free of charge. That night, they ate sushi, then went back to his place to watch *Christmas Vacation*, which led to numerous funny stories about his family Christmases. Sunday, he didn't call. And by ten that night, Ellie felt more than a little depressed. So she called him, making up some lame question about her heater. They ended up talking until one in the morning about everything from Joey's progress with her art teacher to Ellie's miserable high school dates. Monday night, she cooked spaghetti for him. She burned the garlic toast and overcooked the pasta, but he cleared his plate and asked for seconds.

Through all their activities, Matthew never made one sexual advance toward her. Not even an accidental brush of a knee. Even now, he stayed on his side of the couch, the laptop perched on the hard muscles of his thighs and his green eyes tracking over the screen as he read what appeared to be a very long and detailed document.

Ellie should've been happy with the arrangement. After all, the whole platonic thing was her idea. And she was happy. She just wasn't satisfied. Deep inside her, there was this empty space that needed to be filled. And with each passing day, it grew wider.

Matthew glanced up, and his head tipped to the side in question. "What are you reading?"

She looked down at the forgotten book on her lap. "A book written by a Buddhist."

One eye squinted. "No wonder you're bored with it."

"I take it you don't believe in the teachings of Buddha."

"Some, but not an entire book full." He pulled his feet off the coffee table and set his laptop down. "So what's it about?"

She shifted her gaze away from him, trying to hide the

giddy happiness she felt at finally having his full attention. "I'm not going to tell you. You'll just laugh."

"Why would I laugh?"

"Because it's about abstinence."

"Believe me, that is no laughing matter," he grumbled as he leaned back against the cushions and stretched his hands over his head. "So are these yahoos' ideas as crazy as yours?"

"Actually, he's worse. He doesn't believe in having orgasms."

Matthew's eyebrows shot up. "You're kidding?"

She shook her head. "Supposedly, it kills off your inner Buddha."

"Then I guess I'm a mass murderer."

The giggles that erupted out of her mouth didn't surprise her. She had been giggling a lot lately.

Flipping the book on the table, she snuggled back in a corner of the couch. "I probably shouldn't say he doesn't believe in orgasms. He believes that if couples could learn to touch one another without reaching a physical orgasm, they would ultimately experience a more intense and satisfying spiritual one."

"Better than a physical orgasm? The man *is* a nut."

Ellie shrugged. "Maybe. But the book is full of endorsements from people who swear by the man's theories and exercises."

"Exercises? Don't tell me you have to run three miles on the treadmill before you can achieve spiritual orgasm."

"No, it's more metaphysical exercises."

"Definitely a nut."

"I wouldn't knock it until you've tried it."

His eyes narrowed. "Have you?"

"No." She looked away and adjusted the afghan around her legs. "It takes two people. But I'm thinking about asking Sidney and Keith to give it a try."

Matthew snorted. "You mean go without sex? Not likely. Those two haven't come up for air in weeks."

He was right. Sidney showed up at the office during the day but disappeared after work. If it weren't for Matthew, Ellie would've been mad at her friend's defection. But she had no complaints. None at all.

"So you really want to try this lunatic's theories?" he asked.

"Yes, but it's no big deal. If I'm still intrigued after I finish reading it, I can always hire some college kids to try it out." She picked up her cocoa and took a sip, licking off the foamy mustache left behind.

There was a long stretch of silence before Matthew spoke. "What kind of touching?"

"Only knees and palms."

He thought for a moment. "Okay, Doc. I'll be your guinea pig. Just tell me what to do."

"Really? You'd help me?"

"Sure, why not? I'm dying to find out what a spiritual orgasm is like. But I'm not chanting some weird mantra or dancing around with bells on my toes."

Ellie laughed as she set down her cup and pulled the afghan off her legs. "Agreed. No toe-bell dancing." She crossed her legs and then waited for him to follow suit before she scooted closer to him.

"First, we need to take a deep cleansing breath," she instructed. "Try to fill your stomach and diaphragm."

"I knew a woman who used one of those."

"No doubt. I'm sure you've been through the entire spectrum of birth control." She adjusted her knees so they pressed against his. "But I guess that's better than an unwanted child."

"No child of mine would ever be unwanted."

Ellie glanced up to find Matthew looking back at her with intent and serious eyes.

"I'm careful," he said. "But if it did happen...I'd want the child."

She didn't know why the revelation made her feel all mushy inside. Probably because it didn't go with his love-'em-and-leave-'em personality. Of course, in the last few days, she'd noticed a lot of things that didn't go with the playboy image.

Pulling her gaze away, she continued with her instructions. "Try to keep your eyes closed and your breathing even. After a couple minutes, slip your hands over my knees. At that point, I'll cover your hands with mine, and then we lift them up together with palms touching. Your entire focus should be on the points where our bodies touch."

Nodding, Matthew closed his eyes, and Ellie did the same. It was strange, but it didn't take that much work to focus on the points where their bodies touched. Even through the thick cotton of their sweats, his knees felt like tiny little heating pads set on sizzle. Within seconds, she was overwhelmingly hot. She tried to concentrate on her breathing, but ended up concentrating more on his—slow and even breaths that brushed across her forehead and fluttered the bangs of her hair.

His hands slid over her knees, and she almost shot through the roof. Trying desperately to keep her body from going on an inner-Buddha killing spree, she refocused and slid her hands over his. She absorbed his heat into her palms before allowing her fingers to wander over the smooth edges of his trimmed nails to the peaks of his scarred knuckles.

She was surprised at how rough his skin was for a man who supposedly spent most of his time behind a desk. When she got to his wrists, she encircled each one, pressing her index and middle fingers against the pulse that strummed there. The primal rhythm vibrated through the tips of her fingers and coursed through her veins until her heart picked up the beat and thumped in time with his. Wanting to put an end to the exercise as quickly as possible, she released his wrists and lifted his palms to hers.

They were joined in two places. Their knees and their hands. But she felt his touch in every cell of her body. It was like she had found a way to plug into the sun and its endless supply of hot, intense energy. On one hand it was physical, and on the other it was purely spiritual. This was no longer a simple exercise with a friend. At some time during the last few minutes, or maybe the past week, things had changed. Matthew was no longer a harmless playboy who entertained her with his quick wit and clever quips. Now, he was so much more.

The realization scared her, and Ellie opened her eyes.

It was a mistake.

Matthew watched her, his lush green irises reflecting her own deep-seated hunger. She didn't know who moved first, but suddenly their lips touched. It was only a brush, a gentle stroke, but they both pulled back as if burned. He stared at her in confusion and said one word. One word filled with so much longing there was no way to resist it.

"Ellie."

This time she knew exactly who moved first. Although dove would be a more accurate description of her flight across the couch.

Matthew caught her, and they tumbled back on the cushions, their mouths expressing deep satisfied moans as their tongues greeted one another in a frenzied welcome. His hands slid under her sweatshirt to her waist while hers pushed up his shirt to reveal his lean muscles. Pulling back from the kiss, she nipped her way up his stomach to one hard, flat nipple.

"My God, Ellie," he hissed as she sucked it into her mouth.

His desire pushed her on, and she ran her hands down his chest, over his rippled stomach, to the waistband of his sweatpants. Slipping her hand beneath the thick cotton, she closed her fingers around his hard, smooth length. A guttural groan came from deep inside his chest, and his hips lifted off the couch. But just as she got a good rhythm going, he stopped her.

"My turn, baby."

His hands shook as he pulled her sweatshirt up, then unclasped her bra, nudging it aside and covering her nipple with his mouth. He suckled and nipped until she was whimpering with need, then slipped his hand inside her pants. His thumb flicked over the nub that ached with need. Skillfully, he manipulated it until she was milliseconds away from combustion . . .

Then her cell phone rang.

Ellie might've been able to ignore it if the tune Sidney had programmed in wasn't so loud and distinct. But it was hard to ignore the chiming version of Elton John's "The Bitch Is Back." The melody caused Ellie's brain to slam back into her body, and she pulled away from Matthew's magical fingers and scrambled for the phone.

"Hello." Her voice sounded like Kermit with a bad case of the croup.

"Hey, girlfriend. You sick?" Sidney asked.

Ellie tugged down her sweatshirt and sat up. "No. I-I was just reading."

"So what do you think of this weather?" Sidney went on. "Isn't it great? Keith and I got snowed in this morning, and we haven't even gotten out of bed. But you can only stay in bed so long—if you know what I mean. Anyway, we got to talking and thought it would be fun to have a tree-trimming party tonight at your place." She paused. "Keith has another friend he could invite along if you want."

Ellie didn't want to have a tree-trimming party. And she didn't want to meet another one of Keith's friends. All she really wanted to do was crawl back on the couch, strip Matthew naked, and melt into his hot skin.

"Actually, I'm not feeling very—" She caught herself.

What was she doing? Was she just about to lie to her best friend—again—all because she couldn't wait to get back to having sex with Matthew? Yes, that was exactly what she had been about to do. She was willing to lie, cheat, and steal to get just one more fevered stroke from Matthew's warm fingers.

The realization floored her. For most of her life she'd preached abstinence, but this was the first time she realized exactly what she was asking her patients and readers to do. Lust wasn't a weak emotion easily controlled. It was an all-consuming fire that even a strong-willed therapist couldn't handle without getting burned.

And there was little doubt that if she had sex again with Matthew she'd get burned.

She hugged the phone to her ear and took a deep, quivering breath. "That sounds like fun. I'm always up for meeting new people."

"Good," Sidney said, "we'll see you around six." She paused. "You sure you're okay, Elle?"

"Couldn't be better. See you at six," she mumbled before she pressed the button to end the call. As soon as she set the phone down, Matthew spoke.

"Plans for this evening?"

She kept her back to him as she hooked her bra. "Sidney and Keith are coming over."

"Just Sidney and Keith?"

She pulled down her sweatshirt. "Actually, Keith is bringing a friend."

"Ahh, another double date. Hopefully, this one will turn out better than the last." He leaned up and got his laptop.

While Ellie had been all prepared to make light of the Buddhist exercise, she didn't exactly like the thought of Matthew doing the same. Especially when he acted like it hadn't even happened. He just sat there reading his document as if they hadn't almost had sex on his couch. As if she hadn't just told him she had a date with another man.

For some reason, his nonchalant attitude made her angry, and she quickly got up and gathered her things.

"Leaving?" he asked.

"I better get home and get ready."

He glanced at the clock on the mantel, then gave her the once-over. "Yeah, I can see why you might need the extra time."

His words further infuriated her, forcing her to bring up a subject they had no business talking about. "Funny, but you didn't seem to mind the way I looked a few minutes ago."

He shrugged. "I think we covered this in my last therapy session. I have a problem saying no to sex-deprived women."

"Sex-deprived!" Ellie had to fight the urge to throw her cup at him. "You wanted it just as much as—" She caught herself but too late. There was a flicker of something in his eyes, but before he could say anything, she whirled around and stomped to the kitchen. "Never mind."

She should've known that he wouldn't let it go. After she set the cup in the sink, she turned to find him standing in the doorway with a look in his eyes that seemed to burn right through her.

"And just how much do you want it, Ellie?" he asked in a voice barely above a whisper.

She wanted to deny her desire, but it was hard to deny it when just one sultry look had her heart thumping out of control and her breath sawing in and out of her lungs. Luckily, before she had to answer, the garage door opened. There was the thump of boots on the stairs, and then Patrick's booming voice.

"Mattie! You're not going to believe what happened…
Mom kicked Dad out."

"What?" Matthew stepped back into the living room.
"But why?"

"It seems that Mom read—"

Ellie didn't wait to hear the rest before she headed for
the fire escape.

Chapter Twenty-four

If you weren't so damned stubborn, you'd have already apologized and made up with her."

Albert shot Wheezie a sour look over the edge of his coffee mug. "Mary Katherine was the one who tossed me out. Therefore, she is the one who should apologize." He glanced out the window at the snow that stood a good foot high on the bird feeder. "Damn, I planned on flying out this morning to meet with those developers of that new shopping mall. Now it looks like I'll be spending the day at the office."

Wheezie didn't believe in getting involved in marital arguments. Or in taking one person's side against the other. There were always two sides to every story—Cassie's and James's situation being a perfect example. So for the last week, Wheezie had kept her mouth shut in hopes that a little time away from each other would heal all wounds. It wasn't working. And Wheezie figured that she'd stayed out of things long enough.

Picking up the folded newspaper on the table, she reached out and swatted her nephew upside the head.

"What the hell?" Albert glared at her.

Wheezie pointed the newspaper at him. "No wonder Mary Katherine kicked you out. You've forgotten the words that keep a marriage together."

"What are you talking about?" He stared at her as if she had a major case of dementia. "I say 'I love you' all the time to Mary Katherine."

She swatted him again. This time on the shoulder, causing him to spill his coffee on the table. "I'm not talking about 'I love you,' you numbskull. I'm talking about 'thank you.' When was the last time you've said that to Mary Katherine? Because you've been here for an entire week and haven't said it once to me. Not after I fill your big gut with breakfast every morning or have your clean clothes waiting for you at night. All you seem to be interested in is getting back to that company of yours."

"I've got a business to run."

"Bull!" Wheezie got to her feet and might've hit him again if he hadn't scooted his chair out of reach. "You have an entire family to run your business. And all of them would be more than happy to do it, if you'd let them. Instead, they can't make a move without you second-guessing their decisions. A perfect example is that shopping mall you were talking about. Didn't Jacob and Rory just meet with those people and get everything settled?"

Albert scowled. "Yes, but I wanted—"

"You wanted to micromanage." She leaned in closer. "And do you know why, Alby? Because you're terrified of losing control. And I get it. Neill and I had the hardest time letting go of the bar. For close to forty years, it had been our life and the customers our family. And when we sold it, there was this huge void. But do you know what we filled that void with?" She paused a moment. "Each other. That's the fun part about growing old together. You'll always have each other to fill the voids life leaves."

She took his cup from his hand and shuffled over to the coffeemaker. "Once the bar was gone, Neill and I each made a list of everything we wanted to do and hadn't had time for. Then one by one we checked off that list— California wine tours, Grand Canyon hiking, New England in the fall, tango lessons, kayaking, trips to Italy and India." Tears filled her eyes. "And now, looking back, I wish we had sold the bar sooner. I would give just about anything to have one more picture in our photo album. One more adventure with the love of my life."

She turned around to discover Albert sitting at the table with his shoulders slumped and his head in his hands. It was a good sign.

"And you don't think I want some adventure?" he said. "I bought a fishing cabin in hopes that my wife would enjoy weekend trips with me." He looked up. "But do you know what she said when I told her I bought it? She said that she didn't know why I'd want to catch fish when I only want to eat steak. It seems like cooking me a steak dinner has become a huge bone of contention for her— pardon the pun."

"Maybe she wouldn't mind cooking you a steak dinner every once in a while if you were there to enjoy it with her."

"Fine! I'll admit that I'm a workaholic. But I'm not working for myself as much as my family. If M-and-M goes under, do you realize what could happen? The kids would need to get other jobs—jobs that might not be here in Denver. And I won't have my family scattered across the country." He pounded a fist on the table. "As long as I have a breath in my body, Big Al McPherson's family will stay together."

Wheezie couldn't help smiling as she walked over and handed him a cup of coffee. "You've always loved your family, Alby. And I admire you for that. But you are way off base here. This family doesn't stay together because of some construction company. It stays together because of love. And no matter what happens to M-and-M, the McPhersons will remain close, regardless of where they live." She patted his shoulder. "And they'll survive long after you and I are gone. McPhersons are too damned stubborn not to. But what might not survive is your marriage if you don't pull your head out."

She took her chair. "I talked briefly with Mary Katherine this morning, and I think I might have a plan that will get you back in your wife's good graces."

Albert sat up. "What did she say? Is she ready for me to come back?"

Wheezie probably could've lied, but she figured he could use a strong dose of reality. "Not exactly. In fact, she didn't mention you at all. She seems to be pretty busy with planning the shelter's Christmas Eve party. Which is exactly how I came up with my plan."

Unfortunately, before she could give him the details, the stubborn man latched on to something else entirely.

"The shelter Christmas Eve party? What do you mean? What happened to the McPherson Christmas Eve party?"

"We'll still have our party. It will just be a little later."

"Oh, no." Albert shook his head. "There's no way in hell that I'm spending Christmas Eve at some shelter for women. The McPhersons spend their Christmas Eves at home. Mary Katherine bakes sugar cookies with the grandkids while the boys and I play pool, and then the rest of the family comes over and eats before we go to mass. That's what we've been doing for thirty-some-odd years, and that's what we're doing this Christmas." He grabbed the cordless phone that sat on the table. "In fact, I'm going to call the woman right now. This foolishness has gone on long enough."

Figuring it was too late to pull her foot out of her mouth, Wheezie added more sugar to her coffee. "I don't think that's a good idea."

"Now, don't worry, Wheeze." He punched in the numbers. "I appreciate all your advice, but I know how to handle my wife."

"Which is exactly why you're sleeping in my spare room," Wheezie said under her breath. She stirred in her sugar and listened while he dug his grave deeper.

"Mary Katherine, enough is enough." He paced across the kitchen. "Now, I'll admit that I haven't been spending enough time with you. And if you'd like to go to Morton's Steakhouse tonight, I'd be more than happy to take you. We can even go to the healthy yogurt place you like for dessert. But I flat out refuse to spend my Christmas

Eve at some women's—Mary Katherine?" He pulled the phone away and looked at it before putting it back to his ear. "Mary Katherine?"

The dial tone could be heard clear across the room.

"Something wrong?" Wheezie asked.

Albert's face turned as dark as the clouds that hung in the sky. "The fool woman hung up on me."

"Can't say as I blame her. Morton's Steakhouse isn't exactly the way into a woman's heart."

"To hell with a woman's heart!" Albert strode past, tossing the phone down to the table on his way by. "I'm going to work."

"You do that, Alby," she said before taking a sip of her lukewarm coffee. The office was the best place for him until Wheezie could get things figured out. It wouldn't be easy. Not with a man that stubborn. But her Neill hadn't exactly been easygoing, and she'd handled him all right.

She waited for the front door to slam before she reached for the phone. It took a good six rings before Rory picked up.

"Hey, Wheezie," he said. "You need me to come shovel your driveway?"

"No, I don't plan on going out today. But tomorrow I might need you to stop by. And while you're at it, you can bring me that Santa suit you wore last year for the kids."

"You planning on being the jolly ol' elf for Christmas, Wheeze?" Rory asked with a smile in his voice.

Wheezie laughed. "No. But God willing, I might talk a Scrooge into it."

Chapter Twenty-five

Matthew felt like he was coming down with something. He'd closed his laptop hours ago and spent the rest of the day sitting on his couch feeling crappy while he watched the flames roll over faux logs. He hated gas logs. What a pathetic excuse for a fire. They were nothing more than burning gas rolling over molded ceramic. There was no real heat. No crackling, popping wood. Gas logs were nothing more than a gigantic candle.

Without the scent.

He took another sip of his beer. It was the third one he'd had in the last hour. Which might explain why he felt so crappy. Drinking on an empty stomach could screw you up. He should probably make something for dinner. But he wasn't hungry. He rolled the cold beer bottle over his forehead. Yes, he was coming down with something. Or maybe there was a gas leak in the line to his fireplace.

Getting up, he walked over to crack open the window. Instead, he rested an arm on the frame and looked out. It was turning dark outside. The light in the parking lot had come on and reflected off the thick layer of snow. It had stopped snowing earlier, but school would no doubt be canceled again tomorrow, giving kids a few extra days to their holiday break.

As a kid, Matthew had loved snow days. He and his siblings would make big snow forts in the backyard and have snowball wars. Or sculpt snowmen or busty snow-women with flat river rock nipples, which really grossed Cassie out. They'd stay out there for hours, until Mom forced them inside. After pulling off their outerwear in the mudroom, they'd crowd around the kitchen table in their thermal underwear and wool socks and drink hot chocolate and eat oatmeal cookies while a real fire blazed in the huge stone fireplace in the den.

His father was never there. Big Al didn't believe in snow days. In fact, except for a few vacations, Matthew couldn't remember one day of work his father had missed. Not until his heart attack, then only under threat of divorce from his mother. Everyone had thought it was an empty threat...until now.

It was still hard to believe that his mother had kicked his father out. When Matthew had called her to ask her about it, she'd refused to discuss it. But somehow the tone in her voice had said it all. This wasn't a ploy to get his father to take off work and spend more time at home. This was serious.

Matthew wanted to put all the blame on Ellie's book, especially when the woman had acted so guilty by sneaking down the fire escape. But the truth was that Ellie hadn't made his father a workaholic. Her book had just pointed out to his mother the same thing that had been missing in all of Matthew's relationships.

Emotional connection.

And standing there feeling like crap, he had to wonder if Ellie had done him a favor by pointing it out. Now he would no longer be satisfied with a totally sexual relationship. Now he wanted a friend. Someone who yells as loudly as he does at basketball games. Someone who likes lazy afternoons spent on the couch and simple spaghetti dinners at home. Someone who loves art and cries at ballets.

Someone who believed that intimacy should be saved for a person you love.

A rumbling noise drew his attention down to the parking lot just as a monster truck rolled in. It had huge snow tires, a wide-mouthed grille, and mud flaps—each with the silhouette of a naked woman.

Matthew rolled his eyes. What a dick. Was this Ellie's date for the evening? Wait until she got a load of his truck. The prude of a woman would send him packing within the hour.

A few moments later, Keith's SUV pulled into the space next to the truck. He and Sidney got out and walked over to greet the driver, a tall cowboy all gussied up in a black Stetson, Wrangler jeans, and Roper boots. A cowboy who pulled off his hat when Ellie stepped out of her garage in a cute down jacket, too-snug jeans, and furry pink boots that came up to her knees.

She'd curled her hair, and Matthew couldn't help being annoyed that she had gone to the effort for that redneck asshole. Of course, that didn't annoy him as much as the cowboy taking her hand and holding it a little too long. Or maybe what annoyed him most was that Ellie wasn't stopping him. Or sending him packing.

A cowboy? Get real. Surely Ellie didn't have a thing for cowboys. Matthew had dated a woman once who bought him a cowboy hat and boots and wanted him to wear both in bed. Did Ellie like that? It irritated him that he didn't know. Suddenly, he realized that there were a lot of things that he didn't know about Ellie.

He did know a few things. Like her favorite color was red. And she bit her lip when she didn't know the answer to something and cleared her throat when she was uncomfortable. She had trouble making up her mind about things, but once she did, she stuck to her decisions. Because of her father's infidelity, she was screwed up about sex, but beneath the wacky theories was a passionate woman who could set the sheets on fire. She was stubborn and strong willed, but could laugh at herself—

Matthew's breath left his body in a puff of fear. Good Lord, when did he start learning so much about Ellie? And what terrified him the most was that he wanted to learn more.

Did she fantasize about cowboys?

He turned away from the window and stomped into the kitchen.

Who cared? Ellie wasn't his girlfriend. She was just some screwed-up therapist who stumbled into his life one New Year's Eve.

He jerked open the door of the refrigerator. He needed to eat something. And then he would take a shower, or better yet, sit in his Jacuzzi tub with a nice glass of

Chardonnay. Later, he'd head over to Patrick's and play some pool. Or stop by to check on his mom. It wasn't like he didn't have a thousand places to go on a snowy December night. Hell, he might even call one of his lady friends.

But after staring at the contents of his refrigerator until his nose got cold, Matthew slammed the door and headed for bed.

He was coming down with something. He knew it.

Three hours later, he was lying on his bed staring at a muted, cartoon version of *The Night Before Christmas* when a commotion outside caused him to spring to his feet to see what was the matter. Unfortunately, when away to the window he flew like a flash, he didn't discover a lively old fellow and eight tiny reindeer. Instead, he saw Ellie having a snowball fight with the cowboy, and Keith and Sidney were nowhere in sight. In fact, the space where Keith's SUV had been parked was where the cowboy playfully tackled Ellie and proceeded to kiss her.

It was funny, but Matthew didn't remember crossing the room or going down both sets of stairs. Didn't remember opening the garage or feeling the icy wetness that seeped through his socks as he barreled through the snow. His brain only clicked in when he grabbed the cowboy by his jacket and sent him sprawling face-first into the snow piled against the back of the parking lot.

"What the hell?" The cowboy rolled to his feet with fists clenched and snow dripping from his face. "What's your problem, buddy?"

"You." Matthew squared up for a fight, but Ellie jumped in.

"What are you doing, Matthew?" She got to her feet, staring at him in disbelief.

"Do you know this guy, Ellie?" the cowboy asked.

"Yes," she said. "He's my—"

"Boy. Friend," Matthew stated before scooping Ellie over his shoulder and marching back to his condo. His reply must've stunned Ellie because she didn't react until the garage door closed behind them. Then she started struggling and cussing him out. By the time he tossed her onto his king-size bed, she was livid. Which worked out well. Because he wasn't feeling so charitable himself.

"What the hell do you think you're doing?" She glared up at him.

"That's a good question," he said through gritted teeth. "Why don't you answer it?"

"Me? I wasn't the nut who came running out of my house and assaulted someone!"

"No," he said, "you were just the one who was rolling around in the snow with some redneck asshole you hardly know. Have you no morals?"

In the light coming from the hallway, her face turned a deeper red. "Oooo, this coming from a man who has had sex with at least a hundred women."

"All of whom I knew for more than a few hours!"

"Really? I find that hard to believe, especially since you only knew me for about five minutes!"

"Exactly. And look where that got me."

The anger left her eyes, replaced with confusion and something that looked a lot like pain. "Where did that get you, Matthew?"

His anger dissipated beneath the raw honesty of those

big brown eyes, and he slowly released his breath. Never in his life had he lost his temper so completely. Or treated a woman so callously. Sitting down on the bed, he ran a hand through his hair and studied the toes of his thoroughly soaked socks. "Crazy, I guess."

The bed shifted as she sat up behind him. He expected her to chime in with some psychology bullshit about how his actions were really masking a deeper problem, but instead she said something completely mind-blowing. "Me too."

He turned and looked at her. "What?"

Her damp hair curled around her face as she stared back at him. "Ever since I've met you I've felt crazy."

"And just what have you done that's crazy? I haven't seen you showing up at book signings, forcing yourself on dates, or wanting to kick a stupid redneck's ass."

She smiled. "No, I just spent three months calling the hotel in Vegas posing as different people in order to get your name."

"What?" He stared at her with disbelief. "I thought you never wanted to see me again. Especially after your reaction in the bookstore."

Ellie shrugged. "I guess I'm a better liar than you are."

The tight feeling in his chest eased. "So you called the hotel?"

"The very next day."

"And they didn't connect you to my room?"

She shook her head. "No, they said that you'd already checked out."

Matthew nodded, remembering how quickly he'd wanted to get out of the room and all the memories it evoked. He reached out and ran a finger along the back of her hand.

"So why did you want to talk to me?"

Her gaze lowered to his hand resting over hers. "I'm not sure, but I think I might've begged you to take me back to bed."

A smile split his face. "Begged, huh?"

"Don't let it go to your head, McPherson. I was hung-over, disoriented, and suffering from the belief that I would only have sex with a man that I cared about."

"So you cared about me?"

"No. At the time, I barely knew you." She watched as he unzipped her coat. "And you barely knew me. You just wanted to feel my breasts."

"To begin with." He slipped the coat off her shoulders. "But then I wanted more. A lot more."

"Which is why you've been acting so crazy. You're sex deprived."

He tossed her coat to the floor and then took her hands in his. They were ice cold, and he rubbed the heat back into them. "Yes. I want you back in bed with me. I've wanted that for eleven long months. But it's not just about sex anymore, Ellie. I like being with you. I like talking with you. And going places with you." He reached out and smoothed back her hair. "I even like your hair."

She pulled back. "Please don't lie, Matthew."

He moved closer, framing her face with his hands. "I'm not lying. You're beautiful. And not just on the outside. You're beautiful on the inside. The most beautiful woman I've ever known." He leaned in and kissed her, enjoying the warm glide of her sweet lips. But after only a few minutes of heaven, he drew back.

"Why did you kiss him, Ellie?"

She stared up at him, her eyes direct. "I guess I wanted to see if he could make me feel like you do."

"And did he?"

There was only a slight shake of her head, but it was enough to release the knot that had resided in his chest ever since Vegas.

"Good." He reached down and took the edge of her sweater and lifted it over her head. "Let's keep it that way."

He went about undressing her. But instead of a skillful expert who removed each article of clothing with finesse, Matthew turned into a bumbling novice who acted like he'd never seen women's clothing before, let alone removed them. He tugged so hard on one boot he almost yanked her off the bed. He snagged her striped wool sock on a toenail and caused her to cry out in pain. He got the zipper of her jeans stuck halfway down and couldn't get it to budge.

But he was most embarrassed when he tried to take off her bra. Since his freshman year in high school, he could get off a bra with a simple flick of his fingers. The clasp on Ellie's bra took more than a flick. It took a full minute of his undivided attention and then still wouldn't come off.

Through it all, Ellie never laughed at his inept attempt to get her naked. Instead, she tugged off her boots, wiggled out of her jeans, and took off her own bra before helping him out of his sweatpants, wet socks, and boxer briefs.

Once they were naked, they lay on the bed facing one another. His hand rested on the spot where her spine sloped down to her hips, while hers looped up over his shoulders and caressed the hair on the back of his neck.

He wanted her more than he had ever wanted a woman. Yet being there wrapped in her arms seemed to be enough.

He brushed back a strand of her hair, then traced a finger down her forehead, over her freckled nose, and across her lips. He didn't stop until he reached one rose-tipped breast.

"Beautiful," he breathed as he slowly circled the crest with his fingertip.

With a moan, she rolled to her back, allowing him full access. He spent the next few minutes caressing and possessing a wonderland of plump flesh and rigid peaks. When her breath grew uneven and her hips restless, he placed a kiss on her shoulder before nibbling his way to her ear.

"Is there some place else you want me to touch, Ellie?" he whispered. Her jerky nod had him smiling and his hand moving lower. He circled her belly button. "Here?" He moved lower, parting her pubic hair and touching the quivering flesh beneath. "Or maybe here?"

Instead of answering, she covered his hand with hers and guided his fingers to the exact spot she wanted. He strummed her lightly until her hand fell away; then he slipped two fingers deep inside her heat.

Her legs jumped, and she hummed in the back of her throat. He stroked his fingers in and out until her breathing changed and her hips flexed; then he removed his fingers and reached for the nightstand drawer. Once he had the condom on, he turned to find her watching him, her smile soft and seductive.

"Is there some place you want me to touch you?" she said before she took him in hand and led him home. Once inside her, the feel of scorching wet heat and pulsing muscle took his breath away.

"God, Ellie," he hissed, "what have you done to me?"

For an answer, she tilted her hips and took him deeper. He started to move, and everything fell into place. He had been with many women, most much more experienced than Ellie, but not one had made him feel so completely...so completely...complete. The feeling was so intense that when she tightened around him in orgasm, there was no way in hell he could hold back the shower of red-hot sparks that burst over him.

The orgasm lasted. And lasted. And lasted.

Even after his body slumped against her, the pleasure didn't diminish. It just sat inside his heart like a big ball of happiness. He felt no need to get up and get dressed before things got uncomfortable. In fact, he was in no hurry for her to leave at all.

He lifted his head. "Thank you."

Her smile was brilliant. "You're welcome."

He kissed her pert little nose. "Am I too heavy?"

"No," she whispered, but the word came out slightly strained as if she was having trouble catching her breath.

Begrudgingly, he pulled out of her and rolled to his back, discreetly getting rid of the condom. He adjusted the pillows before pulling her into his arms.

Moonlight reflected off the snow on the balcony and spilled through the French doors and across the bed. For a long time, they remained silent as he drew circles on her bare shoulder and she ran her fingers through the hair on his chest.

"Matthew?" Ellie finally spoke.

"Hmm?" Sleep was only a blink away.

"What happens now?"

Matthew's fingers froze on her shoulder. It was a good question. Just one he wasn't ready to answer. Probably because he didn't have an answer. He didn't have a clue what happened next. Every relationship he'd ever had with a woman just sort of evolved on its own. There were no promises made, no expectations to live up to. If he wanted to keep seeing a woman, he did. If he didn't, he didn't.

But he knew that wasn't going to work with Ellie. She wasn't the type of woman who would keep hanging out with a guy who wasn't willing to make a commitment. Who wasn't willing to state his goals and expectations. Who wasn't willing to put his emotions on the line. No, Ellie was the type of woman who wanted everything mapped out. Unfortunately, Matthew had never been in a serious relationship before, so he wasn't real sure where he was—let alone where he was going. All he knew was that he wanted to be with this woman. No, *needed* to be with this woman. He couldn't think about tomorrow or the next day. He would go crazy again if he did. And she had made him crazy enough as it was.

"Go to sleep, Ellie." He brushed the hair back from her forehead and pressed his lips to the spot. "We'll talk about it tomorrow." He encircled her with both arms and snuggled back in the pillows.

Yes, tomorrow he would figure it all out.

Chapter Twenty-six

How long did it take to get the red heart off?" Ellie asked as she sat on the toilet lid, staring at Matthew's divinely naked butt.

The razor halted on the glide up his neck as he studied her reflection in the mirror over the sink. His gaze wandered down to the large amount of cleavage that swelled over the edge of her towel. "A while. Although I didn't work too hard at it."

She smiled. Something she'd done a lot that morning. Of course, it was hard not to be deliriously happy when you were with a gorgeous naked man who knew exactly what made a woman deliriously happy. Like breakfast in bed and an orgasm followed with a hot steamy shower and an orgasm. Although it wasn't just the sexual release that made her feel like spinning around in circles. It was more the way he treated her after the sex. The way he spooned against her as they slept, and the way he absently kissed the top of her head as they watched the morning weather report, and the reverent way he toweled her dry after the shower. It was almost as if she made him as deliriously happy as he made her.

"Why did you do it?" Matthew turned around and leaned back on the edge of the counter, wiping the remaining shaving cream off his face with a hand towel.

It took her a moment to answer with all of his good parts so close to eye level. "I guess I wanted you to remember me."

Something flickered in those deep green eyes. "I didn't need your name to remember you, Ellie."

Her heart did a little stutter step, and she struggled to catch her breath. "You didn't?"

"Nope." He pulled her into his arms. "One kiss just about did it." He kissed her, a deep mating that probably would've led to another wonderful orgasm if they hadn't been interrupted.

"Mattie!" A woman's voice boomed through the door.

It took a second for Ellie's desire-dazed brain to comprehend what she'd heard. It didn't help that Matthew reached out and locked the door, then proceeded to dull her mind further by slipping a warm, skilled hand between the edges of the towel.

"Mattie! Are you in there?"

He nibbled his way to Ellie's ear while he caressed her breast.

"I know you're in there, Mattie! I can hear you breathing."

At this point, even Matthew's experienced touch

couldn't stop Ellie's brain from working. A woman was in his bedroom. A woman who didn't sound like it had been eleven months since she'd last seen him.

Anger quickly overpowered lust. Anger and a whole lot of hurt.

Ellie shoved at his chest, but he ignored her, sweeping back the edges of the towel and guiding her hips up against his erection. The feel of him all hot, hard, and ready took her breath away, but not the woman's who stood just outside the door.

"I'm not leaving until I talk with you, Lover Boy. So stop ignoring me."

Lover Boy? Ellie slid her hands up into Matthew's hair and yanked.

"Owww!" He stepped back, rubbing his head. "What did you do that for?"

The question was so unbelievably arrogant it left Ellie speechless. There was an aggressive woman standing outside the door, a woman who obviously had the security code to his condo, and he thought Ellie was just going to ignore her?

She tried to shove him away, but he refused to let her go.

"Mattie?" The woman's voice came again. "Is someone in there with you?"

Ellie glanced at the door, then back at Matthew. Her eyes narrowed. If she had been the violent type, she might've socked him right in the nose. Especially when a dopey smile split his face.

"You're jealous."

She clenched her fists. But before she could let one fly,

he jerked her against his chest, pinning her arms down to her sides.

His body rumbled with laughter. "It's not so much fun being on the other side, is it?"

"Let me go," she hissed.

"Matthew, I don't have all day!"

He continued to ignore the woman who had the voice of a construction worker who spent too much time behind a jackhammer. "Now you know how I felt when you were rolling around comparing kisses with your cowboy." A wicked look entered his eyes. "Maybe I should open the door and do a little comparing of my own?"

Ellie stopped struggling and glared up at him. "You wouldn't dare."

He released her so quickly she stumbled back against the shower stall. He whipped a towel around his waist and jerked open the door. The woman on the other side squealed in shock as he grabbed her and gave her a resounding smack on the mouth.

"Disgusting, Mattie!" She wiped a hand across her full lips and crinkled her nose.

Matthew turned back to Ellie with the same look of distaste. "She's right. That was a little too sisterly for my tastes."

Sisterly?

Ellie studied the woman. She was huge. Not fat, just tall and very pregnant. But even though her swollen body beneath the black leggings and gray coat looked like it was ready to explode, her face was McPherson beautiful. The bee-stung lips were fuller than Matthew's and Patrick's but the eyes were the same exact shade of wet, green grass. And the color and texture of her long black hair was identical to Matthew's.

Relief washed over Ellie, followed quickly by mortification as those green eyes traveled from the top of her damp hair to the soles of her bare feet.

"Ellie, this is my rude sister, Cassie Sutton." Matthew made the introductions. "Cassie, this is Ellie."

"Nice to meet you." Cassie reached out a hand.

Blushing all the way to her toes, Ellie clutched the cotton towel to her breasts and took her hand. "It's nice to meet you." She squeaked on "you" as her fingers were crushed in a viselike handshake.

"So is there a reason you barged into my house so early in the morning, Big Sister? Or do you just like to be annoying?" Matthew brushed past Cassie and into the bedroom. "And where's your gaggle of geese?"

"Melanie took them sledding on the golf course. So I spent the morning with Mom—which is exactly why I'm here. We need to talk." Cassie followed behind him, giving Ellie time to adjust her towel and look around for her clothes. Unfortunately, her clothes were exactly where she'd left them—strewn across the bedroom floor.

"And you couldn't just call?" Matthew asked on his way into the walk-in closet.

As Ellie tried to discreetly pick up her clothing, Cassie lay down on the bed, her stomach sticking up like the Disneyland Matterhorn. "I tried calling, but for some reason you didn't answer." She peeked around her stomach at Ellie whose face grew even hotter. "Anyway, we need to figure out what to do about this situation between Mom and Dad. Did you realize that their entire argument is centered around that book she gave me?"

Ellie had grabbed the rest of her clothes and headed for the door when Matthew came back out of the closet, looking sexy as ever in jeans and a turtleneck sweater.

"And just where do you think you're going?" he asked. Before she could answer, he turned to his sister. "Ellie's book didn't cause Mom and Dad to break up. The problems in their marriage started a long time ago. When Dad put work before Mom. And a sexually driven relationship before an emotionally driven one."

"What?" Cassie lifted her head. "Don't tell me that you've read that crazy woman's—" Her gaze shot over to Ellie. "Ellie? You're the one who wrote the book? But I thought you were a virgin."

"So what's going on here?" Patrick strode into the room, bundled up in a ski jacket with his face flushed from the cold. His gaze ran over Ellie and the articles of clothing she clutched to her chest and he smiled brightly. "As usual, it looks like my big sis showed up at the wrong time."

"More like too late," Cassie said. "This woman brainwashed Mom and has now moved on to Matthew." She tried to sit up, but it was like watching a turtle on its back. Her arms waved as her feet struggled to reach the ground.

"Easy there, Twiddle Dee." Patrick helped her sit up with a lot more care than his words indicated. "You don't want to break Mattie's bed." His gaze drifted over the messed sheets. "Funny, but it doesn't look like Matthew minded getting his brain washed."

"Ellie didn't brainwash me," Matthew said. "If you had

read her book, you would realize that she isn't against sex. She just doesn't think people should have it before they make an emotional connection."

If Ellie had just been notified that she'd won the Pulitzer Prize, she couldn't have felt more surprised— or happy. Not only had Matthew read her book, but he also had gotten it. While thousands of people hadn't, this one man—who she thought never would—understood. And she couldn't express how much that meant to her. Although the smile on her face must've come close because Matthew's expression softened, and he winked.

"See what I mean?" Cassie said. "Completely brain-wash—"

"Cassie! Are you up there?"

Cassie, who only seconds earlier had looked pissed off, now looked terrified.

"By the way," Patrick stated nonchalantly, "James is looking for you."

"Oooo, I could just kill you, Patrick." Cassie's gaze remained riveted to the doorway.

"Don't blame me. I didn't tell him where you were. It was your huge Suburban parked outside that gave you away."

A handsome man with pretty amber eyes strode through the door. Standing in front of Patrick in nothing but a towel was bad enough, but standing in front of a complete stranger was too much for a modest girl to handle. Ellie clutched her clothes to her chest and backed toward the bathroom. But she didn't have to worry. James only seemed interested in Cassie.

"Have you lost your mind, woman?" he said as he towered over the bed. "I told you before I left for work that I didn't want you driving on these icy streets. It's just plain stupid, especially in your condition."

"I'm not stupid," Cassie grumbled. "And if you were so worried about me, then you should've stayed home instead of going into work."

"You went into work today?" Patrick looked confused. "But I thought Dad said that he was the only one who had shown up this morning."

James cleared his throat. "I spent most of the morning in my office. He probably just didn't notice I was there."

"That seems doubtful given that your office is right next door to Dad's." Matthew took a step closer, his expression reminding Ellie of the way he'd looked last night when he'd wanted to fight Sam the Cowboy. "You didn't happen to see your secretary this morning, did you, Sutton?"

James stared at him. "My secretary? What are you getting at, Mattie?"

Cassie struggled to her feet, positioning herself between the two men. "He's getting at the truth, James. Something I've been ignoring for months because I was too scared to face it." Her voice cracked. "You're having an affair."

James looked like he'd just been punched in the stomach. His expression held so much hurt and pain that Ellie had to wonder if Cassie had her facts straight. Especially when James made no effort to explain. He just stared at his wife for what seemed like an eternity before he turned to the door.

"Can you make sure Cassandra gets home safely, Patrick?" he said. "I need to go have sex with my secretary." He walked out the door.

Once he was gone, an uncomfortable silence fell over the room. It was finally broken by Cassie's sob. Not a soft sob, but a loud wail that had both McPherson brothers looking terrified.

Realizing that someone needed to take charge, Ellie stepped out of the bathroom. "Patrick, why don't you go after your brother-in-law? I'm sure he could use a friend about now. Matthew, make your sister a cup of tea. I think I left a box in your pantry. If not, you know the code to my garage."

The men almost ran into each other heading for the door. Ellie waited until they were gone before she placed her clothes on the bathroom counter and grabbed a box of tissues. Walking back into the bedroom, she sat down on the edge of the bed next to Cassie and held out the box.

Cassie ripped one out and swiped at her eyes. "W-what was I supposed to think when he wants to spend more time at the office than he does with his wife? Especially after getting a beautiful new secretary that isn't close to being as big as a barn." The word "barn" came out in a wail, and she went into another crying jag.

Through all the tears, Ellie remained quiet but supportive by offering tissues and giving Cassie gentle pats on the back. Studies had shown that crying was cathartic. And Ellie had seen the proof in her own practice. A good cry was sometimes better than hours of therapy. Which didn't seem the case with Cassie. Once she stopped crying, she looked like she wanted to punch something—or someone.

"Well, aren't you going to say something?" she said. "I

mean, what's a therapist for if not to make a person feel better?"

Ellie set the tissue box down. "Actually, therapists don't have the power to make you feel better. Their job is to help you figure out what's making you feel bad so you can hopefully fix it yourself."

"Open your ears, Doc," Cassie said, sounding so much like Matthew it was scary. "I'm miserable because my husband is cheating on me. And there's nothing I can do to fix that."

"Hmm? I heard something completely different. I heard you were upset because you think you are as big as a barn while your husband's new secretary is much skinnier."

Cassie leaned closer. "Well, of course she's skinnier. She's not nine months pregnant!"

Ellie nodded. "Exactly."

"Oh, I get it." Cassie stood up. "You think this is just an ego thing. That I'm placing my own hormonal insecurities at my husband's feet. Well, you are wrong, Dr. Simpson." She tapped her chest. "You can ask anyone, and they'll tell you that Cassie McPherson Sutton is a strong, self-sufficient woman who doesn't need a man to stroke her ego. Certainly not some whiny, girlie girl who gets upset because her husband stays late at the office with a woman who is much skinnier than she is."

Before Ellie could even comment, Cassie flopped back down on the bed and started sobbing again.

"Holy crap." Matthew came into the room balancing a cup of tea. "She's still at it?"

Ellie held a finger to her lips, then took the cup and

set it on the nightstand before pulling Matthew into the bathroom.

"Is she going to be okay?" Matthew asked once the door was closed. "Because if she is, I'm going to go beat the crap out of her husband."

"You'll do no such thing." Ellie dropped the towel and reached for her bra. "Especially when I think the man is innocent."

He turned her around. "So you don't think James is having an affair?"

"Don't look so surprised. Just because my father cheats doesn't mean I think everyone does." She swatted at his hands that slid up her waist toward her breasts. "Now let me get dressed before any more of your family shows up and embarrasses me."

He ignored her swats and pulled her closer. "You were embarrassed? Why?"

"How about being caught in your bedroom nearly naked?"

He laughed. "We're all adults, Ellie. I'm sure they didn't think a thing about it."

It was hard not to roll her eyes. "Of course they didn't. I'm sure they're used to finding women in your bedroom." She went back to putting on her bra, but his silence had her looking up.

"You're wrong." His eyes were direct. "You're different, Ellie." When her brows lifted in surprise, he continued. "I'm not going to tell you I've never brought a woman home, but they never spent the night. Ever. You're the first woman to do that."

A loopy fluttering started in Ellie's stomach and

worked its way up to her chest. It wasn't exactly a declaration of undying devotion, but for now it was enough.

"Thank you," she whispered.

Matthew placed a kiss on the top of her head as his arms tightened. "Believe me, sweetheart, the pleasure was all mine."

Chapter Twenty-seven

The Hope House Christmas Eve party had better food, better music, and better company than the art benefit. Unfortunately, Wheezie was too tired to enjoy any of it. In the last week, she'd worked harder than a toothless beaver trying to fix the craziness going on in her family. At the rate things were going, by New Year's, she'd be ready to buy her own casket and call it a life. Of course, she couldn't do that until she found out if all her efforts had worked. Something she was starting to doubt. Cassie and James weren't speaking to each other, and Mary Katherine fluttered around the party like a social butterfly, seemingly unconcerned that her husband wasn't living with her. The only part of Wheezie's plans that was going well was her plan to marry off Matthew.

Ellie looked as happy and lovesick as a girl could get.

"Here you go, Aunt Louise," she said as she handed

Wheezie a paper cup of punch. "I'm sorry, but I couldn't find any scotch."

Wheezie frowned as she accepted the cup. "I thought as much—and call me Wheezie. Aunt Louise makes me sound old and boring." She took a sip of the punch and wrinkled her nose. "Although a good shot could only make this better." Figuring that they only had a few minutes before they'd be interrupted, she got straight to the point. "So I hear you've been seeing a lot of my nephew."

"Yes, we've become good friends," Ellie said. Although her blush said that it was a lot more than mere friendship.

Wheezie hid her smile behind a napkin as she blotted her mouth. "That's good to hear. Matthew could use a friend. Someone to enjoy life with and keep him from being as big of a workaholic as his father."

"I don't know if I'm doing a good job of that," Ellie said. "He was supposed to come to the party with me, but instead he's helping Patrick with some last-minute construction project."

Since the project had been her idea, Wheezie wasn't the least bit concerned. "I'm sure he'll catch up with you later. In fact, why don't you come to the McPhersons' after the party? I know for a fact that Matthew will be there."

"That's a wonderful idea." Mary Katherine came hustling up with a plate of hors d'oeuvres. "We'd love for you to come, Ellie." She gave her a one-armed hug. "I just can't thank you enough for helping Jennifer see the light." She glanced over her shoulder at a woman who was talking with a teenage girl who had way too many knobs and hoops hanging off her face. "I was so surprised to see her and Joey. Especially without a bruise or broken bone between them."

"I didn't do anything," Ellie said. "It was Jennifer who finally figured things out and decided to leave. When I talked with her earlier, she said it had to do with a painting Joey gave her for Christmas. It was an abstract portrait of a woman who couldn't see and had no voice. The painting made Jennifer realize what kind of example she was setting for her daughter. And just the thought of Joey ending up with someone like Anson was enough to get Jennifer to leave."

Mary smiled. "Well, it's a Christmas miracle. And speaking of Christmas"—she turned to Wheezie—"are you sure you gave the man from your Silver Sneakers class the right address?" She glanced at her watch. "He was supposed to be here by now, and the children are getting restless."

"He got the right address," Wheezie said. "I only hope he has enough brains."

"Brains?" Ellie said. "Is Santa suffering from dementia?"

"Only where women are concerned." Wheezie took a sip of her god-awful punch and shivered before setting it down.

Mary glanced at the front door. "Well, I just hope Santa arrives before I have to get back to the house for the family party. And where are Matthew and Patrick? Did you see either of them today, Ellie?"

"Umm, yes." Ellie blushed, making Wheezie all the happier. "I saw Matthew this morning. He had to help Patrick finish up a job but said that he'd try to show up later." She took the tray of hors d'oeuvres. "Here, let me pass these around for you."

When she was gone, Mary looked at Wheezie. "What kind of job would they have on Christmas Eve?"

Wheezie snorted. "How would I know? I've been so busy looking after my house guest that I've had time for little else."

Mary's normally cool expression turned to annoyance. "I'm sure Albert is ecstatic to have someone else to treat as his slave."

A slave? Wheezie wouldn't go that far. She had tried to be a good hostess when her nephew first arrived. But when the stubborn man had refused to see the error of his ways and agree to her plan, Wheezie's hostess skills took a turn for the worse. Every morning she flipped a burned piece of toast in front of him, and every night he got a cold TV dinner. She shrunk his favorite sweater, mismatched his socks, and left his shirts in the dryer until they were as wrinkled as her behind. And to top it all off, she developed poor hearing and made him repeat everything he said at the top of his lungs. Her strategy had finally paid off.

Now all she needed to do was prep Mary. Which called for a little reverse psychology.

"You're absolutely right, Mary. Alby is selfish, arrogant, and controlling. And I don't know how you've put up with him all these years. Just look at how he forced you to have all those kids because he wanted a big family."

Mary's gaze lowered, and she brushed at her holiday apron. "Albert didn't force me to have five children. He wanted two. I was the one who wanted more."

"He still built you that big house and made you move into that snooty neighborhood."

"I chose the neighborhood for the schools. And it was my idea to build a house rather than buy an existing one that didn't have what we—what I wanted."

Wheezie shook her head. "Well, he should've at least gotten you a nanny and a full-time housekeeper."

"He offered to get me both, but I refused to have someone else raise my children." Mary lifted her gaze. "I get what you're doing, Louise. You want me to see that Albert isn't a selfish man. And he's not. He's just a workaholic who loves his job more than he loves me."

"And what about you, Mary? Haven't you loved your job lately more than you've loved your husband?" Wheezie asked. When Mary looked hurt, she continued. "All I'm saying is that, the last time I checked, marriage was a two-way street. A you-scratch-my-back, I'll-scratch-yours kind of deal. And neither one of you have done much scratching lately. You've both been too wrapped up in playing Can You Top This."

Mary's eyes snapped. "All I want is to be treated with respect, instead of like a hormonal woman with nothing better to do than volunteer at what he sees as an insignificant women's shelter."

"He doesn't see it as insignificant. He's mentioned more than once how proud he is of what you're doing here. But he's also jealous of the time it takes away from him. Something you should understand given how you feel about M-and-M Construction."

"So are you saying that two wrongs don't make a right?"

Wheezie smiled. "Something like that. But I'm also saying that two stubborn people won't get things worked out unless someone gives in."

Mary's shoulders drooped. "But why does it always have to be me, Wheeze?"

There was a commotion at the front door. Wheezie couldn't have asked her nephew for better timing. Or for a grander entrance.

"Ho! Ho! Ho!" Albert bellowed as he stepped into the hallway, his face almost obscured by the curly white wig and beard. Even his green eyes were disguised beneath the wire-framed glasses perched on his nose. It was hard for Wheezie to keep a straight face as he tucked his white-gloved thumbs in the wide black belt that encircled his huge stomach. A stomach in the exact shape of Wheezie's chair cushions.

Children and parents flooded out of the living room and into the hallway to greet the new arrival. The McPhersons were mixed in with the residents of the house. Jacob and Melanie with their three children. Rory and Amy with their two—although, now a teen, Gabby couldn't be called a child anymore. Wheezie felt a little guilty that Patrick and Matthew were missing the show. But just like Santa, she needed help achieving her Christmas miracles. And her single nephews were the closest things she had to elves.

The last ones to come out of the living room were James and Cassie. Although they chattered excitingly about Santa to their two children, Jace and McKenna, they completely ignored each other.

"Merry Christmas, everyone," Albert said in a deep voice. "Are there any good little boys and girls in the house?"

A chorus of "Yes" filled the room. Wheezie glanced

over at Mary to see her brow knotted as she stared at Santa's back. Not wanting the surprise to be over too soon, Wheezie distracted her.

"Don't you have a bag of gifts you want Santa to hand out?"

Mary blinked. "Oh, the gifts! Just have your friend sit down in the recliner in the living room, and I'll bring them in to him."

It was easier said than done to get the children to move far enough away so that Santa could move. Once he was seated in the living room, the children swarmed back around him. And it took Mary coming in and taking charge before Santa got some breathing room.

"Children! Everyone needs to form a line if they want to get a gift from Santa. The youngest first and the oldest last."

The children tried to form a line, but it took a lot of grumbling and adult help before it was achieved. The entire time, Mary kept looking at Santa. But when the kids were finally lined up and Santa seated, she left Clarisse to help hand out gifts while she hurried back to the kitchen to get more refreshments.

When she was gone, Wheezie shuffled up on the other side of the chair and Albert glanced over at her through the cloud of white synthetic hair.

"So now what?" he asked.

"Why, you hand out presents, Santa." Wheezie flashed him a smile as the first sticky-fingered little kid climbed up on his lap. "What else?"

He shot her the evil eye before he turned his attention to the children. Wheezie had to give it to him. Once Big Al set his mind to something, nothing stopped him from doing a great job. After a jolly "ho-ho-ho" and a story about what his reindeer liked to eat, he handed out presents and listened to each child's wish list. By the time the gift bag was empty, the younger children were thoroughly convinced that they had been visited by Santa and the older children were having their doubts. The only one who almost exposed the hoax was James and Cassie's daughter McKenna.

The eighteen-month-old, who was usually fearful of Santa, held out her hands and said, "Pop." Fortunately, James and Cassie were in too much of a sulk to notice. And once McKenna was sitting on her grandfather's lap, Al silenced any further toddler babbling with a candy cane. Mary finally returned and directed all the adults into the dining room for refreshments and all the children and their new toys to the playroom.

As the room cleared, she looked at Wheezie. "Could you give me a moment with Santa, Louise? I'd like to thank him personally."

Wheezie smiled, realizing that Mary had known all along. "I'd be more than happy to." She shuffled out of the room, but didn't go far. Too much was riding on the next few minutes. Leaning close to the doorway, she listened as Albert spoke.

"So I guess the beard and glasses didn't fool you."

"After forty years, little can fool me, Albert."

"No, I guess you're right." There was a long pause. "I'm sorry, Mary Katherine. I'm sorry I spent so much time working and ignored the most important thing in my life. I thought I was working so hard for us—for the family. But now I realize I was only doing it for my own ego."

"Me too," Mary said. "These women don't need me here all the time. I've only worked so much to make myself feel more important than I am."

"No. You're wrong, Mary," Albert said. "What you do here is important. More important than I realized until tonight. You've given these families the same thing you gave your children and me. You've given them a home filled with love and laughter, along with hope for the future." He paused again. "I only hope my pigheadedness hasn't ruined our future."

"Oh, Albert." There were tears in Mary's voice, which Wheezie took as a very good sign. "I've missed you."

"Come here," Albert said. There were the muffled sounds of footsteps and a creak of recliner springs. "So tell Santa what you want for your future, Mary Katherine. You want me to quit M-and-M—it's done. You want to travel the world—the world is yours. You want me to become a vegan—I'll plant the biggest vegetable garden you've ever seen. Because the only thing I need for my future is you."

There was a long silence this time, and Wheezie couldn't help peeking around the corner.

Sure enough, Mama McPherson was kissing Santa Claus.

Chapter Twenty-eight

Okay, that was Wheezie, and she said the party is winding down so we need to get a move on."

"Get a move on?" Matthew glared up the stairs at Patrick who was pocketing his phone and paying no attention to the fact that he'd left Matthew balancing the entire weight of the couch while he'd stopped to answer Wheezie's call.

"What's the matter, baby brother?" Patrick took his time lifting his end. "Have all those hours sitting behind a desk made you a weakling?"

"Not hardly." Matthew hefted the sofa higher as they moved down the stairs to the basement. "Although anyone would feel weak after spending the day moving an entire house." Once they set the couch in front of the fireplace, he flopped down on it.

"Stop complaining." Patrick joined him. "You worked

one day, and with a team of professional movers and designers. I've been working here for the last week trying to get everything on the house finished up—with a skeleton crew I had to pull from other jobs."

Matthew looked around the entertainment room and had to concede the point. "It looks great, Paddy. The entire house does."

"Yeah, well, I can't take credit. It was Cassie's plans and James's contracting skills. I just added the finishing touches when James stopped work." Patrick shook his head. "I still can't believe Cassie thought that he was fooling around. That's just one more reason to stay single. Women are crazy to begin with. When they get pregnant, they get even crazier. And Wheezie is just as loony. She seems to think that once Cassie sees the house everything will be great between her and James. But if I did all this work and my wife accused me of having sex with my secretary, it wouldn't be great with me. I'd pack my bags and be out of here."

"You can't do that when you have a family," Matthew said absently as he pulled his cell phone from his pocket and texted Ellie.

Sorry. Got tied up and can't make it. Having fun?

He really hadn't minded helping James and Cassie with their house, but he wished they had finished in time for him to attend the party. Not only because he had gotten attached to the families at the shelter, but also because he didn't like being away from Ellie all day. Especially on Christmas Eve.

"Which is why I'm never having a family," Patrick continued. "Too much work. I have enough problems to handle with my brothers and sisters. Not to mention Mom and Dad." He glanced over. "You heard anything?"

"No, Mom won't talk about it. And I only brought it up once to Dad. He got so wound up that I worried he might have another heart attack. So I haven't brought it up since."

Patrick nodded. "Same with me. Although I never mind winding Dad up." He picked up a magazine that one of the designers had placed on the coffee table and leafed through it. "So it looks like we're the lucky ones, little brother." His gaze lifted. "Unless you've decided to marry your little therapist."

A sound came out of Matthew's mouth that was a mixture of a surprised snort and a nervous laugh. "Not hardly. I barely know the woman."

"I thought you've known her for a year."

Feeling suddenly antsy, Matthew got up and walked over to the fireplace. "Yeah, but we didn't get together until a week ago."

"So you're together?"

It was a good question, one Matthew had been trying to avoid all week. And he didn't know why. It wasn't like he was a dyed-in-the-wool bachelor like Patrick. He hadn't intentionally avoided getting into a relationship with a woman. He just hadn't found a woman he had wanted to be exclusive with.

Exclusive. Is that what he wanted with Ellie?

His phone buzzed, and he pulled it from his pocket and glanced at it.

It would be more fun if you were here.

A smile bloomed on his face, and he texted back.

Later?

"Is the question too hard, little brother?" Patrick said.

Before he could answer his brother, Ellie's text came back.

I can't. Sidney and I planned to celebrate Christmas Eve together. Unless you'd like to sneak down my chimney after she leaves: o)

Matthew's smile got even bigger as he quickly texted back. **Ho Ho Ho! But need to attend midnight mass with the family so won't get home until wee hours of the morning.** He paused for only a second before typing. **Want to come?**

Ellie's reply was disappointing, but probably for the best. Especially with his family. **I'll let you have your family time, but wouldn't mind a visitor in the wee hours. Will have my stocking out and cookies waiting.**

Stocking? Matthew's eyes widened. "Shit!" He turned back to Patrick who was smiling—which would've made Matthew suspicious if he hadn't had other things to worry about. "I forgot to get Ellie a gift." He glanced at his watch. "What stores will be open?"

Patrick rolled to his feet. "At seven o'clock on Christmas Eve, maybe Walgreens." He replaced the magazine on the table. "But I need to warn you. The time I did my shopping there, the spoiled females in our family were not impressed. I take that back—Aunt Wheezie seemed thrilled with the toenail clippers and flowered shower cap. Does Ellie like Chia Pets?"

"This isn't funny." Matthew looked around the room, hoping to discover a vase or knickknack that might work. "How could I have forgotten a gift?"

"Don't freak out. Cassie is the queen of regifting. I'm sure she'll have something you can give Ellie."

"But it can't just be something, Patrick. It needs to be special."

Patrick sent him a knowing look. "Now why would you want to give something special to a girl you've only been with for a week?"

"Shut up." Matthew shoved him.

Unable to let that slide, Patrick shoved him back. "Come on, bro, admit it. You've liked her much longer than a week. Which makes me wonder if it's not 'like' as much as—"

"Don't say it." Matthew drove a shoulder into his stomach and knocked him back into the coffee table. Patrick tripped over it, and they both tumbled onto the couch. But his brother hadn't taken state in wrestling for nothing and, within seconds, was on top and had Matthew in a full nelson.

"No, I'm not going to say it," Patrick said, not even a little out of breath. "You're going to say it. Just say it, Mattie. You love Ellie."

No matter how much blood had rushed to his head, Matthew wasn't about to accept defeat. "No." He tried to work his hand around and grab Patrick's ankle. "I like her. I like her a lot, but I—"

"Love her," Patrick finished for him. "Think about it. She kept you, the ultimate player, from women for almost an entire year. She pisses you off every time she turns around. Once she did let you into her bed, you haven't looked happier. And now you're all upset because you forgot to get her a 'special' gift." His hands tightened, causing Matthew to see dots. "I'd call that love, little brother. You're just too stubborn to admit it."

For a second, Matthew wondered if he was going to pass out. Not so much from Patrick's hold as his words and the annoying fact that they made sense.

"But we're complete opposites," he choked out.

"How so?" Patrick lightened his grip, giving Matthew some much needed oxygen and time to think about his question. It took a while. Especially when he realized that they weren't that opposite. The only thing they had disagreed on was sex. But not anymore. She no longer preached abstinence, and he now understood how much better sex was if you waited to have it with someone you deeply cared about. *Deeply cared about.* Yes, he deeply cared about Ellie, but was that love?

The creak of stairs had them both looking at the doorway. Joey stood on the last step, holding a painting.

"Oh, no," she said in an exasperated voice. "I'm not leaving this here where you two brawling buttheads can destroy it."

Laughing, Patrick released Matthew. "Saved again, little bro." He got to his feet. "So what are you doing here, Squirt? Aren't you supposed to be at the party?"

Joey shot him a belligerent look. "I'm not a squirt, dumbass."

Matthew got up from the couch and cracked his neck, wondering if he'd need to go to a chiropractor. "She's here because I bought a painting for Cassie and James to put in their new house." He turned to Joey. "But I told you that I'd pick it up. You didn't have to drop it by—especially on Christmas Eve."

She shrugged. "I ran into your aunt at the party, and she told me all about the surprise. So I thought I'd drop it by early." Her gaze went to the original painting over the fireplace. "But you're crazy if you think my work is going to go in a house like this."

"Let's see it." He took the painting from her and held it directly under a ceiling light. It wasn't an abstract. It was a painting of snow-laden branches against a steel gray sky. "This is amazing, Joey. So amazing that I don't think I'm going to let my sister have it. I need a gift for someone—"

Joey's face fell. "Yeah, right." She reached for the painting. "Whatever. If it's not good enough..."

"Talk about regifting, Mattie." Patrick took the painting away from both of them, and, within minutes, had the landscape removed and Joey's hung. He stood back and studied it. "Nope this one stays here." He looked over at Joey. "Not bad, Squirt."

"As if I care what you think," Joey said, even though her eyes said something else entirely.

Patrick's phone rang, and he listened for only a second before he said a quick, "Roger that" and hung up. "They'll be here in fifteen." He headed for the stairs. "I'll sweep the second level and make sure everything's good, while you check the main level."

"But how is Wheezie getting them here without letting on about the surprise?" Matthew asked as he followed him.

Patrick stopped on the first stair and turned, flashing his rare smile. "The old bird had her driver disable James's Land Rover, forcing them to catch a ride with her to Mom's house. On the way, she plans to take them on a little Christmas light detour." He shook his head. "I'm just glad she's focused her matchmaking on someone other than me."

"You and me both." Matthew followed him up the stairs.

Patrick laughed. "Somehow I don't think that you've been so lucky, little brother." Before Matthew could ask him what he meant, Patrick took the second set of stairs up to the bedrooms. Once he was gone, Matthew walked across the foyer to the living room.

"Talk about rich." Joey stared up at the twelve-foot lit tree that stood in front of the wall of windows. "Your brother-in-law planned this as a Christmas surprise for his wife? The best gift Anson ever gave Mom was a bottle of cheap perfume that smelled like his dirty socks."

Matthew cringed. Even Joey's stepdad had remembered to buy a gift. He glanced down at the packages under the tree, wondering if he could steal one from James to Cassie. Of course, with his luck, the one he chose would be a waffle maker.

"How was the party?" he asked as he walked into the kitchen. It looked amazing. The designers had filled the granite countertops with bright colored canisters and the glass-front cupboards with matching dishes. They had even put five place settings on the breakfast bar—two regular settings, two in front of the toddler chairs attached to the bar, and one in front of a high chair with a baby plate and silver spoon.

"It was fun. I'm just glad my mom finally woke up. Although Anson is going to be pissed when he finds the note my mom left and realizes we're not coming back."

She picked up one of the oranges from a bowl that sat on the granite counters and studied it. "Wow, this is real. Why would you want an entire bowl of oranges?"

"Did he ever hit you?" Matthew had refrained from asking the question sooner. Mostly because he knew how sensitive Joey was about the subject and he didn't want to ruin their fragile relationship. But now he needed to know.

She tossed the orange back in the bowl. "It doesn't matter, butthead." She twirled around the room like a ballerina. "Because we're free."

Matthew smiled and waited for her to stop spinning before he hooked an arm around her neck and pulled her close. "Come on, let's go before James and Cassie get here."

But Wheezie's clock must've been off, because they had no more than met Patrick in the foyer and stepped out the front door when a car came around the corner. Since the landscaping had yet to be done, they had no choice but to duck behind the giant blow-up Christmas characters Patrick had picked out for Jace and McKenna. Patrick got Frosty. Joey Rudolph. And Matthew the Grinch. Unfortunately, Matthew tripped over the extension cord to the fans that blew up the characters and jerked it from the socket. The characters wilted in a pile of nylon, leaving the three standing there looking stupid as Wheezie's Cadillac pulled up to the curb.

James was the first one out of the car, his gaze scanning the windows of the house and the lights that were strung along the eaves as if he couldn't quite comprehend what was going on.

"Why did we stop?" Cassie struggled to get out of the

backseat. "Whose house is this?" She looked at Matthew and Patrick. "And what are you two doing here?"

Since James wasn't saying anything, Matthew stepped up. "Why don't you take her inside, James, and show her your surprise? We'll follow with Wheezie and the kids in a minute."

Unfortunately, his sister was too much of a control freak to let that happen without getting some answers first. "Take me inside? Why would he take me inside some stranger's—" She paused as her gaze traveled over the house. "Oh, my God." She put a hand to her mouth before turning to James. "This is our house. This is the house we designed together." The Christmas lights reflected off the tears that welled in her eyes. "This is why you've been late coming home. You've been building our dream house. Oh, James." A sob broke loose, and Matthew figured it wouldn't be long until the neighbors called the cops on Cassie for disturbing the peace with her loud wails.

Thankfully, Wheezie finally made it out of the car and took control of the situation.

"No caterwauling, Cassandra," she said. "Instead of sobbing like a ninny, you need to be apologizing to your husband. And you, James"—she pointed a gnarled finger—"should accept her apology. After all, she had cause to be concerned. What was she supposed to think when her normally attentive husband starts working late every night?"

"No, Wheezie, it was all my fault," Cassie hiccupped. "I never should've thought the worst."

"Wheezie's right," James said. "I should've told you from the beginning, instead of trying to surprise you."

Cassie sent him a weepy look. "I love surprises. Especially from the most wonderful husband in the world."

"I love you, Cassandra."

"I love you, too."

"For crying out loud," Joey said, "would you stop with all the mushy crap and take her into the house? Because you haven't even seen the best part yet."

Cassie started up the shoveled path, but James didn't allow her to take more than two steps before he swung her up in his arms. If he felt the burden of carrying a small blimp, he didn't show it. He looked happy and proud. And Matthew figured he had a right to be.

Wanting to give them some time alone, he and Patrick took their time getting the kids out of the car and plugging back in the cartoon characters so they could see them. When they finally walked into the house, Cassie and James were kissing in front of the tree.

Obviously, Wheezie had been right. Again.

The kids loved the house as much as their parents did. McKenna went for the ornaments on the tree, and Jace raced upstairs to his bedroom. Cassie waddled from room to room, stroking the walls, windowsills, and countertops like a cherished pet. She might've done it all night if another surprise hadn't popped up.

While bending over to pull McKenna away from the presents beneath the tree, she stopped suddenly and placed a hand on her stomach. When she straightened, she had a strange look on her face.

"Mattie, do you know if the movers packed the little blue suitcase that was in my closet?" she asked.

"Right, Cass"—he rolled his eyes—"as if I would pay

attention to some little suitcase when I had mountains of furniture to worry about."

James came over and took his wife's arm, gently turning her to face him. "Now?" he asked in a strained voice.

Cassie smiled, her eyes twinkling as bright as the lights on the tree. "What do you think of the name Noel?"

Chapter Twenty-nine

Look, if you want to spend the evening texting, why don't you just say so and I'll go home?"

Ellie stopped checking her cell phone for new text messages and looked up at Sidney who was sprawled on her couch eating one of the chocolate chip cookies they'd just finished baking.

"Look who's talking." Ellie placed her phone down on the coffee table, more than a little disappointed that Matthew hadn't texted her in hours. "At least I don't spend all my time at work texting." After taking a cookie off the plate, she glanced over at Sidney. "Which brings up a good point. Why haven't you texted Keith tonight?"

Sidney grabbed another cookie. "We broke up."

"What?" Ellie set down her cookie and turned to her. "Why didn't you tell me?"

"Because I didn't want you doing what you're about

to do—smother me with sympathy before you start your therapy bullshit." She polished off the cookie in two bites and went for another one, but Ellie picked up the plate and set it on the end table behind her.

"Sugar doesn't help depression, Sid. It only makes you feel worse when you come down from the sugar rush."

"Who said I was depressed?" Sidney refused to meet Ellie's eyes. "Keith and I both went into the relationship with our eyes wide open. And neither one of us was looking for a serious relationship. He just ended it before I was ready, is all."

There were numerous responses Ellie had been trained to say in situations like this, but she realized that Sidney was right. Sometimes therapy was bullshit. Sometimes people didn't need a therapist as much as they needed a friend.

She reached out and took her hand. "I'm sorry."

Sidney squeezed her fingers. "He texted me. I mean, who texts you to break up?"

"Jerk."

Sidney smiled. "Yeah, jerk." Releasing her breath and Ellie's hand, she flopped back on the couch. "But he was good in bed." After a few seconds of staring at the lights on the Christmas tree, she turned to Ellie. "I guess this would be a bad time to ask for a raise."

Ellie laughed and swatted at her. "Yes, it's a bad time. Especially when I just gave you a Christmas bonus."

"That measly check? That won't even cover my trips to Starbucks for a month. And seeing as how your next book on players is going to make twice as much as the one on abstinence, you should be rolling in the dough. So don't be stingy with your best bud." She flashed a teasing smile. "How far along are you on the book, anyway?"

Ellie studied the zigzag rows in her afghan. "Umm, I have a few pages."

Sidney hopped up. "Where's your laptop? I want to see what you've written. Did you write about the sex?" She shot Ellie an annoyed look while she hunted around the room. "Because you sure haven't talked about it with me. I mean, what kind of a friend won't kiss and tell? Especially with a guy who looks like that." She walked into the dining room. "Does he have any sexual fetishes? I knew this guy once who liked to lick my shoes before we—Ellie, where the hell is your laptop?"

"I forgot it at Matthew's."

When Sidney walked back out, she looked more than a little surprised. "Why would you take your laptop over there? Don't tell me you were writing while you were having sex." She headed for the stairs. "Now I definitely have to read what you've written. Isn't your laptop linked to your computer in your spare bedroom?"

Realizing that Sidney wouldn't give up, Ellie told the truth. "You won't find anything on my computer—at least, not anything worth reading." Before Sidney could speak, she held up a hand. "But it doesn't matter because I decided that I'm not writing a book about players."

Sidney came back around the couch. "Why not? I realize you like Matthew, but he doesn't have to know you used him as a guinea pig. And by the time the book is published, even if he figures it out, you'll both have moved on to other people so it won't matter."

Ellie grabbed a cookie and downed it in three bites.

When she glanced over, Sidney was watching her with a speculative look that soon turned to disbelief.

"Shit." She flopped down on the couch. "You've fallen for the guy, haven't you?"

"I wouldn't say that." Ellie spoke over the wad of cookie in her mouth.

"Then why don't you want to do the book about him?"

"Because he's not a player. He's a nice guy who just happened to date—"

"Over a hundred women." Sidney dropped her head back and stared up at the ceiling. "Geez, Elle, you're so damned naïve. I should've known not to let a lamb play with a lion."

Suddenly, Ellie was standing over Sidney and pointing a finger at her. "I am not a naïve lamb. And even if I am, it's better than being a woman with commitment issues!"

Sidney lifted her head. "You're right. I do have commitment issues. Which is exactly why I didn't want you falling for Matthew." She sat up and tapped her chest. "I'm just like him, Elle. I'm just not as good looking. If I were as good looking, I would've hit the hundred mark long ago. So listen to me when I tell you that something inside of us is screwed up. And no matter how much you think you can fix it, you can't."

"You're wrong, Sid." She sat down on the couch. "I know you have commitment issues. And I know it stems from not wanting to be like your mother—a woman who fell in love with the wrong man and dearly paid for it. But one day, you're going to find the right man. Someone who will erase all your fears and help you learn that commitment to a man you love isn't the end of life. It's only the beginning."

Sidney covered her eyes. "Oh, God, you love him."

It was a truth Ellie had been hiding from for days. A truth she had been unable to face until someone else had put it into words.

"Yes," she said. "I love him."

Sidney dropped her hand. "And he loves you?"

As much as Ellie wanted to answer in the affirmative, she knew it would be a lie. She might be the only woman to spend the entire night in his bed, but Matthew didn't love her. If he did, he would've given her an answer about where their relationship was headed instead of hedging around it. And if she was honest, she didn't need an answer. She already knew.

What happens now?

Nothing.

Oh, they would continue to have fun together and great sex. But there would be no white picket fence. No beautiful green-eyed babies. And no rocking chairs on the front porch. Their relationship would end like Sidney and Keith's. Except a plate of cookies wouldn't come close to making her feel better.

When Ellie didn't say anything, it was Sidney's turn to reach over and squeeze her hand. "So when are you going to break it off with him?"

It was the intelligent thing to do. Staying with Matthew would only make things harder. But for once in her life, Ellie didn't want to do the intelligent thing. She wanted to do exactly what every other woman in the world does when she falls in love—she wanted to do the *stupid* thing.

She picked up a cookie and handed it to Sidney before taking one for herself. "I'm not going to break it off." She took a bite and chewed. "I'm going to ride this wave until it's over."

Sidney wasn't exactly happy with her decision. She ranted and raved for a good hour before she finally gave up. Then they ate the rest of the chocolate chip cookies and watched *It's a Wonderful Life* and cried during the phone conversation when Jimmy Stewart kisses Donna Reed and says, "Oh, Mary." Around eleven, Sidney went home, taking every razor Ellie had in the house.

"I get that love is stupid," Sidney said, "and I don't want a repeat of what happened when Riley broke up with you."

"And just how am I going to shave my legs?" Ellie asked.

"Try Nair." Sidney disappeared down the stairs.

With nothing else to do, Ellie turned off the lights and headed to bed. Matthew wasn't coming. If he had planned to, he would've texted her by now. Unfortunately, her brain knew this but her heart didn't. Every time she heard a noise, she ran to the spare room window and looked out. On the fifth trip, she realized that she wasn't going to get any sleep and decided to go over some notes she'd taken on a patient who was experiencing impotency. But when she sat down at her computer and pulled up her files, she saw Matthew's name and couldn't help opening it and reading through the twenty pages of observations she'd written the day after the art benefit.

If one of her colleagues read them, Ellie would be going back to school—or possibly weekly therapy. It was blatantly obvious her theories on Matthew's behavior were just childish attempts to hide her true feelings.

Maybe she loved him even then. Along with half the women in Denver.

Unable to help herself, she got online and looked up his blog page. She was relieved to find no new entries. The last entry was hers. Just another lame attempt to mask her true feelings. She tried to delete it, but the program wouldn't let her. At least she could delete the file she'd written about him. She clicked back and was about to erase it when she heard a car pull into the parking lot below. Quickly shutting down, she hurried out of the room and down the stairs, grabbing a coat off the hook on her way to the garage.

But when she stepped out, she didn't find Matthew pulling his SUV into his garage. Instead a taxicab had stopped in front of his condo and a woman was getting out. Not just any woman, but her mother.

Ellie watched in disbelief as her mom stood shivering while the driver hurried around to the back and pulled her matching designer suitcases out of the trunk.

"Mom?" Ellie called out just as the taxicab driver slammed the trunk.

Her mother looked over. Ellie knew immediately that something was wrong. Her mother's hair was mussed. Her purse didn't match her shoes. Her slacks were wrinkled. Her face was completely devoid of makeup. And her mother never stepped out of the house without a liberal amount of Clinique. Never. Not even to grab the morning paper.

Ellie ran over. "What happened?"

Never one to air her dirty laundry in public, her mother glanced at the driver and shook her head. "Nothing, sweetheart. I just wanted to visit you for the holidays."

She nodded at Matthew's condo. "I guess I got the wrong one."

"I'm right next door." Ellie walked around the back of the cab and took the suitcases from the driver while her mother fished through her wallet to pay him. Once the taxi drove away, she and her mother carried the suitcases through her garage and up the stairs. It wasn't until they were standing in Ellie's living room that she repeated the question. "What happened, Mom?"

Her mother took her time answering. She placed her purse on the coffee table, then took off her coat and carefully folded and laid it across the back of the couch. When she finally lifted her gaze, her brown eyes, identical to Ellie's, brimmed with heartbreaking tears.

"I left your father."

Somehow it wasn't what Ellie expected. She didn't know what she expected, but it wasn't that. Probably because, regardless of her father's infidelity, she assumed her parents would be together forever. It was an infantile belief, but it was true. She wanted her mother to confront her father, but she never wanted her to leave him. Now, as Ellie looked into her mother's devastated eyes, she realized her mistake. Once a person committed to the truth, there was no going back. Not even if the truth made you extremely unhappy. Not even if the truth took away the love of your life.

Her phone buzzed with an incoming text, but Ellie ignored it as she walked over and pulled her mother into her arms.

"What am I going to do, Eleanor?" her mother sobbed.

Ellie didn't know. But crying seemed like a good idea.

Chapter Thirty

Matthew was surprised how busy the hospital delivery ward was on Christmas Eve. He glanced at his watch. Make that Christmas morning. Obviously, babies liked to screw up holiday plans. He pulled out his phone and checked it again. Ellie still hadn't replied to his text. No doubt she was as ticked at his nephew's bad timing as he was. Instead of lying in Ellie's bed surrounded by her warm body, Matthew was stuck on an uncomfortable vinyl couch surrounded by his excited family members.

Although one good thing had come out of his nephew's early arrival—his mother and father seemed to be back together. They sat in one corner of the waiting room, holding hands and whispering like a couple of lovesick teenagers, his father still in his Santa suit—minus the beard and wig.

"What has you looking like a sourpuss?" Wheezie

fidgeted on the couch next to him. "I would think that you'd be happy that your parents are back together."

"I am." He looked at his phone one more time before putting it back in his pocket. "I just would rather be home."

Wheezie smiled. "Seeing as you've never been in a hurry to get back home before, I'd say that this has something to do with Ellie."

Matthew shrugged. "Sorry, Wheeze. I know you wanted Patrick to get with her."

"Patrick and Ellie?" She gave him a sly look. "Why, any fool could see that those two don't belong together."

Matthew's eyes widened as the truth dawned on him. He turned and pointed a finger at her. "You moved her into the condo for me, didn't you? It was never Patrick you wanted to fix her up with." His eyes narrowed on his brother who was sitting at a table across the room playing hearts with Rory and Jacob. "And Patrick was in on it. He helped you plan the entire thing."

"No, I work alone. Although Cassie did agree to rent out her condo to my friend. She just didn't know who my friend was. After she discovered that Ellie wrote the book that prompted your mother to kick your father out, I had to do some fast talking to keep her from tossing Ellie out on her ear."

The realization that he had been manipulated didn't sit well with Matthew. In fact, it made him more than a little belligerent. "Well, don't be thinking about wedding bells, Wheeze. Not when we've only been together for a week."

Wheezie flapped a hand. "A week, a month, or a year, if you love the girl, you love the girl."

"I wish everyone would quit telling me what I feel," he fumed. "It's way too soon to assess my feelings."

"Bull. You've known Ellie for nearly a year, and that's plenty of time to know what your feelings are for her."

"Even if most of that time I hated her."

Wheezie laughed. "You didn't hate her, Matthew. You hated the fact that you couldn't be with her. And that should tell you everything you need to know." She patted his shoulder. "I realize love can be a bit confusing, especially for someone who has spent his entire adult life running from it. I figure your issues have to do with the way your brothers and father teased you about being a mama's boy. Somewhere along the line, you learned that it was wrong to love just one woman but okay to love them all. And while you were young, there was nothing wrong with playing the field. But now that you've found your soul mate, don't screw things up by waiting too long. Marry that girl and marry her quick. Before she figures out what pains in the butt we McPhersons are." She nodded at the nurse who had just appeared in the doorway. "And I'd say we have a new one."

"McPherson?" the nurse said, then looked surprised when more than half of the room got to their feet. "There's a young gentleman who would like to make your acquaintance, but I think it might be better if we kept it to a few family members at a time."

Since Rory and Jacob had to get back to their families before the kids woke up on Christmas morning, their parents and Wheezie let Cassie's brothers go in first. It wasn't the first time Matthew had been in that particular situation. He'd been at the hospital for all his nieces' and nephews' births. Normally, he hurried in, kissed the mother, congratulated the dad, and oohed and aahed over a wrinkly looking baby before making a quick exit. But this time, he let his brothers go first while he stood back and waited his turn. From this angle, he noticed something he had never noticed before. He saw the entire picture: James standing over the bed looking exhausted but happy. Cassie lying there, cuddling her child, looking even more exhausted but somehow serene. The glow on their faces caused Matthew's heart to crack wide open.

This was love. It wasn't perfect, and it wasn't achieved without plenty of effort. But it was beautiful. And Matthew wanted it. He wanted it more than he had ever wanted anything in his life. Suddenly, he realized that he had it. All he had to do was reach for it.

Once again, he congratulated the mother and father and oohed and aahed over the baby. But this time, he really meant it. In fact, he even took a turn holding little Noel who looked up at him with blue eyes that would no doubt turn a startling green. Once he handed Noel back, he made his excuses and headed for the door. He stopped for only a second in the waiting room and said a quick good-bye to Wheezie and his parents.

"I'm assuming you'll be at the house for Christmas dinner," his mother said when he kissed her cheek.

"Yes, but set another place. I'm bringing someone."

His mother's face lit up. "Ellie?"

Wheezie leaned in and gave Matthew a hug. "Now, Mary Katherine, leave the boy alone. He doesn't need help making up his own mind." When she pulled back, her eyes were twinkling merrily. "At least, not anymore."

Matthew didn't remember walking out of the hospital

to the parking garage. His mind was too consumed with thoughts of spending the rest of his life with Ellie. A life filled with her sweet smiles and contagious laughter. Her petite body and bodacious curves. Her quick mind and smart mouth. Just the thought made him want to jump up and punch the air. He had so much energy that, once he pulled out of the parking garage, he could barely keep his Range Rover on the road. He gunned it a little going around a corner and did a three-sixty when he hit a patch of black ice.

When he finally stopped in the middle of the deserted street, Matthew laughed and pounded on the steering wheel.

"I love Ellie."

"I love Ellie!"

The buzzer went off just as Ellie slipped the comforter up over her mother's shoulders. She tiptoed out of her bedroom and hurried down the stairs to answer it, wondering if in her mother's distraught state she'd left something behind in the cab.

She pushed the button. "Yes?"

"I have one question."

Ellie recognized the husky sound of Matthew's voice immediately, but instead of being filled with overwhelming joy, as she would've been only hours ago, a sharp stab of sadness pierced her heart. Sadness based in reality. Her mother's sobs had shattered the belief that she could find happiness in a playboy's arms. She'd spent the last few hours staring reality in the face, and it wasn't pretty. It was tragic and blotchy and filled with pain.

Ellie pressed the button. "What's the question?"

"How come you aren't naked and waiting in my bed?"

Tears sprang to her eyes because she would've given just about anything to be naked and waiting in Matthew's bed. Unfortunately, so would a lot of women. Women who would more than likely find their way back into his bed—whether he was with Ellie or not.

"Ellie?" Matthew's voice broke into her thoughts. "Are you going to open the garage door or do I have to play my rendition of 'Jingle Bells'?"

She closed her eyes and willed the tears back.

Why couldn't Matthew have something else wrong with him? Why couldn't he have a crooked nose or a wart or a really bad sense of humor? She could live with any other shortcoming. Just not infidelity. It didn't seem fair that she would fall in love with a guy who had the same problem as her father. Of course, life wasn't fair. Ellie had learned that early on.

"I'm coming," she said. Then with her insides shaking, she moved down the stairs and stepped out in the garage.

The cold took her breath away and dried the tears at the corners of her eyes. She didn't want to open the door; instead she wanted to go back upstairs and crawl beneath the covers next to her comatose mother. But if she had learned anything from what happened to her mother it was that it was better to face the truth head-on than to wait for it to sideswipe you when you least expected it.

Taking a deep breath, she pressed the button for the garage. It slowly inched up, the rollers squeaking in their metal tracks. The door was only halfway open before Matthew slipped beneath it and pulled her into his arms. The nylon of his jacket was cold against her cheek as he lifted her off the concrete floor and spun her around in a tight circle.

"Merry Christmas," he said, his words muffled against her hair. "I'm sorry I'm late. But Noel decided to come early." When she didn't say anything, he pulled back. "Did you get my text?" She shook her head, unable to get words past the lump of pain in her throat. "Cassie had the baby." He flashed a smile that melted her heart. "Faster than anyone expected, considering how long it took the other two times. But she's doing great. And the baby"— he paused—"the baby is really cute. So cute that I'm thinking I wouldn't mind having one or two."

The pain in her chest grew sharper, and even the cold wind that blew into the garage couldn't keep the moisture from her eyes.

His smile slipped. "Ellie? Are you okay?" He tipped up her chin and looked into her eyes. "I didn't mean to make you cry, baby. Although I know where you're coming from. I got a little misty-eyed myself when I held Noel." He swallowed hard. "And something else happened that I need to tell you about. While I was in the room with Cass, I realized that there is only one woman I want to have children with. Only one woman I want to share all life's special moments with." He pulled her into his arms. "I love you, Ellie."

Suddenly, she understood what a sucker punch felt like. All the air whooshed out of her body and refused to come back in. She wheezed as he pulled back and repeated the words.

"I love you."

A dopey grin split his face. A grin she might've fallen

for if she hadn't known better. But she did know better. Her father said he loved her mother and look where that left her: a fifty-nine-year-old brokenhearted woman sobbing on her daughter's doorstep. That wasn't love. Matthew might believe he loved her, but he didn't. He didn't even know what love was. Love involved trust and honesty and fidelity. Traits a man who had had sex with a hundred different women knew nothing about.

Air rushed back into Ellie's lungs, and she finally found her voice. "You don't love me, Matthew."

Some of the sparkle left his eyes as his grin disappeared. "Excuse me?"

"You don't love me," she stated as she wiggled out of his arms. She moved a few feet away, keeping her eyes on the snow that melted off his boots into watery puddles. "I'm the first woman that you've become friends with. It's very normal to confuse feelings of friendship for something more intense. Especially when coupled with the miracle of birth. When you were at the hospital, Cassie's child brought out the paternal feelings that are in most men, and you immediately transferred those feelings to the last woman you took to bed. Me. Once you've had some time to think things through, you'll realize that what you feel right now is nothing but misplaced emotions."

His voice held disbelief. "Misplaced emotions?"

She nodded but didn't look up. She couldn't look him in the eyes. If she looked him in the eyes, she might start to believe him and that would only get her in trouble. The same kind of trouble her mother was in.

Matthew laughed, but there was no humor in it. "So I take it you aren't having the same misplaced emotions."

"No," she lied. "I can rationalize."

"Well, rationalize this." He reached out and took her arms, pulling her up to meet his descending mouth. The fiery heat of his lips melted any resistance, and she wrapped her arms around his neck and kissed him back as if her life depended on it. He was right. She couldn't rationalize this. Her mind might know he wasn't good for her, but her body craved him like a drug.

Matthew had much more control. He pulled back from the kiss and set her away from him as if he couldn't stand to touch her a second longer. "I don't know what kind of screwed-up ideas you have on love, but there's something more here than just friendship, Ellie. And I suggest you figure it out before you lose it."

He was gone before she completely recovered from his kiss. And along with the overwhelming sadness came a crushing fear.

What if she was wrong?

Misplaced emotions.

Matthew slammed the door of his condo.

Yeah, he had misplaced emotions, all right. He'd misplaced them with the wrong woman. A woman who wouldn't know love if it bit her in the ass. He stomped up the stairs and then stopped suddenly when he got to the top.

His living room looked just as it had when they left it that morning. Ellie's computer sat opened on the coffee table next to her half-full cup of tea, and her ugly knit blanket was spread over the couch partially covering the indention her butt had left on the leather. He stared at the indention while his mind tried to piece together what had just happened.

Could Ellie ever react like a normal woman? He had expected a squeal of delight, or a flood of tears. Instead, she'd treated him like one of her patients and started muttering off all her psychology bullshit. Of course, he didn't believe her. Not for a second. She loved him. She had to love him. What woman wouldn't love him?

He walked over to the couch and flopped down, crushing the knit blanket beneath him. He leaned his head back and rubbed at his temples. Why had he let Wheezie and Patrick put ideas into his head? Matthew McPherson didn't need advice about women. He wrote the book on women. In fact, he shouldn't be worried at all. Ellie would come to her senses. All he needed to do was ignore her for a few days. Possibly flaunt a few of his girlfriends under her nose to make her realize her mistake. By the end of the week, she'd be back at his door begging for his love.

He toed off his boots and settled his feet on the coffee table, accidentally brushing against Ellie's laptop. The screensaver was replaced with a list of her files. He was surprised to see his name on one. Curious, he sat up and opened it. As he read, everything became crystal clear.

Ellie wasn't going to come to her senses.

And she wasn't going to beg.

She didn't love him. Had never loved him. She was only using him as a case study for her next book. *The Players: Emotionally Challenged Men.* Which was why she had called him and set up an appointment. Why she had refused to move. And why she wanted to be friends with him. It had all been part of her plan to get information for her book. Even sex had been part of the plan. No wonder she tried talking him out of being in love with her. She needed an unemotional lab rat, not a blithering idiot spouting love words.

At the bottom of the file was a link to a blog page. He clicked on it, and the muscles in the back of his neck tightened. It was a blog about him. One he didn't even know existed. Where Ellie's observations were unflattering, these women's personal accounts built his ego back up. Until he came to the last entry. It was a tally of how many women faked orgasms with him.

One.

One woman in Vegas on New Year's Eve.

A night that had been nothing but a lie, after all.

Chapter Thirty-one

Her mother slept through most of Christmas morning, which gave Ellie plenty of time for her own sob-fest. Sitting on the couch with her least favorite blanket and a box of Puffs, she sobbed and whimpered through two full-length holiday movies on Turner Classics. She didn't even know what movies they were. She couldn't see them through her tears or hear them over her sobs. It seemed facing reality sooner rather than later didn't make a lot of difference as far as a broken heart was concerned. Ellie felt devastated.

Every time she got a hold of herself, she would see Matthew's sparkling eyes again and hear his voice whisper... *I love you.* And as much as she tried to deny it, there was a part of her that wanted desperately to believe. The part that kept listening for the buzzer and her cell phone. The part that just wanted to see his face again. To touch his warm skin. To snuggle against his chest.

Around eleven o'clock, her buzzer did go off, and she raced down the stairs. But when she opened the garage, Matthew wasn't waiting on the other side. Instead, a pile of plastic and electronics that had once been her laptop sat in the snow. She contributed its battered state to her harsh rejection. Until she opened the envelope that accompanied it and found a check for one laptop and two therapy sessions made out to Dr. E. B. Simpson, author of *The Players: Emotionally Challenged Men*.

Which made her cry even harder.

When she came back up the stairs, her phone rang. She scrambled to answer it, wiping at her eyes and blowing her nose before she pushed the button.

But it wasn't Matthew.

It was her father.

"Merry Christmas, Ellie Belly." When she didn't reply, he cleared his throat. "So I guess you talked with your mother." He paused. "Is she okay?"

"No, Dad," she said. "She's not okay."

He swallowed, the sound surprisingly vulnerable. "So she told you?"

The anger she'd held inside for most of her life sprang up, and this time, she couldn't stop herself from voicing it. "She didn't have to. I've known about the other women for a long time."

There was another stretch of silence before he spoke. "I assumed as much after you wrote that book." He released his breath. "I'm so sorry, Ellie. I'm so very sorry. I really screwed things up, didn't I?"

For years, Ellie had wanted to confront her father with the truth and hear him admit to his mistakes. But now that he finally had, she didn't feel the satisfaction she'd thought she would. She just felt sad and tired. "You need to get help, Dad."

"I know. You know any good psychologists?" He tried to chuckle, but it came out more like a choked breath.

"A few," she said with no emotion in her voice at all.

Another pause. "Do you think I have a chance?"

"Of recovering?"

"And getting your mother back."

"I don't know, Dad," she said honestly. "I guess it depends on how badly you want both of those things."

There was a sound very close to a sob, but since she'd never heard her father cry she couldn't be sure. After a moment, he spoke. "You probably don't believe this, but I love her, Ellie Belly."

The tears that she'd been holding back for most of the conversation leaked from her eyes. "I know."

"Will you tell her?"

She nodded but couldn't speak past the lump in her throat.

"Okay then. I guess I'll let you go." He paused. "And, Ellie?"

"Y-yes?"

"I love you, too."

"Me too, Daddy," she whispered before she hung up.

As she sat there with the phone clutched in her hand, she realized that Sidney had been right. Ellie only saw things as being black or white. Good or evil. Wrong or right. But life held a plethora of colors. Lush reds. Vibrant greens. And somber grays. Because the hard, cold truth was that sometimes people loved you and still broke your heart.

"Was that your father?"

Ellie looked up. Her mother stood in the doorway, an expensive satin robe wrapped around her pencil-thin body. Having taken after the short, big-busted women on her father's side, Ellie had always envied her mother's fast metabolism and svelte figure. While Ellie looked like a soggy frump in her baggy sweats, her mother looked elegant and regal as she moved into the room. Even with no makeup and puffy eyes.

"Yes, it was Dad," Ellie said as she placed her phone on the coffee table.

Her mother stopped a few feet away from the couch. "What did he want?"

"To know where you were and if you were okay."

"Did you tell him I was here?"

"No, but I think he figured it out."

She nodded and fiddled with her sash. "Did he say anything else?"

"He wanted the name of a good therapist," Ellie said. "I have someone in mind who I think will work."

"Good." Her mother nodded. "He needs some help." Then as if that was that, she moved into the kitchen and started looking in cupboards.

Ellie got up and followed her. "What are you doing?"

"I'm making your favorite blueberry pancake breakfast." Her mother pulled a skillet out of the lower cupboard and placed it on the stove. "It's the least I can do after ruining your Christmas. Besides, it will take my mind off all the sluts your father screwed."

Ellie eyes widened. She wasn't sure she was ready for this conversation, but she knew it was something they needed to have. For both their sakes.

After putting on the teakettle, she sat down on a barstool and watched her mother put pancake ingredients in a bowl. "Mom? You really didn't know before this?" she asked.

Her mother stopped whisking and looked out the window at the snow that had begun to fall. "I knew."

"Then why didn't you do something about it sooner?"

She looked back, her brown eyes filled with something Ellie didn't quite understand—a knowledge she had yet to learn.

"Did you know that not a day goes by that your father doesn't tell me how beautiful I am?" Her lips quivered into a smile. "Not one day. And not only does he say it, but he also shows it by constantly touching me and spoiling me with gifts." She pressed her lips together and then released a heavy sigh. "It was hard to believe that he could love me like that and have other women on the side. Or maybe I just didn't want to believe it. Because if I did, I wouldn't be his beautiful wife anymore. I'd just be the sad divorcée who couldn't hang on to her husband. At first, I convinced myself that it wasn't happening. That he couldn't be cheating on me if we had a good sex life and so much fun together. Then, I tried to rationalize it by telling myself that all men went through affairs. Each became just another fling he needed to get out of his system. So I ignored them all. Until my doctor found a lump in my breast."

Ellie sat up. "What? Oh, my God, Mom. Why didn't you tell me?"

Her mother started pouring the batter on the skillet as if she hadn't just dropped a bombshell. "I wasn't about to worry you. Not when you just started a new life in a new city. Besides, it turned out to be nothing but a benign cyst."

"Still, you should've told me."

"It's over now. And it turned out to be a good thing."

Ellie stared at her in disbelief. "Good? How can you say that?"

Her mother shrugged. "It made me reassess my life and realize that, not only am I beautiful, but I'm also intelligent. Too intelligent to stay with a man who can't remain faithful."

"So you really are leaving Dad?"

The pancakes were flipped before her mother spoke. "Yes. But maybe not forever. We both need time away from each other. Your father needs to get help, and I need to figure out who I am." She pointed the spatula at Ellie. "But that doesn't mean I don't love him, Ellie. Or that I can't forgive him."

"Even after all the women?"

"Even then." She smiled. "As your grandmother always said, love conquers all. And to some extent, she's right. We all have a limit of what we're willing to put up with for love. Some people just have a higher tolerance than others do."

Ellie pulled her knee up to her chest and rested her chin on it. "I don't think mine is very high."

"You have been pretty cold to your father in recent years," her mother said as she set a plate of pancakes down in front of her.

"I couldn't stand the thought of what he was doing to you," she said. "How he was playing you for a fool."

Her mother placed tea bags in two cups. "Are you sure it was all about me?"

She paused for only a second before answering. "You're right. It was more about me than it was about you." She cut into the pancakes, even though she wasn't the least bit hungry. "I guess I couldn't accept the fact that my superman father had the same human frailties as other people."

Her mother brought their tea over and took the stool next to Ellie. "For all his faults," she said, "he was a good father, Ellie. He never missed one of your dance recitals, or your piano concerts, or one school function. Not one. Even after you got a chip on your shoulder."

"A chip on my shoulder?"

"A pretty big one, I'd say." She smiled and swiped a hand over Ellie's shoulder. "I'm sure your father's infidelity is responsible for it as much as my avoidance, but at thirty-one, I'd say that it's time to knock it off and get on with your life. What your father does shouldn't control who you are and what you do."

It annoyed Ellie that her mother was still lecturing her, and she got defiant. "What Dad did doesn't control what I do."

One of her mother's perfectly plucked eyebrows lifted as she took a sip of her tea. "Really? Don't tell me you actually believe all the things you wrote in that book?"

Ellie's spine stiffened, and she set down her fork. "Of course I do. Emotion is the most important part of a relationship. It's not just about the physical."

"True. But isn't passion an emotion?"

"Well, yes, but I'm not talking about passion. I'm talking—"

"About love and commitment. Yes, I know." She shook her head. "I've read your book. I just think you've got a few things wrong."

It was one thing to have Matthew question her views and quite another for her mother to question them. Especially in her present situation. "Like what?" she snapped a little too sharply.

"Like your ideas on using abstinence as a way to figure out if a man loves you or not." She shot Ellie one of those all-knowing mother looks. "Love is about giving, Ellie. It's never been about receiving. You love someone not because they love you, but because you can't help loving them. Love is given freely without strings or requirements or pledges of abstinence." She reached over and squeezed Ellie's knee. "Love doesn't have to be proven; it just has to be felt."

The lump in Ellie's throat returned along with the tears that she thought she'd cried out. She sniffed. "It would've been nice if you had told me these things a few years earlier before I gave advice to half the women in America."

Her mother laughed. "I wouldn't worry about it. Women view self-help books like diet books: If it doesn't work for them, they loan it to a friend."

Ellie smiled weakly and nodded. "Maybe Sid will like my copy."

"So I take it your love life hasn't been working out?"

It had been working out until Ellie had gone and screwed it up. Just the thought of what she'd done made her sick to her stomach, and she pushed her plate away. "I wanted proof," she said.

"Aah, and he wasn't willing to abstain from sex?"

"No, that wasn't it."

Her mother glanced over. "He couldn't tell you he loved you?"

With her throat clogged with tears, Ellie shook her head.

"Then what, Ellie?" her mother asked.

Tears dripped from the corners of her eyes and ran down her cheeks. "He couldn't give me proof that he would love me—and me alone—forever."

Her mother placed an arm around her shoulder and pulled her close. "And what about you, my precious girl? Will you love him forever?"

Ellie nodded her head and sobbed louder. Before long, her mother joined in. They were both soggy messes by the time they pulled away. They took one look at each other's red-rimmed eyes and laughed.

"Well, I would say that's enough of that." Her mother slipped off the barstool. "We need to both take a long, hot shower and get out of the house for a little bit."

Ellie shook her head. "You go ahead. I need to talk with Matthew first."

"Matthew?" Her mother smiled. "I've always loved that name." Turning, she headed up the stairs.

Unfortunately, Matthew wouldn't answer her calls, and Ellie refused to make up with him through a text. He had told her that he was planning on spending Christmas day at his parents' house. But what if he hadn't? What if he was sitting in his condo feeling as miserable as she did? Jumping up, she grabbed her coat off the hook and headed down the stairs. The garage door had only rolled up a foot when she saw a man's boots.

"Matthew," she breathed before the door finished opening. But it wasn't Matthew who stood on the other side. It was a man she didn't recognize. A man who held her book in one hand.

"Nope." He smiled, but it didn't remove the cold bleakness from his dark eyes. Or the chill that tiptoed up Ellie's spine. "Guess again, bitch."

Chapter Thirty-two

So does everyone know who their Secret Santa is?" Matthew's mother looked down the long dining room table at the entire McPherson family.

Matthew didn't know who his Secret Santa was, and he didn't care. Nor did he care about the slab of prime rib that sat uneaten on his plate. He was just going through the motions of Christmas Day until he could make an excuse and get out of there. Not that he had anywhere to go. His home was no longer his home. Not when the enemy lived right next door.

"Jacob and I got Rory and Amy and gave them a weekend without kids," Melanie said. "As divine intervention would have it, Rory and Amy got us and plan to take our kids for New Year's."

Amy looked over at Melanie and winked. "Great minds think alike."

"And Matthew got me," his mother said. "And helped out at Hope House. Which I greatly appreciated. You and Ellie have been indispensable. I was so sorry to hear that she came down with the flu."

It was the only excuse Matthew could come up with to explain why she hadn't come with him to Christmas dinner. He couldn't bring himself to tell the truth and let his family know what a fool he'd been.

"Mary Katherine got me," his father said. "And I got Wheezie—"

"Now, wait a minute," Patrick hopped in. "You didn't say what Mom did for you."

His father actually blushed. "That's none of your damned business, boy."

"The children, Albert," his mother warned as she glanced down at the end of the long table where the kids were seated. Most of the younger children were busy talking about their Christmas gifts, but Gabby was all ears.

"Which is exactly why I'm not going to say what you did for me, Mary Katherine." His father tossed his wife a wink, and it was her turn to blush. "Now where was I? Oh, yes, I got Wheezie and dressed up in a ridiculous—" He glanced down at the kids and ended the sentenced there.

"I didn't think you looked ridiculous." His mother leaned over and gave him a kiss on the cheek. "I thought you looked wonderful. But it was more a gift to me and the families of Hope House than Wheezie."

"Having Alby out of my house is gift enough," Wheezie said. "Now can we finish up with Mary Katherine's crazy gift exchange and move on to dessert?"

"I'm with Wheezie," Patrick said. "Let's move this

thing along. James gave Cassie a house. I got James and helped him finish that house. And Cassie got me, and Wheezie talked her into moving in Dr. Simpson." He shot Matthew a sly look. "When that didn't work out, she somehow acquired the deed to Dad's cabin and gave it to me this morning when I went to see her at the hospital."

His father shrugged. "Your mother and I have decided that a fishing cabin is for our later years. Right now, we want to travel the world. And seeing as how you love your solitude so much, Cassie convinced me that you were the obvious one to get the cabin." He pointed a finger. "But don't think you can go up there every weekend. Now that I'll be taking off work more, you'll need to help carry the load." He looked around the table. "In fact, I'm counting on all of you."

"We've always been here, Dad," Jacob said. "And we always will be." He went to push back from the table. "So I guess that takes care of the gift exchange."

"No, it doesn't, Uncle Jake," Gabby said. "You're forgetting Uncle Matthew. Who was his Secret Santa?"

"Wheezie," Rory said. "She asked me to trade her Cassie for Jacob, who I'm assuming she then traded to James for Matthew. So what did you get Mattie, Wheeze?"

All eyes turned to Wheezie, and her eyebrows lifted. "With all my wheeling and dealing, I guess it completely slipped my mind."

"Don't you worry, Aunt Louise," his mother said. "I'm sure that Matthew understands. You've given all the kids plenty over the years."

"She's right, Wheeze," Matthew said. "It's not a big deal."

Wheezie sighed. "Well, I'm sure sorry. I guess it was just too much for an old bird like me to come up with something a young bachelor would like." She sent Matthew a weak smile. "Now how about some of that rum cake, Mary Katherine?"

There was a chorus of agreement, and everyone got up from the table and adjourned to the family room where they would eat rum cake and play games until the kids came down from their Christmas sugar highs and needed to be taken home and put to bed. Matthew wanted to go home and go to bed, too. But before he could think up an excuse, his cell phone rang. He pulled it out of his pocket and looked at the number. He didn't know why he felt disappointed when it wasn't Ellie. Obviously, it would take some time to get over her.

But he would. He had to.

"Hello," he answered.

"Mr. McPherson?" A woman's voice came through the receiver. "I'm so sorry to bother you on Christmas Day, but I got a phone call from my husband that has me a little concerned."

"Who is this?"

"Oh, I'm sorry. This is Jennifer Hastings. Joey's mother."

Matthew moved away from his chattering family and into his father's study. "So what's going on, Mrs. Hastings? Is Joey okay?"

"Yes. She's right here with me at the shelter."

"So I'm afraid I don't understand. Why are you calling?"

She took a deep breath and released it. "My husband,

Anson, found the note I left him, and he's been calling me nonstop since last night. At first, I didn't answer. But this morning, I gave in. And well, he's really lost it this time. I guess he found the book Dr. Simpson gave me and read it. And he now blames her for me leaving him. I tried to explain that it wasn't her, but he wouldn't listen. And I think he might actually hurt her if he gets a chance."

"It's nice that you're concerned, Mrs. Hastings, but shouldn't you be calling Dr. Simpson? Although I don't think you should be too concerned, seeing as how your husband doesn't know where she lives."

"That's just it," she said. "He might know where she lives."

Matthew froze on the way over to his father's desk. "What do you mean?"

"Well, I left her business card with her home number in the book. And I'm worried that if he has her name and number, he can easily get her address. And as angry as hc sounded, I just don't know what he'll do."

Matthew's stomach tightened, but he tried to remain calm. "I'm sure there's nothing to worry about, but I'll check on her just in case. You and Joey are safe, right?"

"Yes. Just make sure Dr. Simpson is."

"I will." Matthew hung up and dialed Ellie's number, no longer caring about the fact that she had used him. Right now, all that mattered was that she was okay. Once he knew that, he could go back to hating her. Or not hating her. He suddenly realized he could never hate Ellie. Not when just the thought of her getting hurt filled him with gut-wrenching fear. And with each ring of the phone, his fear grew.

"What's going on, Mattie?" Patrick walked into the study. "You haven't said more than two words since you got here. Did you and Ellie have another fight?"

Matthew held up a hand until Ellie's cell phone message clicked on. "Shit." He shoved his phone into his pocket and headed for the door. "I think Ellie might be in trouble."

Patrick didn't hesitate to follow him. "We'll take my truck."

A beat-up Pontiac was parked right in front of Ellie's garage. Matthew didn't even wait for Patrick to pull to a complete stop before he hopped out and punched in the security code. Nor did he and Patrick wait until the garage had completely opened before they slipped underneath and headed up the stairs.

He had explained everything on the way over, and just talking about what the guy had done to Joey's mom had deepened Matthew's fear and anger. He didn't know what to expect when he shoved open the door and took the stairs two at a time. But it wasn't a middle-aged woman waving a gun.

When she saw Matthew, she pointed it at him. "Are you friend or foe?"

Matthew held up his hands and looked around the room. "Friend. Where's Ellie?"

Ellie popped up from behind the couch, and the relief he felt was indescribable. Until he noticed her swollen jaw.

"The sonofabitch!" He came the rest of the way up the stairs. "Where is he? I'm going to kill him."

"There's no need for that, young man," the woman said. "We Simpsons can handle things quite nicely without any help." She pointed the gun at the pair of boots that stuck out from behind the couch. "Although I wish I'd coldcocked him before he hit my daughter in the jaw."

Matthew walked over to the man who lay facedown on the floor with his hands tied behind his back. He was out cold. And if the lump on his head was any indication, he'd be out for a while. Since there would be no satisfaction in beating up a hog-tied, unconscious man, he turned his attention to Ellie.

"Are you okay?" He stepped closer and gingerly touched her swollen jaw. "Should we call an ambulance?"

She stood there looking at him with eyes that glistened with unshed tears. And suddenly it didn't matter that she didn't love him. It didn't matter that she had only used him. All that mattered was comforting her. But before he could pull her into his arms, her mother stepped between them and handed Ellie a bag of frozen peas.

"It's probably best if she doesn't talk until we find out how much damage the bastard did." She turned to Matthew. "I already called the police and requested an ambulance." She held out her hand. "I'm Ellie's mother, Jeanette Simpson. And you must be Matthew." When he nodded, she smiled. "Now I understand what changed my daughter's way of thinking."

Matthew might've questioned the statement if the police and ambulance hadn't arrived. While the emergency medical tech checked out Joey's father and Ellie, Matthew answered the police officer's questions. During the questioning, Joey's father finally came to and started getting belligerent with the tech. Matthew moved toward him but was stopped by one of the cops.

"Leave him to us, sir." He nodded at his partner who

quickly handcuffed Joey's father and read him his rights before he was loaded on a stretcher and carried down the stairs. Another ambulance had been called for Ellie. While the tech didn't think her injuries were serious, he thought she needed to go to the hospital for x-rays. Her mother rode along in the ambulance. While Patrick went back to the house to explain things to their family, Matthew followed the ambulance in his Porsche. He was sitting in the waiting room, waiting to hear the results of the tests, when Sidney showed up.

"What happened?" She charged into the room, the tails of her scarf flapping. "I stopped by her condo with Chinese for dinner and discovered everything locked up tight. I wouldn't have known where to look if one of your neighbors hadn't told me about the ambulance." She grabbed him by the front of the sweater. "So help me God, if you've hurt her, I'm going to kick your ass from here to Kansas."

"I didn't hurt her," Matthew said before he calmly explained what had happened. When he was finished, Sidney flopped down in the chair next to him.

"Holy crap. Is she okay?"

"Her jaw is pretty bruised, but they don't think it's broken. They're taking x-rays to be sure."

"I guess her mom is with her?" When he nodded, she shook her head. "Some Christmas Ellie's having. First, her mom leaves her dad and then some jerk shows up."

Matthew sat up. "Her mother left her father?" He hadn't really given much thought to why her mother was there alone, but now it made perfect sense.

"Yeah, I guess her mom finally got sick of him fooling

around on her." She picked up a magazine and nervously flipped through it. "When I talked with Ellie this morning, she'd said her mom was pretty upset when she arrived last night."

"What time did her mother arrive?"

Sidney looked at him. "I left at around ten, so it must've been after that."

Only hours before Matthew showed up. Which explained Ellie's reaction to him telling her that he loved her. She had always compared Matthew to her father. No doubt, she saw herself as her mother. A woman who would one day arrive on her daughter's doorstep a brokenhearted victim.

"Look," Sidney said, "I don't usually get involved in other people's relationships, but I love Ellie and I can't see this thing with you turning out well." She tossed down the magazine. "So do us both a big favor and end it now before she falls even harder."

"And just what makes you think she's fallen for me?"

She hesitated for only a second. "Her refusal to write a book about self-centered players, using you as her subject." Before her words could even sink in, she held up a hand. "Don't get pissed. It was all my idea. I bulldozed her into it, not realizing until it was too late what a stupid idea it was." She gave him the once-over. "I mean, who wouldn't fall in love with someone who looks like you?"

The word "love," coupled with the evidence that Ellie hadn't used him, should've made Matthew ecstatic. Instead, all he felt was depressed. Depressed because he didn't know if love was strong enough to overcome all of Ellie's fears.

"Sidney," Mrs. Simpson said as she came into the

room, "I'm so glad you're here. I was just getting ready to call you."

Both Matthew and Sidney got to their feet.

"How is she, Mrs. Simpson?" Sidney asked first.

"She's fine," she said as she gave her a hug. "The x-rays show no broken bones, but the doctor thought it would be best if she stayed in the hospital for a night so they could keep an eye on her. Although I doubt that she'll sleep a wink after all the excitement. I was just on my way to the gift shop to see about getting her a book or magazine to read." She hooked an arm through Sidney's. "Since I don't have a clue what she would like, you can come with me." She glanced at Matthew and smiled. "Fifth floor."

On the fifth floor, Matthew was directed to a semi-private room. He tapped on the door before pushing it open. An older woman was lying in the first bed watching television. When she saw him, her eyes behind the lens of her thick glasses lit up.

"Santa answered my letter after all." She waved him in. "Well, don't just stand there, you Hot Pocket. Come on in and give me my bed bath."

Matthew smiled and then held up his hands. "I'm afraid I forgot my sponge and body wash."

She snapped her fingers. "Just my luck." She pointed at the curtain that separated her bed from the next one. "If you're looking for a sweet young thing with pretty brown eyes, she's behind curtain number one."

"Thank you." He sent her a wink, which prompted her to sigh.

"Aah, to be young again."

He walked around the curtain and found Ellie lying in

bed. She wore a blue print hospital gown that sagged on her shoulders, and her arm with the IV rested on the sheet and blanket that were tucked neatly across her lap. She attempted a smile, but it turned into more of a grimace.

"No smiles," he said as he moved to the side of the bed. "And no talking." He examined her bruised jaw and got angry all over again. She must've read it on his face because she held up her fingers in an okay sign.

"No, it's not okay, Ellie," he said. "I wish I had been there to stop him." She started to say something, but he sent her a warning look. With a frustrated groan, she reached for her phone on the bed tray, and within a few seconds, his phone was buzzing. He pulled it from his pocket and read the text.

It's not your fault. I'm the one who needs to apologize. I'm so sorry, Matthew.

When he finished reading, he looked up and found her watching him with tear-filled eyes. He sat down on the edge of the bed and took her hand in his.

"Sidney told me about the book being her idea," he said. "And she also told me about your parents splitting up. I'm assuming that your mother's arrival is what triggered your reaction when I told you that I love you."

She nodded, her eyes pleading. He released his breath and ran a hand through his hair. They should wait to have this conversation. Especially after the day she'd had. But he found that he couldn't keep the words in. Not when his entire life hung in the balance.

"I'm sorry that your father cheated on your mother, Ellie." He looked back at her. "And I'm sorry your boyfriend cheated on you." He touched his chest. "But I'm not them. And I refuse to pay the price for their sins. Yes, I've been with my share of women, and I won't apologize for that. I happen to love women. But until you, I've never been in love with a woman." He looked down at their clasped hands. "I love you, Ellie. I want to marry you and spend the rest of my life loving you. But I won't spend the rest of my life feeling guilty every time I talk to a female sales clerk or go to lunch with a female client. If you can't let go of the past and trust me, then there's no future for us."

Tears leaked down her cheeks, and Matthew hated that he had put them there. But he couldn't take the words back. Not when they were true. Getting up from the bed, he placed a kiss on her forehead.

"I'm going to let you get some rest. I'll be back to see you in the morning."

It was difficult to turn and walk away, especially with Ellie's sobs echoing through his heart. Of course, her sobs were much softer than the woman's in the next bed. He came around the curtain and found her glasses on her head and a tissue clutched in her hand.

"That was about the sweetest thing I've ever heard." She blew her nose loudly. "And if she won't marry you, I will."

His cell phone buzzed. He had just pulled the phone from his pocket when Wheezie shuffled in the open door, followed by his entire family—including Cassie who was being pushed in a wheelchair by James.

"She'll marry him," Wheezie said. "She just needs a proper proposal." She held out her hand to Matthew. "Patrick mentioned that you needed a gift for Ellie, and

I figured this would work just fine. It's not much—Neill was dirt poor when he bought it for me—but it should tide Ellie over until you can get her one of those gaudy diamonds."

Matthew looked at the small solitaire ring in the wrinkled palm of Wheezie's hand and shook his head. "I think it's a little premature—"

The curtain was jerked back, and Ellie stood there in her hospital gown. The tears were still there, but now they were mixed with a whole lot of sass. She walked over, maneuvering the IV cart through his family. Taking the phone from his hand, she tapped the touch screen and shoved it up to his face.

Matthew's heart took a leap when he read the words.

I have no future without you.

Then before his lips had even tipped up in a smile, Ellie handed the phone to Patrick and took the ring from Wheezie and held it out to Matthew.

The woman in the bed chuckled. "I think that's a yes."

"Of course it's a yes," Wheezie said. "Only an imbecile would say no to a McPherson."

"I don't know about that, Wheeze." Cassie adjusted Noel on her shoulder. "We're a lot to handle."

"Amen to that," his mother said, which earned her a glare from his father. A glare that quickly turned into a devious smile.

"I guess this would be a bad time to mention the opening in the back of Ellie's gown," Patrick said.

Ellie quickly clutched it closed before sending his brother a warning look.

Wheezie laughed. "I think she can handle us. Now

stop standing there with a silly grin on your face, Matthew, and slip the ring on."

He shook his head. "Nope. Since I only plan on doing this once, I don't want to make any mistakes." He got down on one knee and took Ellie's hand. "Dr. Ellie Simpson, will you allow me to love you for the rest of my life?"

Before Ellie could open her mouth, all the McPhersons answered in unison.

"Yes!"

Chapter Thirty-three

It had been a beautiful wedding. The music rock and roll. The flowers artificial. The dress vintage. And the Elvis impersonator outlandishly funny.

Ellie released a sigh and stretched her hand out to admire the diamond wedding band that perfectly matched Wheezie's ring. "Simply beautiful."

The man lying on his side next to her smiled a smile that had always—and would always—melt her heart. "You are, you know." Matthew leaned in and brushed a kiss over her lips. "Simply beautiful."

She laughed. "I was talking about the ring and our wedding. But thank you, sir. You make me feel beautiful."

He propped his elbow on the red satin pillow and rested his head in his hand. "Are you sure you're not disappointed that we didn't have the big wedding both our mothers wanted us to have?"

"Not at all. Can you imagine the fiasco that would've been? Two seconds after you proposed, my mother and your mother started in about where we should have the wedding. My mom wanted it in Kansas at the country club, and your mom wanted it in Denver in a Catholic church. And neither seemed willing to compromise. Then there was the hassle of deciding who was going to be in the wedding party. All of your siblings wanted their kids in it. Which would've been okay if you didn't have eight nieces and nephews. You should've heard the crazy idea Cassie came up with about Gabby pushing a wedding train of carriages with McKenna, Douglas, and Noel in them."

Matthew laughed. "Everyone was getting a little crazy. And that was only after four days. Can you imagine the hell we would've had to go through if we had waited a year before tying the knot?"

"I don't even want to think about it." She kissed his shoulder. "Eloping was a good idea, Mr. McPherson."

"It was, wasn't it, Mrs. McPherson?" Careful to avoid the bruise on her jaw, he kissed his way to her ear. "It was almost like divine intervention when I got the call from my buddy informing me that The Heat Suite was available on New Year's Eve." He caressed her earlobe with his tongue, and her toes curled into the satin sheets. "Especially when he's never called me before to offer the room. I usually call him."

"Mmm," she hummed as he caressed her breast. "I'm just happy he did."

"Me too, baby." He pushed down the sheet and

replaced his hand with his mouth. But before things could get really good, someone knocked on the door.

"Ignore them, and they'll go away." Matthew's words heated the wet spot he'd just made with his mouth.

The knocking continued, followed by a muffled, "Room service!"

Matthew let out an exasperated sigh and sat up. "I'll be back." He grabbed the robe on the end of the bed and headed for the door. Ellie had just starting thinking about trying out the stripper pole when he came back into the room, carrying a tray with an ice bucket, champagne, crystal flutes, and chocolate-covered strawberries. "Did you order this?" he asked.

"No." Ellie scooted over to the edge of the bed. "Maybe your friend sent it."

Matthew shook his head. "No, I didn't tell Will that I was getting married." He set the tray down on the nightstand. "Did you tell your mom or dad?"

She shook her head. "Mom's celebrating the New Year at your parents' house, and Dad is spending it with his new support group. And I thought we decided we'd call our parents tomorrow and break the news." She leaned over to help herself to one of the chocolate-covered strawberries and noticed the edge of the white envelope peeking out from under the plate. "But there's a card." She pulled out the card and read it.

" 'Happy New Year, Handsome. Enjoy your happily-ever-after. Love, Your Secret Santa.' " She glanced up. "Secret Santa?"

Instead of answering, Matthew burst out laughing.

"Why that wily old bird. And here I thought eloping to Vegas was all my idea."

"Your aunt Wheezie planned this?"

"It would seem that way." He took the bottle of champagne out of the bucket and pulled off the top with a pop and fizzle. "And she has the right idea. We should be celebrating. Especially when it's almost midnight." He poured them each a glass of champagne, then dropped the robe and joined her in bed. Once she had her glass, he clinked it with his. "Happy New Year, my love." He clinked it again. "And happy anniversary."

"One year." Ellie couldn't help the tears that welled up in her eyes as she took a sip. "Little did I know that I'd meet the love of my life in Sin City."

After taking a drink, he took her glass and set them both back down on the tray. "We can't refer to Vegas as Sin City anymore. Now it's just a place where an old married couple comes to have a little innocent fun."

Her eyebrows lifted. "Innocent?"

"Fun." He pushed down the sheet.

Thirty minutes later, he had demonstrated "innocent fun" in ways that left Ellie breathless and begging for more. When the last tingles had melted from her body, he pulled her close and fell asleep. Ellie smiled with contentment, but before his even breathing lulled her to sleep, she lifted her gaze to the mirror over the bed. It was the same picture she had woken up to a year before. Matthew slept on his stomach with his hand on her breast, his body lean, muscular, and beautiful. The only thing that was different was the white bandage on one butt cheek.

It had been his idea. Something he had insisted

on doing right after their ceremony in the little white chapel. Now just the sight made her heart flutter with love. Not because of the bandage, but because of the tattoo beneath. A tattoo of a simple red heart with one word inked inside.

Ellie.

When Cassie McPherson hires
a hunky escort for the company
Christmas party, she can't wait
to unwrap him like a present.
But there's more to her gorgeous
date than meets the eye…

Please see the next page
for an excerpt from

Hunk for the
Holidays

Chapter Two

A few hours later, Cassie wasn't sure if she looked festive or like a desperate hooker. The dress was a *shirt* with a hem and neckline that ran at opposite angles, showing off her right shoulder and a whole lot of left thigh. The "few little Christmas gifts" Amy had left included a strapless bra that shoved her boobs together and a satiny pair of panties that covered very little of the front and none of the back. Then there were the shoes, which weren't shoes at all, but some kind of torture chambers that imprisoned her feet in skinny, crisscrossed red straps that ran from ankle to toes and kept her feet from sliding off the skyscraper spiked heels. Mike would have drooled over these puppies, she thought. Not that his size thirteens would've fit in them.

The entire ensemble made Cassie feel like a tall, flashing red light that said something like SEX FOR SALE; COME

AND GET IT or DESPERATE, SEX-STARVED WOMAN NEEDS BREAK FROM SHOWER NOZZLE.

But Cassie didn't have much of a choice. Her burgundy dress and shoes had mysteriously disappeared from the executive bathroom. Or not so mysteriously, considering how devious Amy was. Cassie could've gone home and changed, but her escort for the evening was bought and paid for and hopefully on his way to the office to meet her. There was no way she was going to dole out five hundred bucks so some college kid could go home and play video games for the evening.

So Cassie did what she always did in a no-win situation—she went with it, applying more makeup than she normally wore and leaving her hair to fall down her back in long dark waves. The only thing she didn't apply was lipstick. Her lips were full enough without drawing attention to them. She gave her reflection in the mirror one last annoyed look. If this wouldn't degrade and undermine her authority in front of all the employees, nothing would.

On the way back to her office, the phone rang, and since everyone else had left for the night except for Juanita the cleaning lady, Cassie wobbled over to the receptionist's desk and picked up the receiver.

She adjusted it around her dangling diamond earring, the only thing she had planned on wearing, and answered, "M and M Construction."

"Hi, Mama's angel. I'm glad I caught you."

"Hi, Mom. What's up?"

"I wanted to let you know that I'm making your father stay home tonight." In the background, Cassie could hear her father ranting something about how her mother and the damned doctor had ruined all his plans.

"Should I come over?" Cassie sat down on the edge of the desk and examined the last of Amy's gifts, a red beaded clutch purse. She fiddled with the rhinestone latch, trying to figure out how to open it.

"No, sweetheart. He's fine. But if he goes to the party, all he'll do is talk business and Dr. Matheson doesn't think it's a good idea." This time Cassie heard exactly what her father thought of Doc Matheson. "Listen, dear, I need to go and calm him down. I'll talk to you later. Have fun at the party."

"Yeah, Mom. I will." Cassie hung up the phone. Maybe it was best if her father didn't come. If talking business didn't give him another heart attack, her outfit certainly would.

Frustrated with the entire evening so far, she yanked at the latch on the purse. It flipped open, spilling its contents all over the floor. Cassie looked down at the pile of red and black foil-covered condoms surrounding her high heels.

She laughed. "I'll get even with you if it's the last thing I do, Amy Walker." She squatted down and began to scoop the condoms back into her purse, heedless of her unladylike position.

A deep and very masculine cough had her teetering on her heels and almost falling backward on her butt. Grabbing on to the edge of the desk, she regained her balance and got to her feet. Although the sight that greeted her had her reaching out for the desk again.

A man stood by the Christmas tree in the foyer. Not a

man really, more like a vision. The clear lights that twinkled around his dark head made him look like something straight out of a dream. A wet dream. Man, Elite Escorts had outdone themselves this time. This was no gangly college boy in an ill-fitting rental tux, but a mature man in a tuxedo that looked made-to-order for his tall, muscular frame.

Like James Bond right before he bopped a shapely beauty, his bow tie was undone and lay flat against the front pleats of the crisp white shirt that was unbuttoned at his tanned throat. He stood looking at Cassie with a slight smile on his firm lips and one brown brow arched over an eye that was the exact color of her aunt Wheezie's favorite Scotch.

Cassie forgot to breathe.

"Hi." The smile deepened, along with two dimples. "I didn't mean to spook you." When Cassie still didn't say anything, the smile dropped and both brows lifted. "Are you okay?"

He walked toward her, and she was reminded of the black panther at the Denver Zoo, his movements sleek and predatory. She swallowed and tried to get her mind off his hot body and back in her head. It was difficult, especially when this wonderful eye candy stood so close and when she and Amy had just been discussing how long it had been since she'd had sex. But hot or not, she needed to remember that this man was one of her employees. She dealt with men all day long. Alpha men. She could handle some pretty boy who worked for an escort service.

She plastered on a smile. "Yes, I'm fine. It's just that you're early."

The quizzical look remained, and he tugged up the sleeve of his jacket and glanced at a watch that looked an awful lot like her father's Rolex. "No, I'm right on time."

She waved him off. "It doesn't matter. You're here." She grabbed the car keys from the desk and brushed past him. He smelled really good, like hot spiced cider and primitive lust. Or was the primitive lust her?

"My truck's down in the parking garage." She kept talking as she headed toward the elevator. "We'll take it. The party's at a house about thirty minutes away, so it's probably good you got here early." She pressed the button of the elevator, then turned to steal another peek.

He wasn't there. He still stood at the receptionist's desk, although his head had turned to follow her. Okay, so he looked great, but he was a little slow on the uptake. No wonder he worked for an escort service at his age. The elevator doors opened, and she pointed at them.

"Are you coming?"

He tipped his head to one side. "Who are you?"

Oh, so that was it. She just hadn't introduced herself. She laughed and held the door of the elevator. "I'm Cassie McPherson, your employer for the evening."

He didn't move. "My employer?"

Back to the mental deficiency theory. She tried talking slowly and clearly. "Yes, I called Elite Escorts and hired you for the evening to take me to my office Christmas party. I paid in advance, so I expect a little service here. Like maybe you getting a move on."

His whiskey eyes twinkled, but he still didn't move. "You're Cassie McPherson, the daughter of Al McPherson, and you called for a male escort?"

"Right. So are you coming or do I need to get a refund?"

"Your father's not here, I take it?"

"Not that it makes a difference, but no. He's at home."

He might be a simpleton, but, man, the flash of those white, even teeth and dimples were flat-out sexy. "Then I guess I'm all yours for the evening." He walked over and reached above her head to hold the elevator door. "Here"—he held up a foil-covered condom—"you forgot one."

Cassie jerked the condom out of his hand and then nearly fell flat on her face as she stumbled over her feet on the way into the elevator. He reached out and steadied her.

"Easy there."

The door closed, and he pushed one of the buttons while she rubbed the warm imprint he had left on her arm. Her heart thumped wildly against the tight band of her push-up bra. And suddenly she worried if all her high-cholesterol lunches and lack of exercise were catching up to her and besides inheriting her father's bad disposition, she had also inherited his clogged arteries. She couldn't bring herself to believe that it had anything to do with the man who so casually leaned back against the rail that ran along the wall of the elevator. Cassie McPherson didn't go all weak-kneed over men. Even re-e-e-e-ally good-looking ones who belonged in magazine ads for expensive men's cologne.

She turned away from the hot picture he presented and took two deep breaths, willing her heart to resume its normal cadence. It was hard to do with those eyes pinned on her with such intensity. Hard, but not impossible. She wasn't called Cast-Iron Cassie for nothing. She never let emotions get in the way of business. And this was business.

Clearing her throat, she explained the terms of his employment. "So here's what I expect." She opened her clutch and dropped in her car keys and the condom. "Keep a low profile. Be attentive, but not clingy. And try not to talk. If you're asked a question about our relationship, simply say that we've just met."

His eyes narrowed, and one side of his mouth tipped up at the corner. Definitely not a smile, more of a smirk. "How about if I just say that I'm not the kind of man who kisses and tells."

Heat flooded her cheeks, but she held it together. "Just stick to the plan."

"It seems you have a lot of plans." He lifted an eyebrow in the direction of her purse. "I'm not sure I can keep up."

Cassie ignored the innuendo and stayed on track. "The old relatives are the worst. They'll try to get you to commit to family gatherings and such. Decline gracefully. Don't drink with my aunt Louise. She'll drink you under the table and then interrogate the hell out of you. She looks very sweet, but she's a barracuda."

The elevator doors slid open, but not at the parking garage. He stepped out and held the door.

"You pushed the wrong button." She punched L for the lower level. "I'm parked in the garage."

He took her arm and gently but firmly pulled her out. "I know, but I'm parked right out front. So we can take my car."

"I'd rather drive," she stated as she caught the elevator door before it closed.

"But then you'd be escorting me, and that's not what I'm getting paid for." He caressed the underside of her arm. The tingling sensation caused her to pull away.

She turned on him as the elevator door slid closed. "You're getting paid to follow my orders."

In her heels, Cassie was only a few inches shorter than he was. So she shouldn't feel intimidated by his size, not with four brothers who were just as tall, if not taller. Yet there was something about this man that had her taking a step back. She wasn't frightened, but she was smart enough to be wary.

"And I bet you're pretty good at giving orders." He tucked her hand in the crook of his arm and tugged her toward the glass doors. "But right now, it's my job to get you to a Christmas party, and I intend to do it. After that, you can order me around all you want to."

She tried to dig in her heels, but she wasn't exactly stable in the sky-high shoes. The slippery marble floor of the lobby didn't help.

"I like driving," she stated through clenched teeth as he pulled her along.

"No doubt." He reached for the large gold handle of the glass door. "But I'm kinda old-fashioned about that. When I take a woman out, I like to drive."

"You've got to be kidding."

He glanced down at her. "Nope. Not at all. I don't like women to pay, open doors, or drive." He shrugged. "Call it a character flaw." He pulled open the door.

"Obviously, one among many. Let's not forget arrogance and stubbornness." The toes of her shoes hit the threshold, and he was brought up short. "I want to drive."

"Ms. McPherson?"

They both turned and stared at the worried face of the security guard who had come up behind them. "Is everything all right?"

Cassie thought about saying no and getting her arrogant, stubborn escort tossed out on his ear. But then she wouldn't have a date for the evening and would have to suffer through all the wives feeling sorry for her and trying to hook her up with some desperate relative. Of course, how much more desperate could you get than hiring an escort for the evening?

She stopped pulling away. "Of course. Everything is fine, Scotty. How is that new baby of yours?"

The tension left Scotty's face, and he grinned. "As cute as they come. Although he's not so cute when he keeps me up on my nights off."

"He'll outgrow it. My nieces and nephews all did."

"I hope so." Scotty moved over to the door. "Let me get that for you, sir."

"Thank you." Her escort flashed Scotty one of his megawatt smiles. "Merry Christmas."

"Merry Christmas, sir." Scotty nodded at her. "Ms. McPherson."

The frigid air hit Cassie like an ice-cold fist in the face. With it came the realization that she'd forgotten her coat. She stopped dead in her tracks. And her wallet. And her cell phone. The wallet she could live without, but she never went anywhere without her phone. It was her lifeline. How could she have forgotten it?

She glanced at the man who turned to look at her, and a shiver that had nothing to do with the cold raced through her body. Great! Now, all because of some pretty face, she was freezing her posterior off with nothing in her purse but her car keys and a gross amount of condoms.

She tried to pull her hand away, and this time he released it. "I forgot my—" Before she could finish her sentence a heat-infused tuxedo jacket slid over her shoulders, along with a very possessive arm. The warmth that enveloped her melted the rest of her resistance.

Maybe she could go one night without her cell phone.

"This way." He led her right out to the street, where a brand-new black Land Rover was parked in the no-parking zone. The locks clicked, and he opened the door and waited for her to slip inside. Once the door closed, Cassie was surrounded by the spicy scent that emanated from his jacket and overcome by a feeling that could be described only as . . . feminine.

Feminine? Cassie McPherson?

She shook her head to clear it. She needed to be careful. This guy was a bona fide gigolo who knew how to make a woman feel like a woman. A sexy, feminine woman. Which was why he could afford to drive a new Land Rover. The man probably had every wealthy housewife in Denver lined up with their wallets and legs wide open. Which brought up the next point. She waited until they had pulled away from the curb before broaching it.

"About sex."

The SUV swerved slightly, and she quickly glanced over at him. He didn't look shocked as much as amused.

"What about sex?"

She stared straight ahead and tried to keep her voice steady. "I don't want any."

"Ever?"

She looked back at him. "No, not ever. It's just that I don't have sex with escorts."

"Why not? You're paying for it."

Suddenly, her reasons for not having sex with escorts didn't seem valid anymore. Why shouldn't she have sex with an escort? Not just anyone, but this one. This tall, hot, arrogant, and slightly dumb escort who probably needed no sexual instruction at all, who probably could make her come just by looking at her.

An expert lover.

Which was the main reason she couldn't have sex with him. The guy had probably screwed half the female population of the city.

Lucky bitches.

"Because I don't want some nasty disease." She mentally kicked herself for blurting out the truth. "Not that you have some nasty disease, but just in case."

"Then why all the condoms?"

"Those are a joke."

"Too bad."

Her head swiveled around to look at him, but his gaze was pinned on the road. "So you hire escorts just for the company?"

"No, believe me. With my big family, I have plenty of company. I hire escorts to keep that big, loving—and sometimes smothering—family from matchmaking."

He glanced over at her. "That bad, huh?"

She laughed, relieved to be on a less intimate subject. "You don't know the half of it. I've been on so many blind dates, I could write a book on the dos and don'ts."

"But it must be nice to have a big family."

She sighed. "Yeah, sometimes. No, I take that back, most of the time. But it would be a lot nicer if I were married."

"And why aren't you?"

"I've been told I work too much. And I guess they're right." She turned in her seat and looked at his profile. He really was perfect. His features were strong and masculine, but not too prominent. "And what about you? And please don't tell me you have a wife and five kids at home."

He laughed. "I guess I've been told the same thing."

"You work too much?"

He tipped his head and winked at her. "A true workaholic."

In Bramble, Texas, Dusty Hicks is the law. That means no leniency for the gorgeous Brianne Cates. But as Brianne proves that she lives to walk on the wild side, Dusty begins to wonder if maybe he has what it takes to tame her...

Please see the next page for an excerpt from

A Match Made in Texas

Chapter One

Elvis was alive and well.

Alive and well, and annoying the heck out of Brianne Cates.

It wasn't his red silk scarf fluttering over the shoulder of his rhinestone western suit that annoyed her. Or the hand with its chunky gold and diamond rings draped over the side mirror. Or the sky-high black hair that defied the stiff west Texas wind. No, it was the fact that the man was going thirty miles an hour in a sixty-mile-an-hour zone, and he wasn't willing to let Brianne pass.

Most folks who knew Bri said she had the patience of a saint, no doubt because she'd survived a childhood with four arrogant and rowdy brothers. But the truth was that Bri didn't have patience as much as the ability to hide her impatience beneath a calm façade and innocent smile.

After spending the last thirty minutes playing a cat-and-mouse game with the big ol' cherry red Cadillac,

Bri wasn't calm. And she sure wasn't smiling. Gritting her teeth, she pushed down on the accelerator for what seemed like the hundredth time and eased into the other lane. But just as she caught a glimpse of one long rectangular sideburn, the Cadillac shot forward, forcing her to let up on the gas and pull back in her lane or end up wallpapered against the grill of an oncoming semi.

She wanted to blast the horn and flip the bird to the King. But if she had learned anything in the last few weeks, it was that everybody and their brother carried cell phones and one defiant act could go viral within hours.

Which explained what Bri was doing on the two-lane highway in the middle of west Texas. This was her punishment for one little act of defiance. Or maybe not a little one as much as a huge one. And while she was being honest, it hadn't been her first act of defiance.

It was just the first act her family had found out about. They had been devastated when they'd discovered that their "sweet little Bri" wasn't as sweet as they thought. And if there was something that Bri couldn't endure, it was disappointing her family. Nor could she endure staying behind Elvis for one second longer. As soon as the oncoming lane was clear, she moved over and floored it.

If she had been in the massive SUV her brother Brant had insisted she drive for safety, she might've been able to pass the Caddy. But she wasn't. She had borrowed her Granny Lou's car in an attempt to ditch her ex-boyfriend who had been stalking her for the past few months.

Both the boyfriend and the car had been bad choices.

The speedometer inched forward at a snail's pace, giving the Caddy plenty of time to pull away. But Bri refused to give up. With pedal to the metal, she continued to accelerate down the wrong side of the highway.

It took a while for her to draw abreast of the Cadillac. And Elvis seemed as surprised as Bri that a Smart Car could hit ninety. He shot her a shocked look before his lip cocked up in a smile-sneer. He said something but with her windows rolled up and the radio on, she couldn't hear what it was. Probably "thank yew, thank yew very much for putting up with my crap for so long."

She sent the man one of her most innocent smiles… while her foot remained smashed down on the accelerator. She probably would've continued driving next to him all the way to her turnoff if she hadn't glanced up to see the car headed straight for her.

Bri slowed down with every intention of pulling back behind the Cadillac. Except Elvis wasn't quite done screwing with her. He slowed down as well, blocking her from getting back into the right lane and forcing her to play chicken with the oncoming car. And not just any car, but a black-and-white with a row of flashing lights on top. Fortunately, it veered off to the shoulder of the road before they had a head-on collision. Unfortunately, there wasn't much shoulder to the road.

In her side mirror, Bri watched in horror as the sheriff's car sideswiped a couple fence posts before coming to a dust-spitting stop. It didn't stay stopped for long. In a spray of gravel and sagebrush, the patrol car whipped around and, with lights flashing and siren blaring, came hauling butt after them.

Or not them exactly.

Elvis quickly slowed and pulled over. Bri was the only one who kept going. And she wasn't sure why. Part of it was that she wasn't willing to cause her family any more embarrassment by getting a traffic ticket. The bigger part was the same thing that had gotten her in trouble in the first place. The screwed-up thing inside of her that seemed to feed on pure adrenaline and danger. And there was no doubt that being chased by the law was adrenaline pumping and dangerous. It didn't help that about then a Miranda Lambert song came on the radio, and Miranda could make any good girl go bad.

Fall in Love with Forever Romance

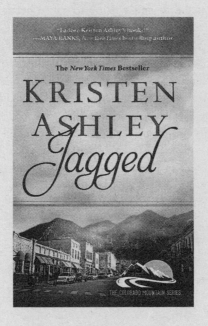

JAGGED

Zara is struggling to make ends meet when her old friend Ham comes back into her life. He wants to help, but a job and a place to live aren't the only things he's offering this time around...Fans of Julie Ann Walker, Lauren Dane, and Julie James will love the fifth book in Kristen Ashley's *New York Times* bestselling Colorado Mountain series, now in print for the first time!

ALL FIRED UP

It's a recipe for temptation: Mix a cool-as-a-cucumber event planner with a devastatingly handsome Irish pastry chef. Add sexual chemistry hot enough to start a fire. Let the sparks fly. Fans of Jill Shalvis will flip for the second book in Kate Meader's Hot in the Kitchen series.

Fall in Love with Forever Romance

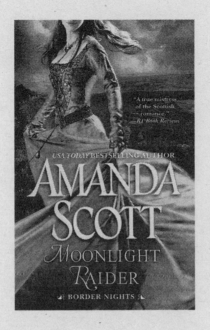

MOONLIGHT RAIDER

USA Today bestselling author Amanda Scott brings to life the history, turmoil, and passion of the Scottish Border as only she can in the first book in her new Border Nights series. Fans of Diana Gabaldon's *Outlander* will be swept away by Scott's tale!

Fall in Love with Forever Romance

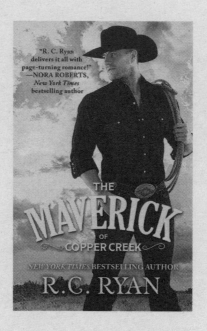

THE MAVERICK OF COPPER CREEK

Fans of Linda Lael Miller, Diana Palmer, and Joan Johnston will love *New York Times* bestselling author R. C. Ryan's THE MAVERICK OF COPPER CREEK, the charming, poignant, and unforgettable first book in her Copper Creek Cowboys series.

Fall in Love with Forever Romance

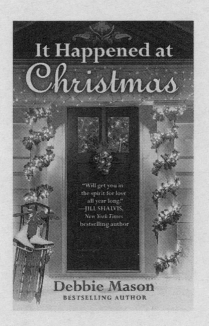

IT HAPPENED AT CHRISTMAS

Ethan and Skye may want a lot of things this holiday season, but what they get is something they didn't expect. Fans of feel-good romances by *New York Times* bestselling authors Brenda Novak, Robyn Carr, and Jill Shalvis will love the third book in Debbie Mason's series set in Christmas, Colorado—where love is the greatest gift of all.

Fall in Love with Forever Romance

MISTLETOE ON MAIN STREET

Fans of Jill Shalvis, Robyn Carr, and Susan Mallery will love this charming debut from best-selling author Olivia Miles about love, healing, and family at Christmastime.

Fall in Love with Forever Romance

Great Low Price!

A CHRISTMAS to REMEMBER

Stories by
JILL SHALVIS, KRISTEN ASHLEY,
Hope Ramsay, Molly Cannon
& Marilyn Pappano

A CHRISTMAS TO REMEMBER

Jill Shalvis headlines this touching anthology of Christmas stories as readers celebrate the holidays with their favorite series. Includes stories from Kristen Ashley, Hope Ramsay, Molly Cannon, and Marilyn Pappano. Now in print for the first time!

Find out more about Forever Romance!

Visit us at
www.hachettebookgroup.com/publishing_forever.aspx

Find us on Facebook
http://www.facebook.com/ForeverRomance

Follow us on Twitter
http://twitter.com/ForeverRomance

NEW AND UPCOMING TITLES

Each month we feature our new titles
and reader favorites.

CONTESTS AND GIVEAWAYS

We give away galleys, autographed copies,
and all kinds of exclusive items.

AUTHOR INFO

You'll find bios, articles, and links to personal websites
for all your favorite authors—and so much more.

GET SOCIAL

Connect with your favorite authors, editors, and
other Forever fans, and share what's important to you.

THE BUZZ

Sign up for our monthly romance newsletter,
and be the first to read all about it.